MIRACLES IN MEDICINE

Life-changing Medical Ideas and Inventions Across the Ages

PRAISE FOR THE BOOK

'The future of healthcare is in the hands of children. India has a huge child population, talented and brilliant, and they can become the providers and caregivers to the nation and the world. Indian doctors are very popular across the world for their empathy and compassionate care.

Roopa Pai has come out with yet another magnificent piece of work, this time covering the history of medicine – occidental and oriental. The book develops into twenty-five fascinating chapters of gripping narrative on modern medicine, surgery, pathology, nutrition and genetics, interspersed with interesting bits of facts. I am sure young minds will be piqued and inspired, by the contents of this book, to take up the medical profession, while even adults will find it informative.'

– Dr Devi Shetty

Roopa Pai, a Bengaluru-based writer, columnist and speaker, is one of India's best-known children's authors. Many of her books are bestsellers, enjoyed as much by adults as by children. Among them is the award-winning, much-translated *The Gita for Children*, listed by Amazon India as one of '100 Indian books to read in a lifetime'. Her TEDx talk 'Decoding the Gita: India's Book of Answers' has received over two million views to date. When she isn't writing, Roopa leads heritage walks around her city with Bangalore Walks, a company she co-founded.

OTHER BOOKS BY ROOPA PAI

The Taranauts Series

The Gita for Children

Ready! 99 Must-have Skills for the World-Conquering Teenager (and Almost-Teenager)

The Vedas and Upanishads for Children

The Yoga Sutras for Children

MIRACLES IN MEDICINE

Life-changing Medical Ideas and Inventions Across the Ages

ROOPA PAI

Illustrations by Mihir Joglekar

hachette INDIA

To healers of every stripe – physical, emotional, spiritual – and to the best doctors, who are all this and more.

First published in paperback in 2019 as *From Leeches to Slug Glue: 25 Explosive Ideas that Made (and Are Making) Modern Medicine*, Puffin Books, Penguin Random House India Pvt. Ltd

This edition published in 2024 by Hachette India
(Registered name: Hachette Book Publishing India Pvt. Ltd)
An Hachette UK company
www.hachetteindia.com

1

Box frames by Sharanya Kunnath

ISBN 978-93-5731-746-7

Hachette Book Publishing India Pvt. Ltd
4th & 5th Floors, Corporate Centre
Plot No. 94, Sector 44, Gurugram – 122003, India

Typeset by Manmohan Kumar, Delhi

Printed and bound in India
by Manipal Technologies Limited

FSC www.fsc.org
MIX
Paper | Supporting responsible forestry
FSC™ C043100

CONTENTS

HOW MANY MEDICAL IDEAS CAN YOU SPOT ON THE COVER?

1. Leonardo da Vinci's Vitruvian Man (Idea 6 –Anatomy); **2.** Human heart (Idea 7 – Circulatory system; Idea 22 – Organ transplants); **3.** Stethoscope (Idea 12); **4.** Mosquito (Idea 19 – Malaria transmission); **5.** Leech (Idea 1 – Ancient treatments for disease); **6.** DNA double helix (Idea 25 – Genetics); 7. Medical syringe* (Idea 11 – Vaccination); **8.** Florence Nightingale (Idea 16 – Nursing); **9.** Capsules** (Idea 21 – Antibiotics); **10.** Microscope (Idea 8 – Microorganisms); **11.** Bacteria (Idea 17 – Louis Pasteur and the germ theory of disease); **12.** Caduceus (Idea 4 – Medical symbols); **13.** Mortar and pestle (Idea 2 – Ayurveda)
PS: Did you spot something we didn't?

** Although the ancients knew about how 'injection' worked, from observing how venom was delivered via snake bites, the medical syringe as we know it today was not developed or used for vaccination until the 19th century.*
*** As for capsules, which have accurate dosages of medication 'encapsulated' inside a gelatin shell, they are considered the most effective form of oral medication and were patented in 1847, well before antibiotics were discovered.*

I DON'T WANT TO BE A DOCTOR. WHY SHOULD I READ THIS BOOK?

It isn't the funnest thing in the world to be ill, of course, but there are always compensations. The biggest, fattest silver lining for us who fall ill in the twenty-first century is, well, exactly that – we've fallen ill in the twenty-first century!

No, seriously. If you had lived even as recently as 200 years ago, you might have received some pretty bizarre, and/or very painful, treatments for your condition.

A physician or barber surgeon (more details given in the box on page x) may have:

- unleashed a whole army of leeches on you, so that they could suck out your 'bad blood' (be warned, this treatment hasn't fallen entirely out of favour, is reputed to have many benefits and may yet make a big comeback);
- drilled a hole into your skull, via a procedure called trepanning, to 'let the evil spirits out' (not even kidding;

also, just FYI, to spare you some really scary nightmares, this procedure isn't life-threatening);

- amputated a limb because it was infected – *without using anaesthesia* (because an effective mixture for numbing pain that didn't send the patient into fatal shock hadn't yet been tested – *ouch*!) and while using surgical instruments that looked more like medieval torture devices than anything else (maybe that was part of the strategy – patients probably passed out from sheer terror the moment they caught sight of the instrument, thus precluding the need for any other kind of knockout drug);
- wrapped you up like a mummy, plunged you into an ice-cold bath and kept you there for hours at a time to treat your 'manic episodes', chained you up and restrained you in a straitjacket for days on end to 'prevent you from hurting yourself', or conducted a lobotomy on you (taken out bits of your brain that they believed to be responsible for madness) – all in an effort to cure you of your 'insanity', which was believed to be a result of 'demonic possession'.

Say whaaaa . . .?

Barber surgeon? Yes! In Europe, for a big part of the last thousand years, barbers doubled as 'surgeons', simply because they were skilled at using sharp tools. Uh-huh. Thank goodness butchers weren't given that honour.

Still, spare those poor physicians a thought. None of them did what they did because they were particularly mean or sadistic – all their treatments were done in good faith and came out of long-held (and as we know now, erroneous) beliefs about what made us ill. Hardly anyone back then understood any aspect of mental illness, and although the treatments have become far more humane now, and great progress has been made, we are still quite some way from truly understanding how – or how much! – the brain is related to the 'mind'. Physical illness, and how the body worked, was better understood, but treatments were often misguided simply because – get this! – until the 1880s, very few people in the world believed, or even suspected, that it was germs that caused disease!

Astounding as it sounds, so many things that we take for granted today about disease and treatment are very new developments in the history of humankind. What we know as 'modern medicine' is arguably the world's youngest science, and seen from that perspective, the massive strides it has made towards understanding and healing the human body (and mind) are nothing short of, um, mind-blowing. We are better-nourished, die far less often from infectious diseases and live way longer as a species today, almost entirely because of advances in modern medicine.

What are some of these eye-popping advances over the last two centuries? Well, among a great many other things, we have:

- almost entirely eradicated some terrible diseases – smallpox, measles, polio – and learnt how to isolate and control the spread of epidemics like cholera and plague, which used to wipe out entire populations in the past;

- extended the average lifespan of human beings to almost double of what it was 150 years ago. Yup, in 1880, the average life expectancy at birth was forty years; today it is closer to eighty. In India, the average life expectancy today is 66.9 years for a male and 69.9 years for a female.
- succeeded in cloning animals (And what is cloning? The process of creating an animal that is genetically identical to another in a 'non-traditional' way, i.e., without fusing sperm and egg. Can you imagine what this technology could do to help revive populations of creatures on the verge of extinction?);
- developed the ability to 3D-print body parts for transplants or replacements. In the future, this will eliminate the long and often fatal wait for organs (for those who need them), and help create hearing aids and prosthetic limbs to perfectly fit your individual ear shape and body type;
- learnt how to tweak things at the DNA level to prevent hereditary diseases from being carried forward instead of treating those diseases after they have showed up. Gene therapy, for that's the name of this still experimental game, has also had some early success in strengthening the immune system and reversing certain kinds of fatal cancers;
- started trials on exciting new technologies like the bionic eye, which consists of a camera that sits on the wearer's head and transmits information directly to their brain. The eye will not restore sight, but it will allow the blind person to lead a far more independent, efficient and productive life;

- begun work on a revolutionary alternative to sutures – glue! – to repair gashes and surgery incisions, inspired by – that's right – slugs! Scientists are now creating a stretchy, flexible, nontoxic, adhesive, using slug slime and algae, which they hope will be able to seal holes in babies' hearts without a single suture in the near future;

. . . and so on and on and on.

Ironically, it is because we live so much longer these days that we are dying from entirely new kinds of diseases. Bunched together as 'lifestyle diseases', they include diabetes, hypertension, cirrhosis of the liver, heart disease and cancer, none of which typically strike the young. Today, doctors and researchers spend far more time and effort managing these chronic conditions than eradicating disease.

This is all very well and very wonderful, but the glorious story of the great advances of the Golden Age of Modern Medicine (which, for the purposes of this book, we shall assume began around 1820) is far from complete. For at the epicentre of this dazzling, dizzying maelstrom, where so many things we once believed to be true about human health have been violently and irreversibly shaken and stirred, stands the true hero of the plot: the all-powerful, all-knowing healer-scientist-counsellor-rockstar-demigod – the hard-working, long-suffering doctor.

But wait! The picture is changing. Even as we watch, the legions of men and women who, through the millennia, have served and treated and healed humankind, and enjoyed in return its unending gratitude, love and respect, apart from gifts of sarees and sweets and farm-fresh vegetables and fruits and fish and fowl – not to forget home-cooked biryani – turn into a blur and disappear.

In their place appears the omnipresent, omnipotent, and omniscient Supreme Doctor – the only one, at least in most of the literate, connected world's opinion, who is truly worthy of the title. And why not? After all, the Supreme Doctor works harder than any other doctor (he's available 24/7, 365 days a year – can your doctor do that?), knows more than anyone else in the world about the most minute symptoms of all manner of fatal diseases (sure, many of them are also the symptoms of non-fatal diseases, but so what?), gives you a whole plethora of drug cocktails to choose from to treat yourself (while informing you of every obscure side effect of each of them, never mind that those side effects have only so far been known to affect one person in 1.2 million – hey, he does his homework!) and recommends a whole battery of tests and procedures to eliminate a long list of possible conditions, vitamin deficiencies, hormonal imbalances, allergies and, most importantly, fatal diseases that you might be harbouring.

His name, of course, is Dr Google.

As you can imagine, most real doctors fervently wish Dr Google would be exiled to Siberia, allowing them get on with their job of healing people. Unfortunately, our dear Supreme Doctor is here to stay.

Fortunately, however, whatever the superpowers of Dr Google may be, we can never substitute the calm, reassuring face of a doctor who has listened to your own particular litany of pain and suffering (and read between the lines), examined you thoroughly (bringing to bear all their years of knowledge and training and experience and intuition and instinct and understanding of human psychology), followed trails, picked up clues, cut through the maze of red herrings on the way and, acting like Sherlock Holmes and Doctor House rolled into one, figured out – or, at the very least, made a calculated, intelligent guess about – how to make you better.

This book is a celebration of doctors like these through the ages, and a tribute to those men and women from entirely unrelated professions, whose vast curiosity fuelled the innovations, inventions and discoveries that have made – and are continuing to make – modern medicine. It contains twenty-five stories – that aren't always stories – about some truly extraordinary people and ideas that helped in small or spectacular ways to irrevocably alter the old ways of doing things, and allowed us to live longer, more disease-free and more pain-free lives.

And that is one big reason to read this book.

But are we truly 'healthier' as a species? Are we 'fitter'? These are difficult questions, because the very concept of what health is, and the understanding of what makes a person 'whole', has changed so much over the centuries. Does 'good health' simply mean being free of physical disease? Is a long life aided by drugs and procedures and artificial implants really as glorious as it is made out to be? Which is better – having an army of specialists, each of whom knows intimately one organ in the body, attending to you, or being examined by a general physician who knows you, your family and your medical history intimately? Is the human obsession with immortality, which leads pharmaceutical companies to put far more money into research on 'anti-ageing' supplements than cheaper life-saving drugs, something that must be encouraged?

Most importantly, did our ancestors, who believed that good health was all about overall balance and moderation – in food, lifestyle, work, emotions, opinions, behaviour – have the right idea all along? Is it the yoking of mind, body and spirit into a harmonious whole that leads to true well-being?

Reading this book, which is an info-packed romp through 2.500 years of human history, development and thought in the field of health and healing, will also make you wonder about questions like these, which are bound to engage you at some point, whether or not you want to be a doctor yourself. Ta-daa! There's your second good reason to plunge in.

That's not even the half of it, though – the book will also equip you with a whole new arsenal of insanely interesting trivia to impress your adults or win quizzes with. More importantly, it will leave you in complete awe of the human capacity for inquiry, innovation and compassion, and awash in admiration at the indomitable human spirit.

Ready to be gobsmacked, entertained and inspired?

Read on!

SECTION 1: 1600 BCE–200 CE

IF MODERN MEDICINE IS ONLY 200 YEARS OLD, HOW THE HECK DID SICK PEOPLE GET BETTER 2,000 YEARS AGO?

Okay, whatever the previous chapter has led you to believe, the truth is that it wasn't all gloom and doom back in 1 CE. In fact, medicine and surgery had developed to quite a degree in many ancient civilizations, and – here's the coolest part – in the inter-civilizational Medical Olympics (if such a thing had existed) India would have been tough to beat on many counts: most advanced surgical procedures, most effective plant cures, best immunity-building herbal supplements . . .

Let's take a quick tour of some explosive ideas in medicine from a very long time ago, shall we? The coolest part? They've endured – to this day!

IDEA 1

A DOCTOR IS, UM, QUITE A LOT MORE THAN A DOCTOR

The First Healers: Priests and Witches, Shamans and Sorcerers

In the earliest civilizations, across the board, while the piddling stuff like colds and constipation were considered unavoidable annoyances that could be treated with ointments, poultices and potions, serious diseases and fatal conditions were seen to be the work of either a malevolent devil or an angry god. No wonder then, that prayers and chants and all kinds of involved rituals were considered part and parcel of the healing process. No wonder also, that whenever one was in distress, whether physically, mentally or emotionally, people turned to someone who knew (or was believed to know) the right prayers (a priest), could cast the right spells (a witch), could communicate with the spirit world and ask for favours (a shaman) or was powerful enough to enslave spirits and make them do their bidding (a sorcerer).

Considering this from the safe perch of twenty-first-century science (which, if you think about it, is just as shaky a perch as any other), it is easy to dismiss these ancient healers as frauds and their treatments as quackery. But if that were true, how did all these healers not only survive but also thrive through the ages, well into our own century? Well, maybe, just maybe, because their methods actually worked (and everyone knows there's no better advertisement for a healer than word of mouth)!

Seriously? Prayers and spells and spirits can cure disease?

Look at it this way: clearly, that was not all there was to it. The men and women involved in the business of healing in ancient times were as much doctors as:

- Scientists, who studied the innards of dead animals, dissected human cadavers, examined skeletons (this meant they usually had a couple of human skulls lying about the house or sitting in their *jholas*, which scared people silly) and more such unsavoury stuff, thus, getting a basic understanding of human anatomy, the ways in which disease damaged the body and how the body healed itself. They also keenly observed the onset and development of different diseases in their patients, experimenting with various treatments at every stage, until they eventually figured out the most effective ways to reverse or arrest some of those diseases.
- Botanists, who, partly by observing which plants animals regularly ate, which they chose to eat when they were

ill and which they gave a wide berth to, and partly by experimenting on themselves, figured out which plants were edible, which ones had healing powers, and which were poisonous. They then used that knowledge to make people better (and also, occasionally, to make them ill).

- Expert psychologists, who realized that treating an illness of the body not only involved treating the body, but also the mind and spirit of the sick person, and often cured people simply by providing a sympathetic ear, a loud 'demon-exorcizing' dance designed to impress the daylights out of the patient and make them believe they were now free of the pestilence, or a draught that had nothing more healing in it than a generous pinch of sugar.
- Detectives, who made it their business to know exactly what was going on in the lives of every single person in their communities, the better to diagnose an illness and cure it. (Let's say A has made a serious enemy of B by saying awful things about him to the village chief. A does not know that B has found out about his treachery, but the healer knows B is fuming. Could A's illness, he wonders, be a result of B having poisoned him last night at dinner?)
- All the above. If you think about it, to this day, the best doctors take their fundamental cues from the ancients – they are the ones able to combine the curious, inquiring mind of a scientist with the ear and heart of a counsellor and the dog-with-a-bone dedication of a detective.

And that's a wonderful thing, because whatever those early healers knew or did not know about the science of healing, they were certainly experts at the *art* of healing.

In God(s) We Trust

The ancients believed that it wasn't just humans who fell ill or got mortally wounded, the gods did too. And it was the physicians of the gods that humans called upon when they found themselves under the weather. Here's a quick round-up of divine healers from across cultures:

- In ancient India, circa 1500 BCE, it was Rudra the Roarer, the god of the storm and the hunt, who was believed to be the great healer. His arsenal of pills and potions earned him the title Vaidyanatha, lord of doctors.
- The Ashwini twins (or the Ashvins) were also believed to be the doctors of the gods, the older twin being the god of health and the younger the god of medicine. The sons of the sun and the clouds, these two – usually depicted as horsemen (or horse-headed men) – have parallels in other mythologies as well. In Greek and Roman mythology, they find a match in the divine twin horsemen Castor and Pollux. Although they have nothing to do with medicine or the sun, Castor and Pollux, like the two stars of the Ashwini constellation, still occupy a place in the night sky as the zodiac constellation called . . . that's right, Gemini!
- In more recent times (circa 500 BCE), a new god of healing joined the Ashvins. This one is believed to have emerged from the cosmic ocean when it was being churned by the gods and demons, bearing a pot of amrit, the elixir of immortality. And since the elixir of immortality is surely the healing potion to beat all healing potions, Dhanvantari

(for that was the god's name) instantly got elevated to the patron god of healing and Ayurveda.

Now, here's the interesting part: in his four arms, Dhanvantari, who is reckoned to be an avatar of Vishnu, traditionally holds a conch, a chakra, the famous pot of amrit, and – hold your

Dhanvantari

breath – a *jalauka*, which is Sanskrit for 'leech'! The next time you are about to diss leech therapy, tread carefully – these little guys count the gods among their fans.

- In Roman mythology, Apollo the sun god doubled as the god of healing. In Greek mythology, it was his son Asclepius who was cast in the role. With Asclepius, the whole healing thing was clearly a family business – his daughters were Hygieia (the goddess of sanitation and cleanliness), Iaso (the goddess of recuperation), Aceso (the goddess of the healing process), Aglaea (the goddess of the glow of good health) and Panacea (the goddess of universal remedy).

- Ancient Egyptians revered the warrior goddess Sekhmet as the divine healer. Sekhmet, who was depicted as a lioness, the fiercest hunter known to the Egyptians, was also the protector of the pharaohs and the one who led them into battle. Not to be outdone in the gender-equality stakes, the Mesopotamians had their own goddess of healing – Anahita.

IDEA 2

PREVENTION IS BETTER THAN CURE

Disease Is Not Heaven-sent Punishment, Yo! You Bring It upon Yourself!

Seriously? *That* was a revolutionary idea? That prevention is better than cure? Yes! You see, if you believed that you got sick not because of anything you did wrong (or could have done better) but because a sadistic demon had decided to curse you, you also believed, clearly, that you could not prevent it from happening (except perhaps by giving someone a lot of money to make you a talisman or chant you some spells). That's why, for thousands of years, across the world, healers focused only on the so-called 'cure'.

Except for our bright boys of Ayurveda (What's Ayurveda? Find out in the box at the end of this chapter), who were among the first in the world to insist that many diseases could be prevented simply by making sure that one's lifestyle was 'aligned with Nature'.

It was these ancient rationalists who made the mind-blowing (if only because they went so far against the general belief system) declarations that (1) the causes of disease were earthly ones (all the way over in Greece, Hippocrates of Kos was saying similar things, but more about him on page 30), and (2) it was only by a keen examination of the patient – how their face looked, how their skin felt to the touch, how their senses reacted to stimuli and so on – that a doctor could accurately diagnose the illness, before prescribing the proper treatment.

The specific text that talked about all this, in circa 300 BCE (or 100 years before that, or 200 years after – it's insanely hard to lock these ancient texts down to a particular date, or even to a particular century), and set the foundation of all Ayurveda, was the 120-chapter-long *Charaka Samhita* (CS). The person believed to have composed it is the great physician of old, Charaka, often referred to as the Indian Father of Medicine.

Educated at the university of Takshashila (today in Pakistan), Charaka is credited for contributions to the understanding of human anatomy (How many bones are there in the human body? What are the different organs? How are they positioned in relation to each other?), physiology (How do the different systems inside the body work? What happens during digestion? How is the air that is breathed in distributed to every part of the body?), embryology (How does a baby develop in the womb?) and more.

Charaka the physician

Some experts, who have studied the text, believe there wasn't one Charaka, but several (*charaka* is Sanskrit for wanderer). These charakas, they say, were scholars who had chosen to make the science of healing their specialty, and went from village to village using their extensive knowledge of pathology (the causes of disease), clinical examination, diagnosis, and medicinal herbs and minerals to make sick people better.

Charaka's count for the number of bones in the human body was 360, whereas modern medicine has it at 206. How come? Was Charaka pulling his numbers out of a hat, then? Not at all. It was just that he chose to count each of the teeth (and teeth sockets), all the fingernails and toenails (and their corresponding nail beds), pieces of cartilage (which he classified as *taruna asthi*, or 'tender bones') and more, as individual 'bones'.

What exactly is the CS's take on a good, disease-free life? If, says the *Samhita*, you are good about (1) eating recommended foods (which would be different for different regions in specific seasons), (2) washing and cleaning your body regularly (not just the outside – bathe, bathe, bathe! – but also the inside – nose, ears, mouth, fingernails, respiratory passages, digestive tubes), (3) keeping your body strong and supple (with yoga and massage), and (4) following the recommendations on how much, and when, you must rest (which would change depending on the season) – you will be less likely to catch disease. Simple. The remarkable thing is how modern the whole thing sounds, for today's doctors and nutritionists would tell you the same things, using these terms: (1) eat fresh, local and seasonal foods, (2) maintain strict personal hygiene, (3) exercise regularly, and (4) get plenty of sleep. See?

Oh, and the CS has a great deal to say about the qualities of an ideal medical student as well. 'He,' it begins (feel free to substitute that gendered pronoun with 'she', or anything else, and forgive the charakas for not being inclusive – this was written over 2,000 years ago, when women did not train to be doctors, more's the pity), 'should be of a mild disposition, noble by nature, never mean in his acts, free from pride, of strong memory and liberal mind, one who is devoted to truth and likes solitude, of thoughtful disposition, free from anger, of excellent character, compassionate, one fond of study, devoted to both theory and practice, who seeks the good of all creatures.' (*Charaka Samhita*, Book 83). Whoa! Tall order! But hey, no one said it was easy being a doctor, then or now.

Right, back to our core idea: prevention is better than cure. Remarkably, even after the *Charaka Samhita* had put that idea down so clearly, it would be over 1,500 years before that idea was revisited with any rigour. When it was, it led to the explosive idea of vaccination as a way to prevent disease, but how that came about is an entirely different and utterly fascinating story, and one that we will explore later in the book (page 114).

The Science of Medicine? Naah, We Call It the Science of Life

> 'He who hath store of herbs at hand, assembled like kings amid a crowd of men – Physician is that sage's name, fiendslayer, chaser of disease.'
>
> *Rig Veda*, 10.97.6,
> from the translation by Ralph T.H. Griffith

Among the most ancient texts of India, the Vedas, is one called the Atharva Veda. Unlike the other three Vedas, which mainly comprise songs of praise to the gods, a large chunk of the Atharva consists of magic charms and incantations for all kinds of wonderful – and sneaky – things: warding off rivals, keeping a soldier safe at war, putting a crying baby to sleep and, of course, healing illness! It's a veritable book of spells! What's more, it contains actual recipes for medicines – pastes, potions, unguents, ointments, poultices and more.

It's from these ancient fact sheets of healing herbs, roots, leaves, seeds, metals and minerals that the Indian science of healing, Ayurveda, emerged over 2,000 years ago.

Ayurveda clearly has something going for it – despite all the progress modern medicine has made, this ancient science continues to remain popular in the land of its birth. In the twenty-first century, as mistrust of the potent chemical mixtures in modern pharmaceutical drugs has skyrocketed, it has even seen a huge resurgence not just in India but globally.

— āyurveda —

The five elements of Ayurveda – earth, water, fire, wind, space

So, what is Ayurveda all about? What is its approach to sickness and healing? Here's a quick 101.

Let's start with the word itself. Knowing that the word *veda* means knowledge, can you guess what Ayurveda could mean? The knowledge of disease? The knowledge of medicine? The knowledge of healing? None of the above! *Ayur* comes from *ayu*, which simply means 'life', so Ayurveda simply means 'the knowledge, or the science, of life itself'! So much more holistic- and hopeful-sounding than 'the science of disease', don't you think?

Like other ancient medical systems, Ayurveda believes that the five elements that make up the universe – air, fire, earth, water, space – are the exact same elements that make up the human body. While ancient Greek and Roman systems of medicine believed that the body was filled with four humours or bodily fluids, Ayurveda believes it is made up of three kinds of doshas or 'energies' mapped to the elements: vatha (the moving energy of air and the space in which it moves), pitta (the consuming energy of fire) and kapha (the binding energy of earth and water). Just like the Greeks believed that an imbalance of the humours led to illness, Ayurveda believes that imbalance of the doshas leads to disease.

According to Ayurveda, each person is born with a different proportion of each dosha, and it is the maintenance of that balance that is vital; there is no 'ideal' proportion. And, therefore, the treatment also has to be customized to each person (three different people's headaches cannot be cured by prescribing the same aspirin to all three). The treatment also has to be 'holistic', i.e., it should attempt to heal not just the body but also the mind and spirit. Ayurvedic doctors, therefore, will not only prescribe oral medication but also a diet that will ensure good digestion and excretion, along with a strict regimen of yoga and exercise, sunlight and air, and massage (to open 'blocked channels' in the body, which are also thought to lead to dosha imbalance) and meditation (to calm the mind and spirit).

All of which makes a lot of sense. Medical experts warn, however, that far too many Ayurvedic drugs and mixtures in the market today have never had their contents scientifically tested. Of those which have, they say, some have been shown to contain high levels of heavy metals like lead, mercury and arsenic, which modern science believes are dangerous for the body. Ayurvedic texts – and doctors – counter that claim by insisting that it is in how it is *processed*, and *how much* of it is used, that a metal or mineral – or indeed, plant product – becomes toxic. They claim that the ingredients in Ayurvedic medicine have all been processed in a way that they heal, not harm, the body. The jury is still out on that one.

Be that as it may, there's no reason why you shouldn't take the core advice of Ayurveda for good health: eat right, poop regularly, sleep early, wake up at dawn, do some yoga in the early sunlight, pause several times a day to take deep and long breaths, be disciplined about exercise, spend some quiet reflective time with yourself each day and, yes, whenever you have the time, get a massage!

IDEA 3

ONLY ONE WAY TO FIND OUT WHAT A HUMAN BODY CONTAINS – OPEN IT UP AND SEE!

The Birth of Anatomy

Once again, this idea seems like a no-brainer today, and no surprise. After all, we are more than a couple of centuries into the so-called Age of Enlightenment, or the Age of Reason, which brought scientific thinking – observation, experiment, analysis, hypothesis, proof – centre stage in eighteenth-century Europe.

It wasn't always that way. In ancient Egypt, even though the high priests and embalmers had figured out how to extract organs from the dead pharaoh's body (it was important to do this to stop decomposition) before stuffing it with medicated rags and linens, they did not actually ever open the body up entirely. How come? Wouldn't that have been a simpler way to clean up the pharaoh's innards? Sure, but remember that the ancient Egyptians believed their kings and queens would wake up and lord it about in the afterlife as well! Surely, then, they would need their physical bodies to be in tip-top condition.

How did they actually extract the organs, then? Evisceration, or the emptying of the abdominal and chest cavities by removing organs like the liver, lungs, stomach and intestines, was carried out through a small incision made on the left side of the body. These individual organs were washed out with chemicals and oils and placed in separate Canopic jars by the side of the mummified body of the king, so that they could find their way back into it once he 'woke up'.

Brain removal, on the other hand, was done in this (extremely gross) way: first, a hook-shaped tool was used to break through the bone of the skull; second, another tool was used to blend the brain tissue into mush; and last, that mush was drained out through the nose.

(Fun fact: the first people to identify the brain and give it a name were the Egyptians – it seems that their word for 'brain' is the first word for 'brain' in any language!) The heart was not removed from the body, because the Egyptians believed that it (and not the brain) was the seat of thought and intellect, and reckoned their royals would need it to be in place if they needed to function with any authority in the afterlife.

So, although the Egyptians knew a lot about human anatomy – they had not only identified many human organs but also figured out that the heart was the meeting point of a number of tubes and channels that transported fluid (except they thought the fluid was not just blood but also urine and tears!) – they didn't know what the inside of the body looked like. We know this from a famous document called the Edwin

Smith Surgical Papyrus, which dates back to – hold your breath – 1600 BCE!

This scroll describes forty-eight cases of bodily injury – fractures, wounds, dislocations, tumours – starting from the head and going downwards, and includes information, in each case, about how the patient is to be examined, what the likely diagnosis is and a calculated guess as to whether the injury will heal and the patient will survive (this is called prognosis). According to the document, the prognosis helps the physician classify the injury into one of three types: 'an ailment which I will treat' (i.e., which I'm fairly certain I can cure); 'an ailment with which I will contend' (i.e., which I will try my luck with); and 'an ailment not to be treated' (i.e., uh-oh). For injuries that did not fall into the 'uh-oh' category, the papyrus also includes detailed instructions on how they are to be treated.

Treatments include sutures (for closing up open wounds), bandaging, splints, honey as a cure for infection and pressing down with raw meat to stop bleeding. The papyrus also records, in detail, conditions such as paralysis (including which side of the body is affected when the wound is on which side of the head), spinal injuries (also noting which motor movements are affected because of trauma to which part of the spine) and more. In short, it demonstrates a far deeper and greater understanding of injury and treatment than the writings of the Greek scholar Hippocrates, who is considered the Western Father of Medicine. The one big drawback in the Egyptian system? Yup, these guys had never opened up a human body and examined it!

***

Cut to (unfortunate, unintended pun) a thousand years later, to the ancient Greeks and the ancient Indians. First off, let's find out what the Greeks were getting up to.

Between 500 BCE and 200 CE, the Greeks figured out a bunch of things about human anatomy. They understood the human skeleton well, and also how the muscles, bones and joints worked together. They gave the optic nerve (the nerve that connects the eyeball to the brain) its name and began to get a glimmering of what the function of the kidneys was. They discovered that our ears were connected to our respiratory system via a canal they called the Eustachius (We still call it the Eustachian canal. In fact, most of the Western medical terminology in use today comes to us from the ancient Greeks.). They began to understand the circulatory system a little better (even though they believed the heart was the central organ of not just the body's blood distribution system but also its air distribution system) and differentiated between arteries (the tubes that carry blood away from the heart) and veins (the tubes that bring blood back to the heart).

Around 400 BCE, the Greek thinker, philosopher and scientist Aristotle, in a bid to create a more scientific and empirical (something that can be verified by observation or experience, as opposed to pure theory and conjecture) system of understanding human anatomy, began to dissect animals in a methodical way and, willy-nilly, founded a new branch of science that is today called comparative anatomy. (Comparative anatomy is the study of the similarities and differences in the anatomies of different species; as you can guess, this is a very important part of evolutionary biology.)

But the Greeks had still not opened up a real human body!

Until, early in the third century BCE, the emperor Ptolemy (who took over the Greek Empire after the death of his friend Alexander the Great, and went on to conquer Egypt, which his dynasty would then rule for 300 years) finally gave delighted Greek physicians, who had been begging for it a long time, the permission to perform dissections on humans (only dead ones, mind!), and handed over to them the bodies of executed criminals to mess about with.

Herophilos, a Greek physician today hailed as the founder of anatomy, was the biggest gainer of this royal decree. Having moved to Alexandria in Egypt as a child for his education, he went on to become one of its most famous residents, performing dissections at the world's first college of anatomy there. His scientific approach led him to fresh and startling insights about how the human body worked. It was he, for instance, who first declared that the brain was the 'seat of intelligence', thus overturning an age-old theory from Egyptian times that it was from the heart that all thought was generated.

Noticing how the blood moved in the arteries and veins, he figured out a way to measure the pulse, and used that information to diagnose if a person was healthy or not. He was also something of an expert on the female reproductive system and wrote a book on it to help midwives understand the processes of pregnancy and childbirth.

Yup, Herophilos was quite the hero, except that in some ways, he really, um, wasn't. In later years, his contemporaries would accuse him of gaining his revolutionary insights from performing dissections on – grab your jaw before it hits the ground – *people who were alive*, the better to be able to observe the workings of the various body systems!

These live dissections (the correct word for which is vivisections) were performed only on condemned criminals, no less than 600 of them if his fellows are to be believed! Herophilos's logic was that since they were all going to be executed anyway, he might as well use them for the furthering of human knowledge (and if that noble enterprise meant their deaths were hastened, well . . . *shrug*.)

Charming chap, that Herophilos.

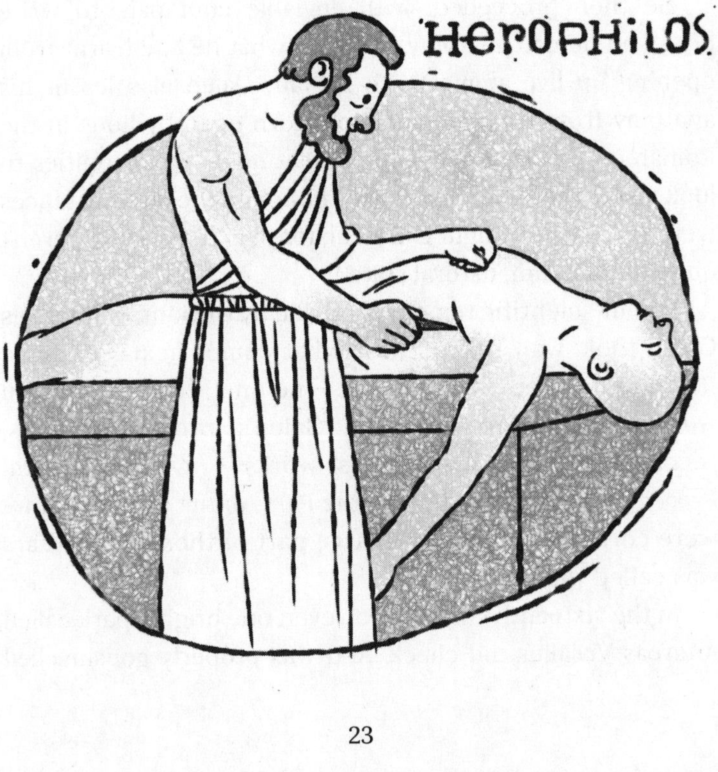

And now to the last great anatomist of ancient Greece, Galen, who lived in the second century CE. Galen compiled all the different anatomical texts available at the time, and did his own independent research as well, except, because the dissection of human bodies was absolutely forbidden by the Roman religion (Greece was now part of the Roman Empire), he performed dissections and vivisections on animals instead. Reckoning that animal anatomies – particularly those of Barbary macaques, which are more closely related to apes than to many other monkeys – could not be very different from human ones.

He then proceeded, with enviable chutzpah, to write books on human anatomy, applying what he had learnt from opening up live animals! (To be fair, Galen also learnt his anatomy from treating gladiators torn open by lions in the Roman circus. That gave him a great many opportunities to look inside the abdominal cavity, although the circumstances weren't what you might call ideal; for one, the organs weren't quite in their, um, natural state.)

If your scientific temper is rattled by the kind of liberties Galen took, wait till you hear what comes next. For some 1,300 years after Galen, no one – no one! – in the Western world thought to check if Galen's pronouncements, recorded in his two famous works – *On Anatomical Procedure* and *On the Uses of the Parts of the Body of Man* – were correct! No wonder a large part of those 1,300 years was called the Dark Ages!

In the sixteenth century, however, one bright spark called Andreas Vesalius did check. And was properly gobsmacked by what he found. To find out more, go to 'Idea 6: Maybe, just maybe, that old Greek Galen got it all wrong' on page 51.

***

Moving on. To India, this time, and to 200 years before the Greek story (i.e., circa 600 BCE).

Remember Charaka, the rock-star physician of ye olde Takshashila? (If you've forgotten him already, shame. Now go refresh your memory on page 10.) Well, a couple of centuries before he arrived on the scene, and over a thousand kilometres from Takshashila, a physician called Sushruta was busy compiling the other trailblazing work on Ayurveda, the *Sushruta Samhita* (SS), in the fabled city of Kashi (aka Varanasi). As with the *Charaka Samhita*, the SS is also believed to have been composed over several centuries, with different people adding their own expertise to it along the way. The SS deals with similar subjects as the CS, and often has similar views – including the belief that good hygiene and regular exercise can help keep illness at bay – but what makes it different is the number of details it includes on surgical procedures (along with the names and descriptions of a variety of surgical instruments). That's why, while Charaka is celebrated as the Indian Father of Medicine, Sushruta is hailed as the Indian Father of Surgery.

What kinds of surgeries? Well, cataract surgery, for one! Yes, over 2,000 years ago, surgeons in India had figured out how to help people whose vision had become cloudy or non-existent (because the lenses in their eyes had become opaque) to regain a large part of their vision, making them the pioneers in this field! They also knew, among a hundred other things, how to extract teeth, perform amputations, extract kidney stones, remove tonsils, and suture wounds, using wine and the heady fumes of certain kinds of incense to sedate the patient somewhat. The SS even describes a procedure for rhinoplasty – reconstruction of a damaged or destroyed nose – and otoplasty – reconstruction of a ripped or torn earlobe, or construction of an entirely new earlobe in people born without it – using flaps of skin from another part of the body, usually the cheek. This makes Sushruta the world's first plastic surgeon.

Now, where did Sushruta stand on dissection? Well, he was quite the trailblazer there – he insisted that every student of surgery dissect human bodies to teach himself anatomy before he ever attempted a surgery. He also suggested that his students practise their incisions on gourds and squashes that resembled different body parts, or fluid-filled leather bags and bladders of dead animals, to simulate the real thing.

But where did Sushruta and his students find cadavers to work on? Many people in India cremated their dead, and the prevailing religious and social mores at the time forbade anyone from desecrating the body of a dead person by putting a knife to it.

Like every good Indian, however, Sushruta found a workaround. In the SS, he details the method of preparing a body for dissection as follows:

1. Choose the body you are going to dissect with care. Make sure the man or woman has not died of poisoning or suffered from a chronic disease, and is less than 100

years old (People lived that long in old-timey India? Well, enough of them seem to have done, or Sushruta would not have put that down as a rule.).

2. Once a suitable body has been found, wrap it in grass and bark, lay it inside a cage and lower the whole body into a gently flowing river, making sure to choose a dark part of the river, away from sunlight.
3. After seven nights, pull the cage out of the river. Now extract the body, which has by now partly decomposed, and begin to brush away the skin with brooms made of rough – but also fragrant, and you can guess why – roots (Look, Ma! No knife!).
4. Voila! The first layer of the body's innards is now ready to be observed.
5. Once you have poked about inside (NOT using a knife, mind!), and made your drawings and notes, press your broom into service again, to reveal more and more layers.

Smart, huh? Also, it appears there was no religious injunction against cutting open bodies of children under two, so Sushruta and his students also peeked into a lot of very young humans. Some scholars think that this is the reason the count of human bones according to the SS is 300 as against the modern count of 206 – babies are actually born with 300 bones, some of which fuse with each other to give us the adult count of 206!

Be that as it may, the fact that Sushruta believed that a deep understanding of anatomy was paramount for an aspiring surgeon, and that he found such a clever way to further human knowledge without contravening any social laws, makes him a great candidate for the Father of Anatomy title, don't you think?

Cataract Surgery, Ye Olde Desi-Style

What is a cataract, with reference to the eye? In simple terms, it is a clouding of the lens. The lens, as you probably know, is positioned between the pupil – the opening in the eyeball through which light enters our eyes – and the retina – the membrane or 'screen' lining the inside of the back of the eyeball. The retina is chock-full of photoreceptors, or light-capturing cells, which intercept the light entering through the pupil and send it to the brain, where it is interpreted as images of what we see. A cloudy or opaque lens, therefore, means an almost total loss of vision! Clearly, this vision loss cannot be corrected using glasses or contact lenses.

What is to be done, then? These days, cataract surgery involves removing the faulty natural lens and replacing it with an artificial lens, which restores full and clear vision to the sufferer. In Sushruta's time, since artificial lenses had not been developed, surgeons in India used a technique called couching. Inserting a specially designed instrument into the eye, they simply pushed the faulty lens out of the line of the pupil and retina and into the vitreous humour – the gel-like substance that fills the eyeball and helps it keep its shape.

Of course, the patient would not be able to see perfectly after such a surgery – the image would not be so sharp anymore because the lens, which focuses the light, was missing now – but since the light entering their eye was now

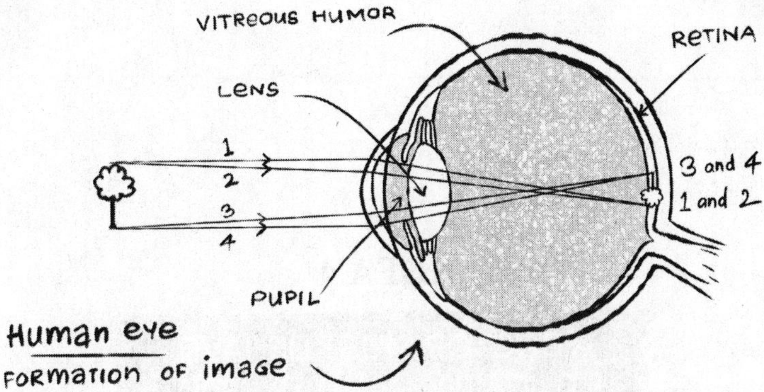

reaching the retina, they certainly would be able to make out colours and shapes, and differentiate between light and darkness, be able to move around independently and live a more or less full life. Which, you will agree, was way better than being completely blind.

Given that, even today, doctors who help restore vision are considered demigods, is there any wonder Sushruta was so highly revered back then?

IDEA 4

A DOCTOR MUST BEHAVE ETHICALLY – AND, BY GOD, HE MUST SWEAR TO IT!

An Introduction to Some Choice Medical Oaths

It's true! From ancient times and all the way to the present, newly minted doctors have been required to take an oath, promising to practise their science according to a strict code of ethics and good, moral behaviour. And the first person who comes to mind when we talk about a medical oath is the Greek physician Hippocrates of Kos, whose name has been immortalized in the Hippocratic Oath that doctors across the world take, even today, at their graduating ceremonies.

Hippocrates lived in the fifth century BCE and has long been regarded in the West as the Father of Medicine, but very little is known about him. His fame rests on a vast body of medical literature from ancient Greece called the Hippocratic Corpus, but most scholars agree that very little of it, if any, was composed by Hippocrates himself.

His real legacy, then? He was the first, in his part of the world, to consider medicine as a separate discipline and a separate profession, not an offshoot of religion or philosophy. Priests and philosophers had their place, said Hippocrates, but they *were* not, *should* not and *could* not be doctors.

Remarkably, many of the things he believed were very similar to what Sushruta and Charaka did: diseases are not the result of divine or demonic intervention, a good lifestyle of healthy eating and exercise can keep illness at bay, the body has the power to heal itself of many illnesses, and so on. And since Hippocrates could have been a contemporary of Sushruta's, many scholars have suggested that (1) the Indians borrowed their ideas from the very advanced Greeks, or (2) the Greeks borrowed their ideas from the very advanced Indians.

But on to the Hippocratic Oath. The text of the original, in this translation by W.H.S. Jones, goes as follows:

> I swear by Apollo Physician, by Asclepius, by Hygieia, by Panacea and by all the gods and goddesses, making them my witnesses, that I will carry out, according to my ability and judgement, this oath and this indenture.
>
> To hold my teacher in this art equal to my own parents; to make him partner in my livelihood; when he is in need of money to share mine with him; to consider his family as my own brothers, and to teach them this art, if they want to learn it, without fee or indenture; to impart precept, oral instruction and all other instruction to my own sons, the sons of my teacher and to indentured pupils who have taken the physician's oath, but to nobody else.

Hippocrates and his famous oath

I will use treatment to help the sick according to my ability and judgement, but never with a view to injury and wrongdoing. Neither will I administer a poison to anybody when asked to do so, nor will I suggest such a course. Similarly, I will not give to a woman a pessary to cause abortion. But I will keep pure and holy both my life and my art. I will not use the knife, not even, verily, on sufferers from stone [i.e., kidney stones], but I will give place to such as are craftsmen therein.

Into whatsoever houses I enter, I will enter to help the sick, and I will abstain from all intentional wrongdoing and harm, especially from abusing the bodies of man or woman, bond [i.e., a person in bondage, a slave] or free. And whatsoever I shall see or hear in the course of my profession,

> as well as outside my profession in my intercourse with men, if it be what should not be published abroad, I will never divulge, holding such things to be holy secrets.
>
> Now if I carry out this oath, and break it not, may I gain for ever reputation among all men for my life and for my art; but if I break it and forswear myself, may the opposite befall me.

What can we deduce from this oath? That even though Hippocrates believed that gods did not cause disease, he still considered the divine physicians necessary witnesses to the oath and hoped for their grace in the practice of his craft. That he believed that teachers should be held in the highest esteem, that he was firmly against abortion, that although he was most certainly not a surgeon ('I will not use the knife'), he was willing to allow a trained surgeon to intervene when needed, and that he considered it his sacred duty to keep his patients' medical, financial and domestic affairs confidential.

Great. Now here's something most people don't know – the *Charaka Samhita* also has its own, quite different, oath of initiation, and it is far more detailed – and, far more 'Indian' – than the Hippocratic Oath! Here it is, edited a little for size.

> The teacher should instruct the disciple in the presence of the sacred fire, Brahmanas [i.e., men of knowledge, priests] and physicians, saying:
>
> 'You shall lead the life of a celibate, grow your hair and beard, speak only the truth, eat no meat, eat only pure food, be free from envy and carry no arms.

There shall be nothing that you will not do at my bidding except hating the king, causing another's death, or committing an act of great unrighteousness or acts leading to calamity.

You shall act without arrogance, with care and attention and with undistracted mind, humility, constant reflection and ungrudging obedience.

If you desire success, wealth and fame as a physician and heaven after death, you shall pray for the welfare of all creatures, beginning with the cows and Brahmanas.

Day and night, however you may be occupied, you shall endeavour for the relief of patients with all your heart and soul.

You shall not desert or injure a patient for the sake of your life. You shall be modest in attire and appearance.

You shall treat no persons who are hated by the king or who are haters of the king or who are hated by the public or who are haters of the public. Similarly, you will not treat those who are wicked, and of miserable character and conduct, those who have not vindicated their honour, those who are on the point of death and women who are unattended by their husbands or guardians.

You will accept no offering of presents by a woman without the express instruction of her husband or guardian. While entering a patient's house, you shall always be accompanied by a man who is known to the patient and who has his permission to enter. You will have no other thought than that of being helpful to the patient.

You shall not make public the peculiar customs of the patient's household. Even knowing that the patient's span of life has come to its close, you will not mention it in the presence of the patient.

You shall not boast of your knowledge.

There is no limit at all to the science of life, Ayurveda. So, you should apply yourself to it with diligence. The entire world is the teacher to the intelligent and the foe to the unintelligent.

Knowing this, you should listen and act according to the words of instruction of even an unfriendly person, when his words are worthy and of a kind as to bring to you fame, long life, strength and prosperity.'

Thereafter the teacher should say this – 'Conduct yourself properly with the gods, sacred fire, Brahmanas, the guru, the aged, the scholars and the preceptors. If you have conducted yourself well with them, the precious stones, the grains and the gods become well disposed towards you. If you should conduct yourself otherwise, they become unfavourable to you.'

To the teacher that has spoken thus, the disciple should say, 'So be it.'

***

What can you take away from *this* oath? One, that it is exactly in line with the Vedic school of ancient Indian practices and beliefs: at every important ritual, the fire is the witness, cows and Brahmanas are to be held in high esteem, all creatures are to be considered equal, the *guru-shishya* relationship is the most sacred of all, the aged and the wise are to be respected, vegetarianism is recommended, one should never stop seeking knowledge... Two, that loyalty to the king was non-negotiable. Three, that a doctor must consider a patient's life more sacred than his own.

Right. Now, in both oaths, you may have noticed clauses that may be problematic, unscientific, religious, politically incorrect, or irrelevant now (for this reason, doctors in many countries use an 'updated' version of the Hippocratic Oath, which makes no mention of God; or a very different 'modern' oath, of which there are many). As an activity, why don't you formulate your own oath for doctors, borrowing the best from both of these and then adding what you feel is missing? Once you've done that, go and check out 'The Hippocratic Oath Updated' for Indian medical students on the website of the Indian Journal of Medical Ethics here: https://ijme.in/articles/the-hippocratic-oath-updated/?galley=html.

Two more questions to think about:

1. Do you think Indian medical students should consider taking an updated version of the *Charaka Samhita* Oath, instead of the Hippocratic Oath, given that both oaths are of similar vintage? Why or why not?
2. Do you think students of every other profession should also be made to take their own oath of ethical behaviour?

Two Rods Don't Make a Right

Remember Asclepius, the Greek god of medicine (If you don't, go back to page 6 to check out 'In God(s) We Trust')? Well, he carries a rod – a sort of walking stick, around which a snake is entwined. Now, if you're an observant, curious person, you've probably noticed that the symbol of medicine today – found on doctors' letterheads and hospitals and pharmaceutical company logos, particularly in the US – is a rod too, except this one has wings and has *two* snakes entwined around it. The correct name for this winged rod is caduceus – and this is the rod carried by the Greek messenger god Hermes, who

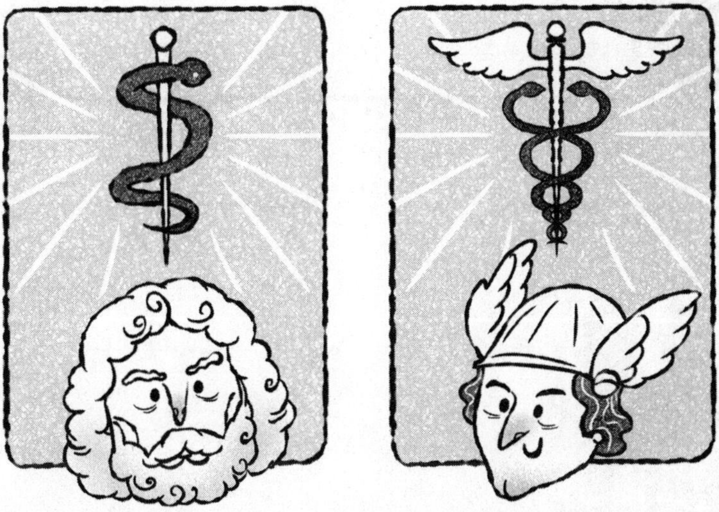

Asclepius and Hermes, with their respective snaky staffs

has nothing whatsoever to do with medicine. So how come this one became the symbol of modern medicine?

Actually, it was the rod of Asclepius – the one-snake rod – that was traditionally – and correctly – associated with medicine. Around the year 1851, however, someone high up in the design department of the US Army mixed the two rods up, and the caduceus began to appear on the uniforms of the staff at army hospitals. Since these hospitals were everywhere, and were government institutions to boot, that mistake was replicated over and over until the caduceus became the 'official' symbol of doctors in America. As America's global influence grew, so did the mistake. So much so, that if you saw the rod of Asclepius on your doctor's door today, you'd probably wonder where the other snake had got to.

SECTION 2: 200 CE–1700 CE

LEARNING, UNLEARNING, RELEARNING

Between the last great Greek anatomist Galen's death in 210 CE and the coming of age of the Schola Medica Salernitana, the world's first 'medical school', in Salerno, Italy, in the eleventh century, 800 years later, the world had changed quite dramatically.

While Western Europe descended, in the fifth century, into its 1,000-year-long Dark Ages, marked by little or no intellectual progress, the Near East and North Africa – Arabia, Tunisia, Syria, Persia, Baghdad – welded together, in the heat of religious fervour, into the Islamic Empire, came into their own, and great strides were made by their brightest and best in astronomy, optics, mathematics, art, architecture, engineering and – ta-da! – medicine.

How did power – political, economic, cultural and intellectual – shift so dramatically from the West to this part of the East during the first millennium, the period that saw two great world religions – Christianity and Islam – capture the human imagination?

It happened in stages. With the fall of the Western Roman Empire in the fifth century, the action moved first to the Gupta Empire in north India. A few centuries later (between the eighth and twelfth centuries), it shifted again, to the Rashtrakutas and Cholas in south and west India, and around the same time, to the glittering city of Baghdad (in today's Iraq), the capital of the new and happening Islamic Empire.

Under the Guptas flourished great astronomers and mathematicians like Aryabhata, who, among other things, declared that the earth spins on its axis and, like the other planets, goes round the sun. Also, the astronomer-astrologer Varahamihira, who described what actually happens during reflection (back-scattering of particles) and refraction (change in the direction of light as it passes from one medium to another of different density) of light. Their works were commented and built upon by mathematicians like Bhaskara I, who was the first to write numbers as figures – 1, 2, 3 and so on, up to 9 – and created what came to be called the Hindu decimal system. It had ten symbols including zero, and, again, it was Bhaskara who first represented zero as a circle. There was also Brahmagupta, who laid down a set of rules that specified how to calculate using the zero.

In the ninth century, the great mathematician Mahaviracharya refined Brahmagupta's work under the patronage of the Rashtrakuta kings of Karnataka, separating mathematics from astrology and writing the earliest Indian text devoted entirely to mathematics, the *Ganitasangraha.*

He is credited with giving names to geometrical concepts like the circle, semicircle, rhombus, isosceles triangle and equilateral triangle. In the same period, under the Chola kings of Tamil Nadu, great innovations were made in art (the famous Chola bronzes) and architecture (as seen in the spectacular Brihadeeshwara Temple in Thanjavur). The Cholas also influenced and impacted world trade hugely by connecting China (their trading partners in the East) with the Islamic world, centred at Baghdad (their trading partners in the West). In Gujarat, the great Indian metallurgist and alchemist Nagarjuna was composing an early treatise on the pharmaceutical branch of Ayurveda, Rasa Shastra, with recipes for sophisticated drugs for specific ailments.

Although the Arabs themselves always referred to the ten numerals as Hindu numerals (Hindu was a word the Persians used for the people of the land beyond the River Indus), Europeans, who were introduced to them by the Arabs around the ninth century, wrongly referred to them as Arabic numerals, and the name stuck.

By this time, however, the focus of the world's attention had shifted to glittering Baghdad. Let's travel there now, at the far end of the eighth century, for a ringside view of the period that would later be hailed as the Islamic Golden Age. The Golden Age would last 600 years, and the creative ferment it generated would bring about an explosion of new ideas in every field.

Historians date the beginning of the age specifically to the establishment of the House of Wisdom, an intellectual centre / university / spectacular library set up during the reign of the great caliph Harun al-Rashid, who ruled from 786 to 809 CE. Here it was, in the House of Wisdom, that the so-called Translation Movement (What was that? Check out Idea 5 on page 43 for more details) reached its full flowering.

One of the later scholars who benefited from the Translation Movement was a self-taught Persian polymath (this lovely word simply means someone who is curious about and has a great level of expertise in a vast variety of seemingly unrelated subjects) from Bukhara (in today's Uzbekistan). The medical encyclopaedia he completed in 1025 CE, *Al-Qanun f'it-Tibb* or The Canon of Medicine, was born out of his studies of the ancient Greek, Persian and Indian medical texts, and would go on to become the standard medical text across Europe and west Asia for the next 600 years. The name of this towering intellectual, respected equally by both the Eastern and Western worlds, was Ibn Sina.

Ibn Sina was called Avicenna by the Europeans, and that is the name more commonly used for him in most non-Arabic texts, so for the rest of this book, we will switch to Avicenna too.

IDEA 5

DON'T KNOW HOW TO PROCEED? GO BACK TO START!

How the Islamic Empire's Translation Movement Spurred a New Age in Medicine

Sure, the Greeks had done all that great work (not all of it correct, as we know now) on anatomy, physiology, medicine, and surgery well before the Common Era (CE) began, but over the first millennium CE, all those texts were gradually sidelined and quite forgotten in Europe. One of Avicenna's big achievements was introducing the great classical medical texts of Europe . . . back to the Europeans! How did Europe, specifically Western Europe, lose sight of all that wealth of classical knowledge?

Remember how, by the time Galen wrote his great works on anatomy in the second century, Greece was part of the Roman Empire? By 395 CE, the empire had become so vast and clunky and so difficult for one emperor to administer that two equal-status emperors were appointed to do it. One emperor would rule the western provinces, or the Western Roman Empire, of which Italy was a part, and the other would rule the eastern provinces, which included Greece.

When the Western Roman Empire fell in 476 CE to Germanic hordes, all the old Greek texts fell into disuse, not only because that's what usually happens in the aftermath of a terrible war, but also because very few people on the western side knew Greek well enough to read them.

More importantly, the new rulers in place either looked down their noses or actively hated everything that the old regime had produced, respected or loved. Within a few decades, Western Europe had slipped into the Dark Ages, a 1,000-year period of little or no cultural or scientific progress.

> The language barrier (which led to Western Europe's collective amnesia about the Greek texts) was also one of the main reasons why the ancient Sanskrit works of medicine and surgery did not become known around the world for so many centuries.

As for the Eastern Roman Empire, it continued to flourish from its capital in Constantinople (today's Istanbul) for another 1,000 years (called the Byzantine Empire, because Constantinople's old name was Byzantium). Classical Greek works continued to be studied here, and new developments in medicine and surgery were made. One of those developments was uroscopy – the practice of examining a patient's urine for blood, pus and colour – which became very important in Byzantine medicine as a way to diagnose disease. In the seventh century, the Byzantine physician Paul of Aegina wrote his *Medical Compendium in Seven Books*, which was a compilation of all the medical knowledge of the Western world. Some 300 years later, in what was probably a first, conjoined twins were surgically separated in Byzantium.

However, there was still a huge gap in knowledge – no one had yet made a study of the collective medical wisdoms of the East and West. That giant leap was made possible by what is today called the Translation Movement, which began in Arabia in the eighth century. Here's how that played out.

You probably know that Islam was founded by Muhammad the Prophet in Mecca, Arabia, in the early seventh century. After the Prophet's death in 632 CE, his political and religious successors, the Caliphs, continued to expand their territories as he had done, spreading the word of the Quran into the rest of the Middle East, northern Africa and Europe.

As the Islamic Empire grew, it absorbed into itself lands and peoples that spoke a variety of different languages – Persian, Syriac, Hebrew and more. The official language of the empire, however, remained Arabic.

It was a heady, exciting time for scholars of every stripe. Since the Quran placed great value on education and the acquiring of knowledge, they had the full encouragement and patronage of the Caliphs. As they met and interacted with fellow scholars from far-flung parts of the empire, there grew a great eagerness to learn from each other. The only

House of Wisdom – the great Abbasid Library

challenge was language – they could neither understand each other nor read each other's manuscripts!

And thus was born what we now call the Translation Movement, in the second half of the seventh century. The Syriacs, the only ones in the region who spoke Arabic and Greek fluently, were the first to jump in, and translations of classical Greek texts into Arabic began in right earnest. While they were at it, other translators who knew Persian or Sanskrit began translating classical works from Persia and India into Arabic as well.

The Translation Movement reached its peak under the Abbasid Caliph Harun al-Rashid, who established the great library in Baghdad called the House of Wisdom in the late eighth century. Every translated work, besides rare books and collections of Arabic and Persian poetry, found a place on its shelves, making it one of the greatest collections of human knowledge in the medieval world. In the next few centuries, building on this knowledge, Muslim scholars made great strides in every field of human development – astronomy, law, engineering, art, philosophy and, yes, medicine.

***

From the House of Wisdom, copies travelled to other great libraries across the East. One of those libraries was in our Avicenna's Bukhara, which, in the tenth century, was giving Baghdad a run for its money as the cultural capital of the Islamic world.

Avicenna was born in a village near Bukhara in 980 CE. (At this time, Bukhara was not part of the Islamic Caliphate; it was the capital of the Persian dynasty of the Samanids.) His brilliance shone through from his very childhood – by the age of ten, he had memorized the Quran; by fifteen, he had learnt Indian arithmetic from an Indian vegetable seller called Mahmoud Massi (no, seriously), read plenty of philosophy (struggling especially hard with Aristotle's works) and taught himself a few ways to treat the sick by observing wandering healers. At sixteen, he began to study medical theory, and was delighted to find that it was way easier to grasp than maths and metaphysics. By the age of eighteen, he was a fully qualified physician (eat your hearts out, modern-day medical students who take so much longer than two years to get there)!

With his very first job, he hit the jackpot – he was appointed physician to the emir (ruler), Nuh II. Almost immediately after, the emir fell dangerously ill, but made a full recovery under Avicenna's care. As a reward, the grateful emir threw open the royal library of the Samanids to the talented teenager. Delighted, Avicenna plunged into reading translated works on Indian, Persian, and Greek medicine. Unfortunately, the library burnt down soon after. A few years later, the Samanid dynasty itself came to an end. Avicenna was forced to move from place to place looking for the right job for his many talents, but there were great libraries everywhere he went, and he never lost an opportunity to educate himself.

A few years later, he began writing his groundbreaking work, *The Canon of Medicine*. Avicenna went on to write over 450 works (of which only about 240 survive, forty of them on medicine) on subjects as varied as theology, geology, philosophy, psychology, chemistry, astronomy, physics, logic and even – hold your breath – poetry (told you he was a polymath!). Of all the surviving works from the Islamic Golden Age, his works alone account for around 50 per cent! But *The Canon of Medicine* remains his greatest work, if only because it consolidated, and built on, all the existing medical knowledge in the world up to that time. It was this magnum opus that would renew interest in the classical texts, and spur the next round of innovations in anatomy, medicine and surgery as Europe emerged from the Dark Ages in the fifteenth century.

One tragic, concluding note, on Baghdad and the House of Wisdom: In 1258 CE, the Mongol armies, looking to extend their empire, surrounded the city in the famous Siege of Baghdad for twelve days. When Baghdad fell, the Mongols executed the caliph, Al Musta'sim, massacred thousands of

Avicenna

people, and sacked the city. They destroyed all its libraries, including the House of Wisdom. Every last book (remember this was a time when every single book was written by hand and there were only a few copies of each) was dumped into the River Tigris.

The Islamic Empire ruled by the caliphs, which had, at the height of its glory, extended from Spain and Portugal in the west to the River Indus (in today's Pakistan) in the east, sandwiching large swathes of North Africa in between, never recovered from the body blow. The Islamic Golden Age, which had begun with the establishment of the House of Wisdom, came to an emphatic end with its annihilation.

Asia bowed out of the world stage, making way for a resurgent Europe to claim its place in the sun.

Avicenna Still Lives! In India!

Although it has no place in allopathic (modern medicine is also called allopathy – find out who named it that and what it means on page 139) hospitals today, Avicenna's *Canon of Medicine* still plays an important role in Unani medicine, a traditional form of Persian-Arabic medicine, which became popular in India during the Mughal period and is still practised today. Several Indian universities offer undergraduate degrees in Unani medicine, just as they do in other traditional systems of Indian medicine. We even have a Ministry of Ayurveda, Yoga (and Naturopathy), Unani, Siddha and Homoeopathy (AYUSH), which monitors higher education in these disciplines, supports scientific research on traditional medicines and has a vast digital library with details of hundreds of thousands of traditional drug formulations, to ensure that no one else can take a patent out on any of them and claim it to be their own. There is even an Ibn Sina Academy of Medieval Medicine and Sciences in Aligarh, which was founded in 2001!

Also, unrelated fun fact: there is a crater named after Avicenna on the moon. Now you know.

IDEA 6

MAYBE, JUST MAYBE, THAT OLD GREEK GALEN GOT A LOT OF IT WRONG

In Which Europe Wakes Up, and Begins to Question Everything

The House of Wisdom, the great library and intellectual centre of the Islamic Empire, went down in 1258 CE, but all was not lost. For over 300 years before this, copies of works in Arabic – both translations and originals – had made their way from there to Europe, a great number of them through the port of Naples, which was at the crossroads of Europe, the Middle East and Asia. These treasures had been lapped up greedily – and gratefully – by scholars, scientists, academics and curious readers hungry for knowledge and fresh, new ways of looking at the world. Their imaginations fired by what they read, this brigade would lead their fellows into the Renaissance – Europe's great intellectual and cultural reawakening – in the thirteenth century.

A mere 100 kilometres away from Naples was the town of Cassino, home of the hill known as Monte Cassino. On top of the hill was the fortified monastery (aka abbey) founded by Benedict of Nursia, a Christian saint today considered to be the patron saint of Europe, in 529 CE. The monks who lived and worked there were called Benedictine monks after their founder, and the order (i.e., a community of monks or nuns that follow the same religious, social and moral rules) came to be called the Benedictine Order. The rules the monks were supposed to live by were written down by St Benedict himself, in a book called (rather unimaginatively) *Rule of Saint Benedict*. Among the most important rules in the rule book was this one: 'Before and above all things, care must be taken of the sick, that they be served in very truth as Christ is served; because He hath said, "I was sick, and you visited me."'

In keeping with this rule, St Benedict ensured that a hospital was part of the abbey right from its founding (today, that hospital is considered to be the very first in 'modern' Europe). Several other Benedictine monasteries were set up in the surrounding areas during Benedict's lifetime, and every single one of them had a hospital attached. When Arabic works began to arrive from across the Mediterranean Sea into Naples, guess who was calling dibs on the ones that dealt with medicine? The Benedictine monks, of course!

Not all the Benedictine monks knew Arabic, but the ones that did quickly began to translate the works on medicine (many of which had themselves been translated into Arabic from Greek) and other subjects into Latin, a language which was understood by anyone with a college degree in

Western Europe. In the scriptorium (a room in the monastery meant exclusively for writing, copying and embellishing manuscripts), other monks – the scribes – wrote these translations down in beautiful calligraphy and compiled them into manuscripts, which were further 'illuminated', i.e., decorated with drop capitals, borders, illustrations and cover art, and often with gold or silver leaf. Finished manuscripts became part of the abbey's already extensive library.

By the turn of the second millennium CE, there were over 200 monks in the scriptorium at Monte Cassino, furiously producing illuminated manuscripts and turning the monastery library into one of the biggest and best in Europe. As you can imagine, the monks who worked on medical manuscripts became something of experts in the field. They began to put their knowledge to use on the sick in the monastery hospital and were soon getting good results with new treatments and procedures. Impressed, medical men from all over Europe, Asia and Africa began to flock to the library, turning Monte Cassino into an informal medical school. By mid-tenth century, that informal academy had moved to the seaside town of Salerno, famous for its invigorating, salubrious climate, and reinvented itself as the Schola Medica Salernitana, celebrated today as the world's first medical school.

***

In the thirteenth century, a new kind of thinking began to sweep across Italy, first only in pockets, and then, as it gained momentum, across the whole country. It was called humanism, and it believed that the purpose of education was to create citizens who were not only experts at philosophy, maths, theology or medicine but were also capable of thinking 'critically'. Humanists rejected the notion that an entity called God (and attendant angels and demons) controlled things in the human world, and insisted that humans were entirely capable of fashioning their own destinies. The idea, which seems so irrefutable to us now, shook European society up in such fundamental ways that it would be over 300 years before it was truly accepted.

To understand why humanist education was such a revolutionary concept then, we should examine the system of education that had been in vogue for several centuries before that – scholasticism. As you can tell, the word 'scholastic' itself came from *schola*, the Latin word for 'school'. In scholas of all kinds, including the Schola Medica in Salerno, education involved reading the old texts, committing them to memory and believing implicitly that they were the last word on the subject. Questioning and debating the pros and cons of the theories was not discouraged, but only entertained up to a point, and since it was mostly monks who were the teachers, a belief in God's omnipotence was mandatory.

Humanism proposed the exact opposite – that everything should be questioned, taken apart and examined for flaws using the great human gift of reason, and that independent thinking, both in classrooms and outside of them, must be actively encouraged. That kind of approach, it declared, would help people truly live with dignity, without feeling they were mere pawns in some cosmic game, with no agency of their own. It was only when humans believed that they could use their own considerable talents to deal with human concerns, and solve them with no help from a supernatural power, said humanists, that a robust society could be created, where every individual fulfilled his or her true potential.

To equip citizens to be able to think independently, express their opinions and, more importantly, be able to cogently defend what they believed was the truth, while appreciating (but respectfully countering) opposing points of view, humanists suggested that education – even so-called 'professional' education, like medicine – be broadened to include what we today call the humanities (grammar, logic, rhetoric, history, poetry, moral philosophy). What they were saying was that it was time for society to get out of the stranglehold of organized religion, which had dominated human thought for over a thousand years, and go back to the time before that – when independent thinking, and a tradition of questioning, truth-seeking and debate had been the norm, especially among the ancient Greeks and Indians.

The debate still rages around the world: are students better served by university syllabi that focus purely on science (engineering, medicine, pure sciences, statistics), humanities (literature, psychology, economics) or business studies, or by syllabi that include a bit of everything, at least in the first couple of years? What do you think?

Humanism took its time to catch on, but once it did, there was no looking back. Over the next three centuries, Western Europe was swept up in a whirl of exciting new innovations in art, literature, music, architecture, exploration, navigation, the sciences, governance and ways of doing business. Historians refer to that glorious period in European history – between the thirteenth and seventeenth centuries – as the European Renaissance. All the innovation that happened during this time – in ideas, inventions, warfare, engineering and, yes, medicine – would help Western Europe dominate the rest of the world right to the middle of the twentieth century.

PS: Any guesses as to how this 'new' idea called humanism had suddenly popped up in Italian minds? Yup, because of the renewed access to ancient thought they had suddenly received through the hard work of Arabic translators! Not to mention all the advancements made in so many fields by thinkers and artists from the Middle East and North Africa. You see why it is so short-sighted to believe that one culture, geography or people are somehow intrinsically superior to, or genetically 'cleverer', than others, simply because they are dominating the world at that point?

***

Did the culture of questioning 'received wisdom' shake up medicine too? But of course! Let's see how that went.

With original works by Arabic scholars of medicine like Avicenna, Rhazes, Ibn Imran, Ibn Suleiman and Ibn al-Jazzar (all translated into Latin by the great medieval physician

Constantine of Africa – more on him in the box on page 66) to help their thinking along, doctors and others began questioning the theories of the Greek anatomist Galen, that holiest of holy cows! (Remember how he had written his authoritative work on human anatomy without *ever* having dissected a human body, and yet been studied by European medical students unquestioningly for over 1,300 years? Yup, *that* Galen.)

One of the first people who questioned Galen's conclusions was not really a physician, or even a medical student. He was one of the most famous artists in history, and he was interested in anatomy simply because he wanted to present human musculature accurately in his drawings of human figures. His name was Leonardo da Vinci (Did you say, 'Oh-oh, I know, the *Mona Lisa* guy!'? Uh-huh, the very same.).

Many historians and scholars see Leonardo, who lived between 1452 and 1519, as the ultimate genius and Renaissance Man, the perfect poster boy for humanism, because of the breadth and depth of his curiosity, expertise and innovation in a mind-boggling number of fields, including engineering, palaeontology, botany, music, history, cartography and human anatomy. Quickly becoming an expert at drawing visible anatomical features like muscles and tendons, he rose to enough prominence as an artist to request and receive permission to dissect human corpses at the Hospital of Santa Maria Nuova in Florence (founded in 1288, and still active!).

Working with a doctor there between 1510 and 1511 CE, Leonardo, who was now in his fifties, dissected rapidly decomposing bodies (no refrigeration, remember?) through the night (after finishing his day job), by lamplight, made over

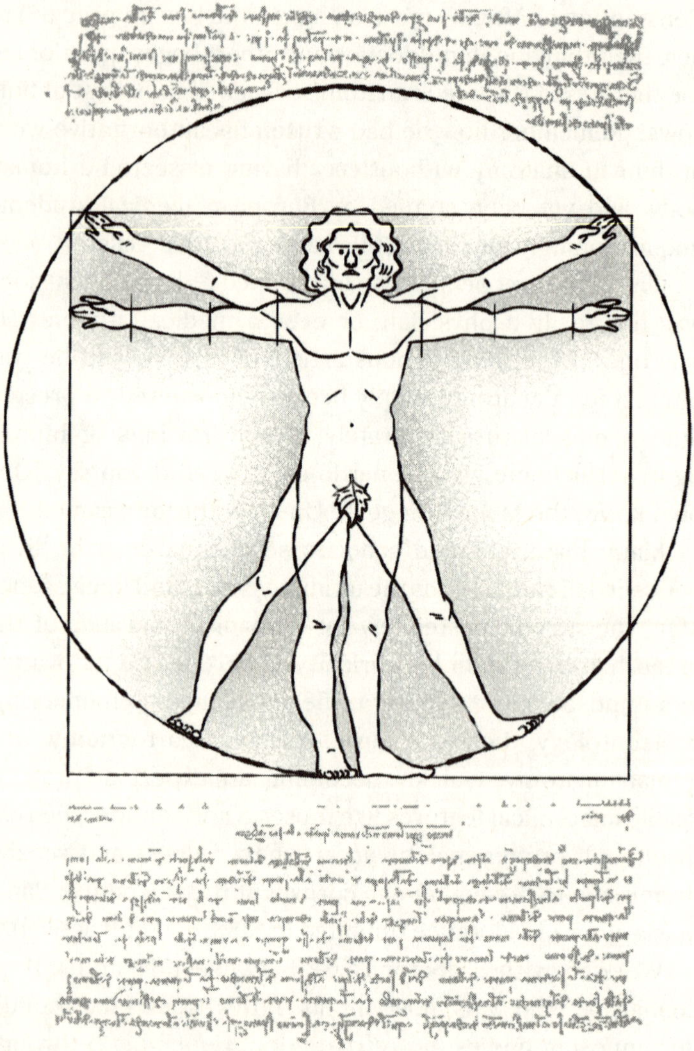

Leonardo da Vinci's Vitruvian Man

240 detailed drawings and left copious notations on each. (He had to have had a spectacular visual memory to be able to reproduce what he had seen at night in the morning!) He even wrote some 13,000 words for a book on anatomy that was far ahead of its time. Sadly, he died too soon to see that project through, and his heir, Francesco Melzi, could not have his drawings and notes published, or even properly organized, before he himself died fifty years later, thus depriving sixteenth-century medical science of a huge treasure.

Among Leonardo's genius contributions on the human body was a drawing he called 'The Proportions of the Human Body According to Vitruvius'. It was based on the work of the ancient Roman architect, Vitruvius, who believed that the best architecture came from following the proportions of the ideal human body, as designed by Nature. (For instance, such a body was one whose full height was exactly eight times that of its head). Leonardo drew a man according to Vitruvius's proportions and superimposed two images of him – one inside a circle and the other inside a square. We know that perfectly proportioned drawing today as 'Vitruvian Man'.

However, it was his anatomical drawings that were a revelation. He is credited with making the first-ever accurate drawing of a human foetus inside the uterus. He also contradicted Galen entirely on three counts, insisting that (1) the heart was a muscle just like any other muscle, (2) both veins and arteries originated from the heart, and (3) both carried plain old blood. (What had Galen said about all of this? See the box 'Dr Galen's Gory Story' at the end of this chapter.)

***

Andreas Vesalius (actually, his name was the more pedestrian Andries van Wesel, but it was the fashion for top-notch scholars in those days to Latinize their names) was only five when Leonardo da Vinci died. As a child growing up in Brussels, in a family of doctors, he could not have imagined that his name, like Leonardo's, would one day be inscribed in golden letters in the history of mankind (except for one minor difference – while Leonardo's would feature in the 'all-time greats' list, his would be among the 'all-time *medical* greats').

What makes Dr Vesalius so important? Consider this: sure, Leonardo disproved some of Galen's conclusions by relying on his own experience with dissecting, but since he wasn't a doctor himself, he did not have to challenge Galen publicly. Vesalius, though, was very much part of the medical establishment, which believed implicitly in Galen and his faulty theories. And yet, at the risk of being ostracized by his own fraternity and even facing persecution, Vesalius went ahead and declared Galen wrong. Here's how it happened.

In those days, dissections in medical colleges were done by barber surgeons according to the instructions of the professor, while the students gathered around and watched. Physicians – the ones who went to college and learned to treat disease – considered themselves far too posh for something like dissection or surgery; that was the job of the unlettered barber (how the tables have turned; today, surgeons occupy the highest rung of the medical ladder). No one, neither the professors nor the students, considered confirming Galen's conclusions by doing dissections themselves.

To Vesalius, who believed in a hands-on, direct-observation approach to learning (he was a true child of humanism), this whole practice seemed entirely ridiculous. As the head of the department of anatomy and surgery at his alma mater, the University of Padua in Italy (he was offered the post on the day he graduated!), he began doing dissections himself, and encouraged his students to do the same, urging them to observe the human cadaver's innards with fresh eyes, draw their own conclusions and propose their own theories. Based on what he himself observed, he created six large woodcut posters that proved so popular with his students that he put them all in a book – *Tabulae Anatomicae Sex* (The Six Anatomical Pictures) – in 1538.

In 1541, entirely by chance, Vesalius discovered that Galen had never actually dissected a human body; he had only ever worked on Barbary macaques, reasoning that since the apes were very close to humans in their physical structure, their anatomy must match the human one. Shocked and stunned, he called out Galen to the blissfully oblivious medical community, receiving mostly abuse for his pains (no one likes to be made to look like a fool!). In 1543, he published his groundbreaking seven-volume anatomical masterpiece, *De Humani Corporis Fabrica* (On the Fabric of the Human Body), commissioning a student of the great Italian Renaissance artist Titian to do the (often creepily posed, but always very detailed and accurate) illustrations accompanying it.

So beautifully was it produced, and so brilliant its content, that it was soon being pirated everywhere. Very quickly, it dislodged Galen's works as the last word in human anatomy.

At the ripe old age of twenty-eight, Andreas Vesalius had arrived – and how!

Our friend Vesalius also has the distinction of being the one responsible for the oldest surviving 'anatomical preparation' – a complete human skeleton which he assembled in 1543, after completing the public dissection of the body of a convicted felon in Basel, Switzerland. 'The Basel Skeleton' stands to this day in the Anatomical Museum of the University of Basel.

Vesalius went on to demolish many of Galen's theories, most famously the one about the 'invisible pores' in the dividing wall between the right and left sides of the heart (See point no. 4 in the box 'Dr Galen's Gory Story' at the end of this chapter). By the simple expedient of pouring water – and other fluids of different densities – into the right ventricle (one of the four chambers of the heart; Galen had believed there were only two) and waiting to see if some of it would move to the left ventricle through the 'invisible pores' – they did not – Vesalius proved conclusively that, well, *there were no pores*! And Vesalius being Vesalius, he did not hesitate to say it out loud either.

It was a true 'But the emperor has no clothes on!' moment in medical history. In one fell swoop, everything we thought we knew about human anatomy and physiology became suspect. Among other things, new theories for how blood circulated in the body had to be proposed – and proved. Luckily, even though Vesalius himself could not come up with a satisfactory alternative explanation, there were other bright sparks waiting in the wings for just such an opportunity.

Dr Galen's Gory Story

Poor Galen. In the sixteenth century, after some 1,400 years of ruling the roost as Europe's greatest anatomist and Explainer-in-Chief of What the Body Contains and How It All Works, he was about to get his long-overdue comeuppance from people like Andreas Vesalius and William Harvey (Idea 7, page 68).

So now is a good time to find out what the old Greek actually believed about things like blood (aka gore), the heart, the veins, the arteries, the lungs – in short, about the respiratory and circulatory systems.

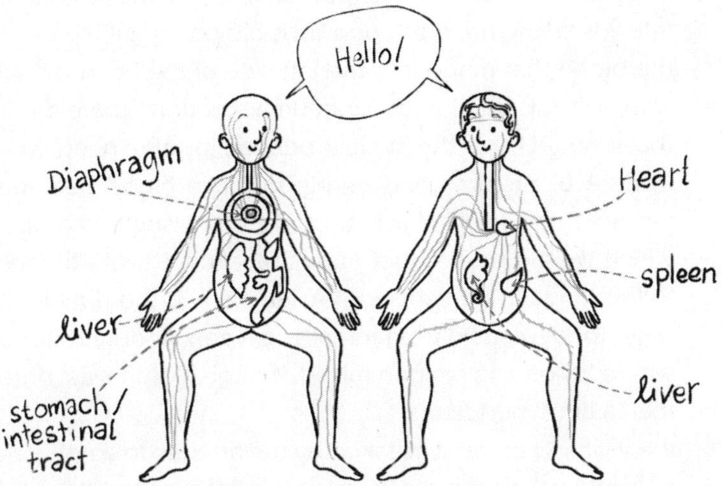

Anatomical drawings of veins and arteries from 1165 CE

According to Galen:

1. there were two separate blood systems in the body – one involving the veins, the other involving the arteries (wrong – they are both part of the same system);
2. blood was continuously produced and continuously consumed in the body; it was not circulated (SO wrong);
3. purple 'nutritive' blood was produced by the liver from the food we ate, and carried to the right side of the heart by the veins, which originated in the liver; that purple blood was meant for the growth of the body (nope, blood is not produced by the liver, nor do veins originate there);
4. from the right side of the heart, part of the purple blood went into the lungs to nourish them. In the lungs, it gave out 'sooty vapours', which were released from the body when we exhaled. Another portion of blood moved to the left side of the heart through 'invisible pores' (NOT!);
5. the blood that made it to the left side of the heart mixed with a 'vital spirit' called pneuma, brought there from the lungs. Using the heat produced by the heart, the mixture of pneuma and purple nutritive blood became red 'vivifying' (or life-giving) blood. More sooty vapours, which were a by-product of this reaction, travelled back to the lungs to be exhaled (We-ell, he had the right idea here. Today we know 'pneuma' as oxygen. About how and where blood and oxygen mixed, though, Galen was more than a little muddled.);
6. the vivifying blood was taken by the arteries to a network of blood vessels at the base of the brain called the rete mirabile (or 'the marvellous net'), from where it was

distributed to different parts of the body through the nerves to be consumed (Because many warm-blooded mammals have a rete mirabile, Galen assumed that humans did too. They do not.);

7. both nutritive blood and vivifying blood were needed by the body, but while nutritive blood was attracted by different parts as and when they needed it, vivifying blood had to reach all parts of the body and be consumed continuously, to keep the body alive (hmmmm ....).

Yup, given what we know today, Galen's conclusions sound pretty darn ridiculous, but spare that old Greek a thought. He knew nothing about oxygen and carbon dioxide, had no access to a microscope, could see that there were two different colours of blood, and was trying to imagine the workings of a human body while looking at the inside of an animal cadaver (because human dissection was frowned upon)! Given those circumstances, Galen did a pretty good job. If you're still not convinced, visualize yourself in a situation where you are asked to look at the innards of a machine from outer space that has been cut off from its power source, and then explain the function of each part and how they connect to each other to make some other machine work. Pretty flummoxing, right?

Constantinus Africanus, Healer from – duh! – Africa

In 1077 CE, a newly ordained Benedictine monk became part of the Abbey of Monte Cassino. This monk was not young, and the biographies written about him suggest that he had had a chequered career – born in Carthage (part of modern Tunisia; if you don't know where that is, go check now! When you do, make sure you notice how close to Italy this North African country is), this Saracen (the European moniker for Muslims from North Africa) had in fact begun life as a merchant and trader who moved to Sicily for better business prospects. Not knowing Italian, he had found himself an interpreter – a fellow Tunisian called Abbas of Curiat, who practised as a doctor in Italy.

A few years into his move to Sicily, Constantine fell very ill and was treated by his friend Abbas. Having always been curious by nature, and having, therefore, quite a decent knowledge of medicine as practised in the Islamic Empire, Constantine was aghast to find that not only did Abbas not ask for a sample of his urine to diagnose his disease (remember we talked earlier about how uroscopy was a big part of Eastern medicine – see page 44 to refresh your memory), he actually seemed to know very little about new advances in healing. Desperate, Constantine asked for books on Italian medicine, and discovered that there were precious few. Luckily for him, and for all of us, he recovered from his illness after having had an epiphany, on his sickbed, as to the purpose of his life. The moment he was well enough to travel, Constantine returned to his native land, where he spent several years educating himself about medicine and collecting books on the subject. He is also believed to have travelled extensively in India, Babylon and Ethiopia, observing and learning from healers there.

Towards the end of the eleventh century, Constantine returned to Italy, to Salerno this time, where the Schola Medica had already begun to gain a following, carrying with him his precious cargo of knowledge, experience and books. His vast understanding, not just of medicine but of so many related and unrelated fields, was so intimidating, it is said, that he was seen either as a great wizard or an evil sorcerer. But the rulers of Salerno loved him, and with their patronage, Constantinus Africanus went on to become one of the most famous physicians in the Schola Medica, single-handedly raising its profile as a great school of medicine.

A few years later, Constantine converted to Christianity (it is likely he took the name Constantine at this time – his original name, sadly, is lost in the mists of history) and became a Benedictine monk. He spent the rest of his days at Monte Cassino, translating medical works from Arabic to Latin. Many of those translations were used as textbooks in Europe right up to the seventeenth century.

IDEA 7

THE BODY'S 'BLOODY' SECRET, REVEALED!

At Long Last, an Understanding of the Circulatory System

In his alma mater, the University of Padua, young Andreas Vesalius had a colleague (or teacher, or student, no one is quite sure) in the department of anatomy and surgery called Realdo Colombo. Vesalius and Colombo started off as very good friends, but somewhere along the way, they turned into bitter rivals. Unlike Vesalius, Colombo believed in vivisection, saying it was the only way to truly figure out the workings of the heart and lungs. He criticized Vesalius for only doing his dissections on dead animals and people, saying that for all his denouncing of Galen's methods, Vesalius was no better than the old Greek master.

Moving to Rome in 1548, Colombo started working on a text on anatomy to rival Vesalius's masterpiece *De Fabrica*, and even commissioned the great Renaissance artist Michelangelo (yup, the same guy who made the famous sculpture of David and painted the ceiling of the Sistine Chapel!) to illustrate his book. Unfortunately for all of us, that work never saw the light of day (maybe because Michelangelo was already seventy by the time Colombo started working on the project), but after Colombo's death in 1559, his sons published his writings, among which were some truly explosive discoveries about the heart, lungs and blood, in a text called *De re Anatomica* (On Things Anatomical).

What mistakes did Colombo point out in Galen's theories (see the box 'Dr Galen's Gory Story' on page 63) that Vesalius had not? For one, that the purple blood did not in fact become red in the heart as Galen had believed. Instead, said Colombo, the blood made a 'pulmonary transit' (pulmonary simply means 'relating to the lungs') – it was pushed out of the right side of the heart, made a detour through the lungs and then came back into the left side. It was in the lungs that the purple blood gave up the so-called sooty vapours and turned red. Secondly, said Colombo, the heart did not expand with each heartbeat as previously believed; instead, it *contracted.* Before each heartbeat, the heart filled with blood; then, contracting, it *squeezed* the blood out through the arteries into the lungs and the rest of the body.

Seventy years later, it was these two landmark findings by Colombo that helped the English physician William Harvey not only discover that blood circulated through the body instead of being consumed, but also explain how exactly it did so. (Colombo never figured out circulation – he still believed, like everyone before him, that blood was continuously produced and consumed in the body.)

Almost exactly twenty years after Colombo's death in Rome, William Harvey was born in the picturesque port town of Folkestone on the east coast of England. In 1599, at the age of twenty-one, he enrolled as a medical student at the University of Padua, the very same institution that had produced medical greats like Andreas Vesalius and Realdo Colombo. After being elected to the Royal College of Physicians back in England, Harvey went on to become the physician in charge at London's famous St Bartholomew's Hospital (founded in 1123 and still going strong), a position he held for most of the rest of his life. His dedicated and brilliant work there saw him go from strength to strength – in 1618, he was appointed Physician Extraordinary to King James I.

How did Harvey go from there to discovering the process called the 'pulmonary circulation' of blood? Like Colombo, Harvey believed that it was only by observing a living, beating heart that one could have an accurate understanding of how it worked. To this end, he performed hundreds of vivisections on a variety of animals, but it was frustrating work simply because of the rapidity of the heartbeat (the human heart contracts seventy-two times a minute on average!). '. . . I found the task so truly arduous,' he writes in his book *De Motu Cordis* (On the Motion of the Heart), '. . . that I was almost tempted to think . . . that the movement of the heart was only to be comprehended by God.'

One thing he did realize was that the heart clearly pumped out a LOT of blood every minute. But exactly how much?

Methodically, Harvey measured the volume of the ventricles (the two lower, larger chambers of the heart from where blood was squeezed out with each heartbeat), the amount of blood they pumped out per heartbeat and the number of heartbeats per minute, and calculated that the heart pumped *at least* between 0.5 and 1 litre of blood per minute (today, we know that the actual amount of blood pumped per minute is 4 litres; Harvey had deliberately used the lowest possible values in his calculations). That meant the heart pumped out close to 30 litres of blood every thirty minutes.

That value gave Harvey his 'Eureka!' moment: the human body, he knew, contained an average of 5 litres of blood; there was no way that a whopping 30 litres of blood could

William Harvey

be produced (by the liver) or consumed (by the rest of the body) in half an hour! The only explanation was that blood was not being produced or consumed – it was merely being circulated through the body!

Excited, he set out to find out exactly how blood circulated.

He already knew, from Colombo's work, that the lungs were involved; now he applied himself to finding out more about how exactly blood entered and left the heart. Now, did the arteries fill the heart with blood or empty it? What about the veins? To find out, Harvey did experiments like tying up the veins and arteries of live snakes and fish to see what modifications occurred in the heart. When he tied up the arteries, he found, the heart became engorged with blood and swelled up ('That means the arteries take blood away from the heart!'); when he tied up the veins – that's right – the heart emptied of blood ('That means the veins bring blood back to the heart!').

Harvey repeated the same experiments on live human beings (don't panic – he did it without cutting them up!). When he tied a flat band tightly around the upper part of a person's arm, thus choking both the surface veins and deep-seated arteries, he noticed that the part of the arm below the band turned cold and pale, while the part above the band became warm, red and swollen. When he loosened the band slightly, the arteries inside opened up, allowing blood from the heart to reach the lower arm. But since the veins were still choked by the band, blood could not flow back to the heart. Now the lower arm swelled up, and the veins there, now full of blood, stood out like purple cords under the skin. (Ever wondered why when a nurse wants to draw blood for a blood test, they tie a band tightly around your arm? Yes, because your veins then fill up and stand out, making it easier for them to see where to poke!)

The other thing Harvey noticed was that when the veins swelled up, there were little bumps all along them, a few centimetres apart. Instantly, he recognized them as the 'valves' that Hieronymus Fabricius, his favourite teacher in the University of Padua, had described in one of his books.

Not sure what a valve is? Well, it's a 'gateway' that allows movement (of fluids or gases) in only one direction in a tube or channel. Can you guess why veins, which carry blood back to the heart from all parts of the body, need to have valves? Yes, so that the blood that is pumped upwards to the heart from the parts of the body below it doesn't flow back down the veins because of gravity! Valves in the veins only open to allow blood to flow upwards, not downwards.

When he put all of this together, Dr William Harvey, FRCP (Fellow of the Royal College of Physicians, if you must know), could take a very calculated guess at exactly how the blood circulated through the human body. But because he could not demonstrate it, he knew it wouldn't be easy to get other doctors, most of whom still believed in Galen's theories, to accept what he was saying. Still, unwilling to keep the truth to himself, he published his seventy-two-page book, *De Motu*

Cordis, in Frankfurt (in today's Germany) in 1628, releasing it just in time for a famous annual book fair there, to ensure that the largest number of people got to know about it.

Expectedly, there was a huge amount of criticism, with many eminent physicians declaring that they'd 'rather err with Galen than proclaim the truth with Harvey'. It took twenty years for the establishment to come around, but by the end of Harvey's own lifetime, his theory on the circulation of blood had been embraced by doctors and scientists everywhere.

What makes Harvey's achievements particularly significant is that he did all his work against the background of severe political upheaval in England. In 1625, when King James was succeeded by Charles I, Harvey became his personal physician as well. He was particularly loyal to the king, so when the English Civil War broke out in 1642, he was squarely cast on the side of the Royalists – the chaps who supported the king. That automatically put him at loggerheads with the Roundheads, who wanted more power for the English parliament. During one particular raid by the Roundheads, a vast number of Harvey's notes were stolen and scattered – a huge personal and professional loss. In 1645, the university town of Oxford, where Harvey had moved with the king, fell to the Roundheads. In 1649, Charles I was executed, and the parliament became very powerful in England. Completely ostracized from public life, Harvey spent his remaining years in quiet study until his death in 1657.

Today, over 350 years later, William Harvey is celebrated as one of the most influential figures of the second millennium.

Be Still, My Beating Heart – Not!

How does the heart work to circulate blood? Here's a refresher.

The heart has four chambers. The right atrium sits above the right ventricle, and between them is the tricuspid valve that allows blood to flow only from the atrium to the ventricle. The left atrium sits above the left ventricle, and between them is the mitral valve that, again, allows blood to flow only from the atrium to the ventricle.

Red blood, freshly loaded with oxygen from the lungs, comes into the left atrium through the pulmonary vein and passes through the mitral valve to the left ventricle. When the left ventricle is full, the heart contracts, squeezing red blood (which is blood that is full of oxygen) into the aorta through the aortic valve. The red (or oxygenated) blood flows through the aorta and its branches, the arteries, which become finer and finer until they are fine enough to enter every last cell of the body. When the blood reaches the cells, it gives up its oxygen to the cell and picks up carbon dioxide (sort of like giving the cells their lunch and picking up the trash at the same time).

Now purple, the blood returns to the heart through the right atrium through a series of larger and larger veins, which finally enter the heart as the superior and inferior vena cava. This blood moves from the right atrium to the right ventricle through the tricuspid valve. When the right ventricle is full (which happens while the left ventricle is full), the heart contracts, squeezing purple blood out of the right ventricle into the pulmonary artery through the open pulmonary valve.

The pulmonary artery carries the blood to the lungs. (See what happened there? Exactly! The pulmonary transit!)

In the lungs, the purple (or deoxygenated) blood gives up its 'sooty vapours' – which we exhale as carbon dioxide – refreshes itself with oxygen from our next inhalation, turns red and flows through the pulmonary vein back into the left atrium, completing the cycle.

And what is the heartbeat? The 'lub-dub' sound you hear through a stethoscope placed on the left side of the chest? Well, the 'lub' is the sound of the tricuspid and mitral valves closing, to ensure there is no backflow into the atria (plural of atrium) when the heart squeezes the ventricles. The 'dub' is the sound of the aortic and pulmonary valves closing immediately after, to prevent the blood from the aorta and the pulmonary artery from flowing back into the ventricles.

Now, try saying 'lub-dub' seventy-two times in a minute! Can't do it? Well, thank your lucky stars your heart can!

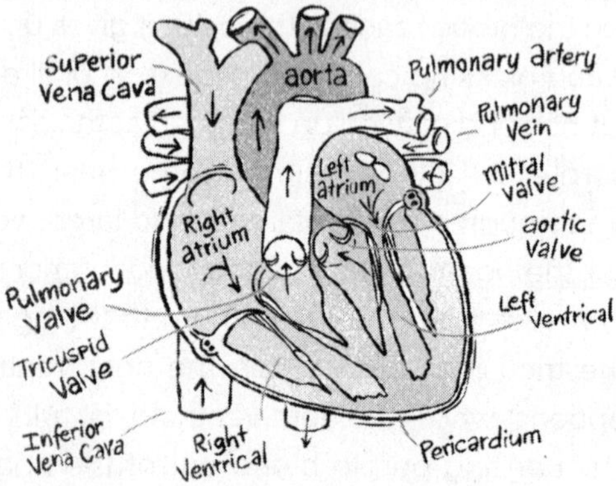

A Rough Diagram of the Human Heart

I'm Sorry, Dr Vesalius, but the Arabs Were Here First

Almost 300 years before Vesalius pointed out that there were actually no pores in the thick wall of tissue between the right and left sides of the heart, and Colombo discovered that blood made a pulmonary transit between the two sides of the heart, a brilliant physician from Damascus, Syria, had already figured out both those things. His name was Ibn al-Nafis, and he even wrote his theories down in a book called *Shahr Tashrih al-Qanun*, Commentary on Anatomy of (Ibn Sina's) Kitab al-Qanun, which was published in 1242 CE, when al-Nafis was only twenty-nine. Unfortunately, no one in the West noticed this work until the 1930s, 700 years after it was written. It was a young Egyptian doctor who discovered al-Nafis's manuscript in a library in Berlin while working on his thesis and announced it to the world. Oh well, better late than never, right?

The Breath of Life

It was the Father of Chemistry, Robert Boyle (Have you studied Boyle's Law in science yet? Yup, this is the same guy. If you haven't, don't worry – you will most likely encounter it before you're done with tenth grade.), who first demonstrated in the late seventeenth century, through experiments, that 'common air' (i.e., air that surrounds us all, the atmosphere) contained a certain 'something' that was necessary for life. He did this by putting several different creatures – butterflies, bees, birds, mice – into a container, reducing the amount of air in it and observing the effect it had on each creature. They all became listless and droopy, staggered around unsteadily and/or died. When he put a lit candle inside the container and reduced the amount of air, the same thing happened to the flame – it guttered and died – leading Boyle to suspect that it was the same 'something' in the air that also caused a flame to burn brightly.

A few years later, his fellow countryman, the English physician Richard Lower, had his own *aha*! moment: purple blood become red in the lungs, he realized suddenly, because of exposure to that exact 'something' in the air. But we had to wait almost another century for that something to be winkled out of 'common air' and named. In 1774, English chemist Joseph Priestley noticed that when mercuric oxide was burnt, it produced a gas that not only helped a fire burn strongly but was also important to sustain life. When he exposed a mouse to the gas, the mouse perked up visibly – it became far more active, and eventually lived much longer than average. Priestley spoke about his discovery to French chemist and nobleman Antoine Lavoisier, who had been doing his own experiments on combustion (burning). Lavoisier christened this life-giving, combustion-enhancing gas oxygen.

And that's when, at long last, we began to see glimmerings of *why* blood circulates in the body – to distribute this life-sustaining oxygen, which it picks up from the 'common air' breathed in by the lungs, to every last cell in our bodies.

IDEA 8

OMG! A WHOLE NEW WORLD – OF ITSY-BITSY TEENY-WEENIES!

The Microscope Opens Up a Dazzling Place We Never Knew

So William Harvey was a rock star, but he still didn't get everything about circulation. While he was able to explain *how* blood circulated, he never did crack *why* blood circulated. We now know it circulates for two reasons: to pick up oxygen from the lungs to distribute to all the cells in the body, and to bring back carbon dioxide from the cells on its way back to the lungs. At that time, though, no one even knew that there was such a gas as oxygen or had even figured out the actual link between air and life. (To find out who finally made the connection, see the box 'The Breath of Life' on page 78.)

The other thing Harvey could not for the life of him explain was this: if blood circulates, and there is only one network through which it does so, there must be some point at which the arteries *become* the veins, and some way for arterial blood to become venous blood. For some years, there had been a theory that the arteries kept dividing into smaller and smaller branches until the branches became very, very fine (at that point, the theory said, the branches were called capillaries). Harvey accepted that theory like everyone else did, but he actually had no proof of it – capillaries were too small to be seen by the naked eye, and there were no microscopes around yet. In any case, the capillary theory did not explain all the other stuff that needed explaining.

It was only when the microscope made its quiet entrance on the world science stage that things got kicked up several notches. Sure, lenses had been around for thousands of years, and magnifying glasses (also called simple microscopes) at least since the thirteenth century. But the first time a compound microscope, i.e., an instrument that combined two lenses – an objective lens (which collects light from the object being observed and focuses the light rays to create an image) and an eyepiece (which magnifies the image created by the objective lens) – through which the observer looks at the object, entered scientific records was only in 1620.

What's more, although many people in the following years have been credited with its invention – some of them were true masters in the science of optics, like Dutch spectacle-maker Hans Lippershey and his countryman and rival Zacharias Janssen, both of whom also claimed to be the inventors of the telescope; others were engineers and inventors of great repute like Cornelis Drebbel, also Dutch,

The First Microscopes

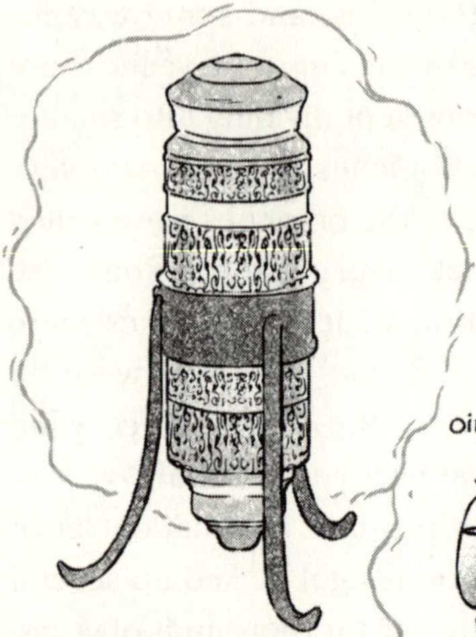

Galileo's microscope

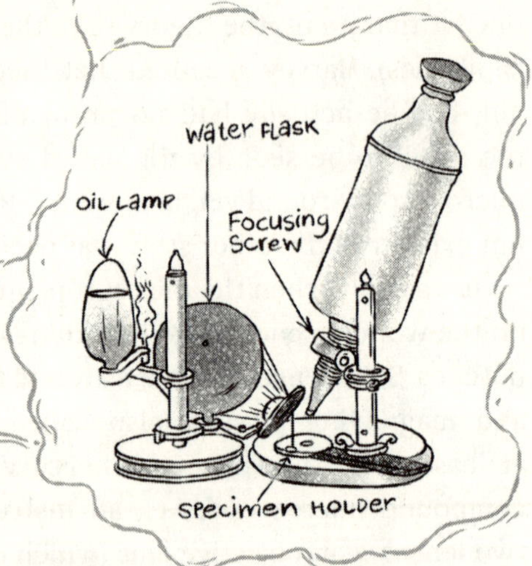

Hooke's microscope

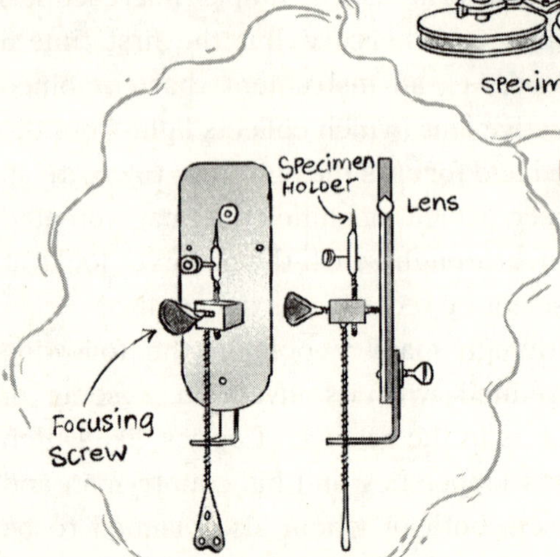

Leeuwenhoek's microscope

who built the world's first navigable submarine; another strong contender was the great Italian astronomer, inventor and polymath Galileo Galilei – in short, we don't really know who the inventor of the compound microscope was.

What we do know is who first gave this instrument its name. That happened in 1625, after Galileo created an improved version of the compound microscope and presented it to the nobleman Federico Cesi, founder of a famous institute of science in Rome called Accademia dei Lincei (Academy of the Lynx; in Greek mythology, lynxes are believed to have supernaturally good eyesight – in other words, they don't miss a thing). Galileo – who often signed off as Galileo Galilei Linceo (Galileo [of the Academy of] the Lynx) – was the intellectual heart of the academy, and it was his colleague there, Giovanni Faber, a celebrated botanist, who christened Galileo's new instrument the 'microscope' (from the Greek words *mikros* – 'small' – and *skopos* – 'to see'; it matched nicely with 'telescope', which had also been named by the Linceans). Just FYI, Galileo himself had called his creation 'occhiolino', that is, 'the little eye'.

***

However, the microscope continued to be a novelty until the 1660s and 1670s. Its possibilities as an instrument to expand our understanding of the universe, in the opposite direction from the telescope, escaped most people until *Micrographia*, the very first book to carry illustrations of insects, plants and more *as seen through a microscope*, exploded into the public imagination in 1665. The book was written and illustrated by the spectacularly gifted 'English Leonardo', the scientist, architect, mapmaker, surveyor, inventor, geologist and overall genius Robert Hooke. It was also the first publication of the Royal Society, the modern world's oldest academy to practise experimental science, which had itself been founded in 1660. The book contained such fascinating, never-even-suspected-they-existed details about the fundamental building blocks of familiar things, that it soon became the world's first scientific bestseller.

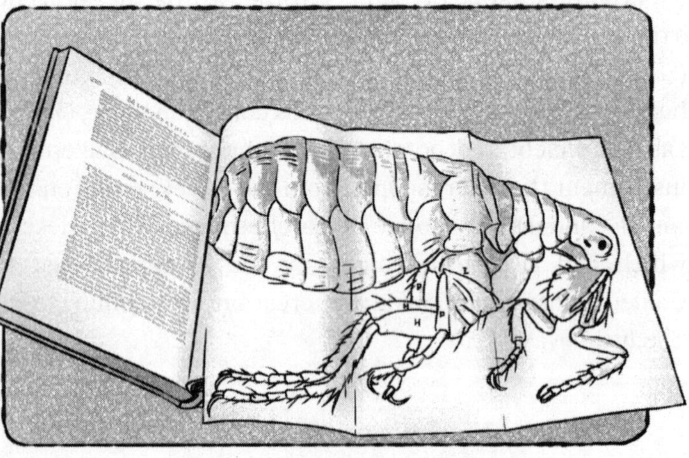

Robert Hooke's *Micrographia*

Fun fact: The president of the Royal Society from 2015 to 2020 was Indian-born Venkatraman Ramakrishnan, the 2009 Nobel Prize winner in Chemistry.

Micrographia is also significant for biology and medicine in one specific way – while researching for the book, Hooke happened to look at a thin slice of cork under a microscope and noticed an irregular but continuous pattern of small compartment-like structures in it. When he observed plant tissue, he noticed a similar pattern there. Hugely excited, he wrote his impressions down. '. . . I could exceedingly plainly perceive it [the slice of cork],' he wrote, 'to be all perforated and porous, much like a honeycomb, but that the pores of it were not regular . . . these pores, or cells, were indeed the first microscopical pores I ever saw, and perhaps, that were ever seen, for I had not met with any writer or person, that had made any mention of them before this.'

Now, can you guess what makes this particular passage so significant? Yes, it was the first time anyone had used the word 'cell' to describe the building blocks of living tissue! As you know, the name stuck.

***

From the moment *Micrographia* hit the stands, there was no looking back for microscopy. But even before Hooke put insects and plants under his microscope, others across Europe had begun looking through their eyepieces at all kinds of interesting stuff – blood, human tissue, pond water, fabric (yes, fabric, and thereby hangs a tale – read on!).

Two people, particularly – the Dutch draper and inventor Antonie van Leeuwenhoek (say 'Lay-oo-ven-hook') and the Italian biologist and physician Marcello Malpighi – helped make huge strides forward in medicine simply because of their curiosity (and let that be a lesson to you, boys and girls – never, ever stop being curious!) about the world.

Let's talk about Malpighi first. Born in Bologna, Malpighi was a devoted son who would return again and again to his native town to live and work, despite all the inducements offered to him by other universities across Italy (a grateful Bologna commemorated him with a tomb in its main church, with the inscription 'Great genius, a life honestly lived, a strong and tough mind, a daring love for the medical art').

The 'daring love for medical art' part is particularly apt in Malpighi's case – he challenged so many long-held theories about the human body that envious and disbelieving colleagues were constantly dissing his findings. Looking through his handy-dandy microscope, he discovered that invertebrates breathed not through their lungs but through holes in their skin called tracheae; that plants, similarly, breathed through holes in their leaves (they were later given the name stomata); that skin got its colour from a layer of mucus just below its surface (we now know that it is cells called melanocytes found in this layer that give our skin and hair their colour); and that blood got its red colour from a particular kind of cell that it was packed with (today we call them, well, red blood cells).

But his most important finding happened in 1661, when he put the lung tissue of a frog under a microscope, and became the first person to see . . . yes, the famous capillaries! In that piece of lung tissue, Malpighi saw the network that connected the tiniest arteries to the tiniest veins and was able to declare with conviction that that was *exactly* how –

and where – arteries became veins, i.e., how blood was passed from arteries to veins in all animals. At long last, the last missing link in the circulation of blood had been found. For all his groundbreaking work on tissues, Malpighi is today considered the Father of Histology (histology, as you can guess, is the microscopic study of tissues).

***

On to seventeenth-century Netherlands, and to Antonie van Leeuwenhoek's cloth shop! History doesn't confirm for us exactly why a draper was so keen on microscopes, but the story goes that Leeuwenhoek created his brilliant and very compact microscopes (the largest was no longer than 5 centimetres) simply to be able to observe the weave of a fabric better before he bought it, to confirm that it was really as fine as the weaver insisted. Leeuwenhoek's microscope consisted of only one lens – a tiny glass sphere (and we all know, from looking through a fishbowl, how a glass globe full of water magnifies things) – sandwiched between two metal plates riveted together, but it was ten times more powerful than the best compound microscope of the day! In fact, no one was able to create a microscope with better magnification for over 150 years after Leeuwenhoek!

Once he had got his own copy of *Micrographia*, one of the first things the fascinated Leeuwenhoek did was to put the same things Hooke had observed – the leg of a louse, the stinger of a bee – under his own homemade microscope. What he saw was what no human in the world, ever, as far as we know, had *ever* seen: a first glimpse at a whole invisible universe – that pulsated with Lilliputian life! It was a goosebump-y, *Horton Hears a Who!* moment – Leeuwenhoek had discovered microorganisms (aka microbes, aka creatures too small to be seen by the naked eye).

Leeuwenhoek shared his findings with his good friend, the physician Regnier de Graaf (who himself made great contributions to the study of reproductive biology), who urged him to write about the *diertgens* (*dier* is Dutch for 'animal', and 'diertgen' simply means 'small animal') to the Royal Society in London. At first, Leeuwenhoek was hesitant – he thought of himself simply as a businessman, someone with no literary or scientific background, but on de Graaf's insistence that he be more confident about his work, he finally did write that letter in 1673, and received many congratulations and much adulation in return.

There was more to come. In 1676, while examining green algae in a sample of pond water under his microscope, Leeuwenhoek saw something that truly blew his mind – creatures that were at least 1,000 times smaller than anything he had seen before! Yes, Leeuwenhoek had discovered single-celled organisms!

He wrote enthusiastically to the Royal Society – as always, composing his letter not in scholarly Latin but in colloquial Dutch – about the wayyyy smaller diertgens, but what he was saying was so incredible that it was met with severe scepticism. Leeuwenhoek defended his findings so steadfastly, however, that the society finally sent a committee to his town, mainly to check if he was in his right mind. In

1677, when the committee reported that he was, the society finally capitulated and accepted his findings. In 1680, they even elected him a fellow of the Royal Society.

Leeuwenhoek was surprised and pleased at the honour, but he neither attended the induction ceremony in London nor ever attended a single meeting of the society. A shrewd businessman, he knew that the scientific community would never truly accept him as one of them, and he was happy instead to continue his exploration of the invisible world from right where he was. He continued writing letters to the Royal Society, however – including details about the symptoms and progression of a rare disease he had contracted in his late eighties, which caused his midriff to move uncontrollably. In honour of this inveterate scientist and precise chronicler, that disease is today called van Leeuwenhoek's disease.

IDEA 9

THE BODY IS NOT MYSTICAL, IT IS A MACHINE!

How the New and Exciting Science of Biomechanics Came to Be

It was in the seventeenth century that the European Renaissance, which had begun in Italy in the thirteenth century, came to its glorious climax, both despite and because of all the stuff that was happening in the background. Stuff like what? Well, for one, since the concept of a nation state (which simply means a territory ruled by a centralized government, in which a majority of people share the same culture; most countries today, including India, are nation states) hadn't yet been invented, kingdoms were constantly at war and borders shifted continuously. Secondly, global exploration, which had begun with those doughty sea dogs Christopher Columbus and Vasco da Gama a century before, had proved conclusively that the world was round, created the new science (or art?) of cartography or map-making and sent European powers scrambling for their share of the luscious, suddenly accessible wealth of far-flung continents, paving the way for centuries of exploitation and colonization. And so on.

As far as science was concerned . . . actually, let's pause here for a moment and take a little detour to talk about what 'science' meant in the seventeenth century.

Let's talk about all those towering thinkers and intellectuals of the seventeenth century that we today describe as mathematicians, physicists, biologists, *scientists*. Now here's a fun fact: they themselves never thought of themselves in those terms. Simply because . . . yes, those terms did not exist in their day! Instead, they called themselves 'natural philosophers', people who were curious about Nature (i.e., the physical universe, the human body, and everything else we call 'matter') and the human spirit (the soul, or what we call 'energy'), and thought deeply about how they all worked, and how – or if – all of them fit together. All the greatest thinkers in human history, from Aristotle and the sages of the Upanishads to Leonardo to Galileo to Isaac Newton, were natural philosophers. It wasn't until the nineteenth century, by when many things about Nature and the universe had been figured out, that we needed separate branches of study for each. That was when words like 'biology' and 'physicist' were created, and the concept of 'modern science' arose.

Perhaps it was because they did not confine themselves to boxes labelled 'botanist' or 'astronomer' or 'chemist' that these 'generalist' thinkers were able to see connections that a 'specialist' might have missed. Perhaps that ability was helped along by the other thing that was common to most natural philosophers – a deep and abiding faith in God. In fact, through history, some of the greatest natural philosophers came from the ranks of the clergy and the priesthood. Many others had studied theology at university. Today, we tend to think of science and spirituality as being at loggerheads with each other, but these deeply spiritual men (across the world, women did not receive formal education until very recently, and so did not make it into the history books as 'thinkers') saw no contradiction in applying reason and logic, and later, experimental and empirical methods, to solve problems while still retaining a sense of wonder and awe at the handiwork of the Great Designer as well as gratitude for the 'divine grace' that had helped them see further than others. End of detour.

***

Back to the topic at hand, and to the great French mathematician and scientist René Descartes (say 'Dei-kaart') – yes, the guy who simply and emphatically declared, 'I think, therefore I am', and the guy who gave us Cartesian geometry (aka coordinate geometry – if you haven't studied it yet, you will at some point if you stick with maths).

Descartes believed that the body and mind were two separate entities that were not connected to each other (today, many of us connect the physical organ of the brain to the mind, seeing it as the generator and keeper of thoughts, ideas, memory and emotion, although we have no conclusive evidence of that either). He saw the body as a mechanical object, and compared bodily organs to non-living objects: the brain was like a reservoir, he said; the eyes functioned like lenses (and so all the laws of optics – reflection, refraction, etc. – would apply to the eye as well); and the heart worked like a steam engine – according to him, blood evaporated due to the heat of the heart and its vapours spread through the body, condensing some way down the line back into liquid blood, just like water vaporized into steam in a steam engine. As you can guess, many of Descartes's views were wrong, since they were not always based on having seen how the organs worked; but the very fact that he was thinking of the body as a machine was revolutionary for the time.

You see, until then, the body had been thought to be something that was completely mystical and divine, because it had 'life'. Comparing the body to a machine – something humans could devise – was seen as a slur against God. It was this kind of thinking, in fact, that was responsible for holding back progress in medicine – if you thought of the body as a machine, you could think of ways to 'repair' it just as you did a machine, but if you didn't, there was no straight way forward. Descartes was roundly criticized for his views by many of his contemporaries, but the idea that the body was a machine had come to stay.

With Isaac Newton (born 1642) figuring out the physical laws of the universe, thus introducing the idea that the universe itself was a huge machine (designed and created by

God, perhaps, but still a machine) that behaved in a predictable fashion, more and more people began to study the mechanics of the human body. How did the joints work? How did the muscles help us move? How did the kidneys filter urine out of blood? That single shift in approach had a huge impact on medicine. How? By creating entire new fields of medicine like iatrophysics, iatromechanics and iatrochemistry (*iatro* in Greek means 'healer', so iatrophysics, literally, is 'the doctor's physics', a way to apply the laws of physics to the human body; you can work out what the other two 'iatro' sciences are by yourself). One of the most influential iatrophysicists was the Italian mathematician and physicist Giovanni Borelli, who took over as head of the department of mathematics at the University of Pisa a few years after Galileo had quit the post. It was in that university that Borelli met Marcello Malpighi, and, fascinated by the muscle fibres, red blood cells, tendons and ligaments Malpighi showed him under the microscope, began his own exploration into the science of animal movement.

To begin with, Borelli observed joints – in mammals, birds, reptiles, insects, humans – closely, and fabricated several simple machines to model exactly how each worked. He also compared the heart to a piston and, through the laws of mechanics, figured (correctly) that if the piston had to work, the arteries would have to be elastic (capable of returning to their original size and shape, after expanding, to accommodate the rush of blood each time the heart contracted and shot blood through them). He measured the volume of air inhaled and exhaled by the lungs and figured

Giovanni Borelli

out that the two were not equal – the lungs were never fully evacuated during exhalation. He was also the first to discover the different ways in which muscles hooked to bones and put forward several theories on how they worked to produce movement. He put all his findings on animal movement into a book of two volumes, called *De Motu*

Animalium (On the Motion of Animals), borrowing the name from Aristotle's 2,000-year-old work on the same topic. For his groundbreaking work on the subject, Borelli is today hailed as the Father of Biomechanics.

Not only joints and muscles, but even physiological functions – circulation, digestion, excretion – began to be seen as happening in a mechanical way, and as being connected with the working of the piston that was the heart (until then, the thinking had been different; for instance, it was believed that parts of the body 'attracted' blood to themselves only when they needed it). According to the new thinking, good health resulted when the bodily fluids and secretions – blood, urine, digestive acids, sweat – flowed as they should; disease happened when (1) fluid movement was obstructed in some way, (2) when the amount of fluid or secretion became too much or too little, or (3) when the fluids stagnated at some point in the body. (Doesn't it all remind you a little of the flow of the Greek humours and the Ayurvedic doshas through the body? The ancients were not so far off the mark, after all.)

With a never-before perspective on the human body as a fabulously designed, well-oiled machine, and the new-found ability to take a closer look at everything through the microscope, medicine was poised for the next big leap.

You Say Chemistry, I Say Chymystry

We have spoken of iatrophysics, but what of iatrochemistry, or the 'healer's chemistry'? Oh, that has been around ages! It has its roots in the ancient science of alchemy (also called 'chymystry'). Since time immemorial, natural philosophers had been engaged to create a fabled substance (in Europe, it was called the philosopher's stone – hmm, brings a certain book to mind?) that had the power to do many magical things – convert base metals into gold, generate the 'elixir of immortality' and/or be 'the panacea (remedy) for all ills'. These seekers were called alchemists, the science they practised alchemy (or chymystry) and their collective efforts the Magnum Opus (Great Work). Alchemy was necessarily undertaken in great secrecy (you would not want your enemies to find your recipe for immortality, would you?) and was associated with sorcery and magic, but some of the greatest scientists of the seventeenth century, including the great Sir Isaac Newton himself, were alchemists!

The original iatrochemists – people who believed that the body was made up of chemicals and that ingesting certain substances could change the body's chemical composition were the ancient Greeks (who worked with the notion that there were four fluids or humours in the body) and the Indian Ayurvedic masters (who said there were three energies). Both were pretty firm that disease was the result of an imbalance of these humours or energies. However, while the ancient

Greeks focused on surgery, simple remedies like mud baths and peppermint and chamomile teas, and creating facilities which had a soothing and conducive environment for the body to heal itself, certain Ayurvedic physicians, who were really alchemists, had a whole dossier of sophisticated healing concoctions that were made not only from plant parts (some of which were toxic), but also animal parts and small amounts of suitably processed and purified metals – gold, silver, copper, mercury – and non-metals like sulphur.

These medicines were part of a pharmaceutical and alchemical tradition called Rasa Shastra and the recipes for preparing them began to be written down around the eighth century.

In Europe, the idea of using metals and minerals in medicine began to be talked about in the thirteenth century, but captured the European imagination only in the sixteenth century. Its most famous proponent was the brilliant and temperamental Swiss alchemist and astrologer called Paracelsus. Declaring that it was 'poison in the system' that caused disease, and believing that only poison could remove poison, he created medicines that included all kinds of chemicals, even toxic ones like arsenic, antimony, mercury and lead. Paracelsus was very popular and his medicines were considered effective in his time, but they fell out of favour after his death, owing mainly to his disorganized notes on the subject, which made it difficult for anyone else to research further on the topic.

What Paracelsus did achieve, however, was to set off a way of thinking that led to more and more research on how – and why – certain drugs worked on the body in the ways they did. This paved the way for the modern science of biochemistry,

SECTION 3: 1700 CE–1900 CE

HERE COMES MODERN MEDICINE: 200 YEARS OF GLORIOUS INTELLECTUAL FERMENT

What the Renaissance sparked in Europe – the rejection of received wisdom, the belief that human beings were not mere pawns to be moved around by a whimsical divine power but creatures of intelligence who could fashion their own destinies, an insatiable curiosity to discover more and more about the wondrous universe we had been gifted and had the privilege to be part of – the so-called Age of Enlightenment, a huge creative drive to come up with ways to make human life more comfortable and productive, which spanned roughly 200 years, brought to a head.

In Italy, Germany, France, Britain, the Netherlands, Sweden – everywhere, everywhere – the brightest men and women were observing, studying, deducing, analysing, researching, experimenting and educating themselves on exciting fields of human knowledge. With the dawn of the

Age of Imperialism – the time when European powers divvied up the rest of the world between themselves like a large and luscious chocolate cake and proceeded to devour it, making themselves rich beyond their wildest dreams in the process – these bright minds were also travelling like never before, absorbing new experiences, seeing exotic new landscapes, trees, animals and birds, and learning a great deal about how different people lived and worked.

These men and women (mostly men, it must be said – a very large percentage of women still did not receive the benefit of a formal education or work at jobs outside the home) did not see themselves as inhabiting boxes labelled 'physicists' or 'chemists' or 'biologists'; in fact, they didn't even see themselves as 'scientists', because science was itself, at that time, undefined. Instead, they called themselves natural philosophers – people who were simply curious about how Nature worked, whether they were talking about the stars or the seas or the human body. Their cerebral and mechanical endeavours got an extra boost – of funding, patronage, creativity, urgency – with the coming of the Industrial Revolution in England towards the end of the eighteenth century.

With the world as their oyster, the natural philosophers of Europe led the inexorable, dazzling march towards the Age of Modern Medicine.

IDEA 10

THE MENTALLY ILL ARE PEOPLE TOO – BE KIND

How Do You Say That Again? Sy-ky-uh-tree!

Here's a quick question: In which ancient text is mental illness, and treatments for it, first described? Go on, take a guess. Done? Now, did you guess that the text was the *Charaka Samhita*, one of the two chief handbooks of Ayurveda, written way back in the second century CE? If you did, you are absolutely right! (If you didn't, this is a good time for a tip: when it comes to 'first mentions' in medicine or surgery, Ayurveda is a safe horse to back. Now you know.)

Although mental illness has been around just as long as humans have been, it has been understood very differently through the ages. In Ayurveda, which draws from the ancient Indian belief that body, mind and spirit are inextricably intertwined with each other, mental illness was thought to be as much a disease of the body and spirit as it was of the mind. The most fundamental treatment, therefore, included change in diet (to include foods that were thought to be calming to the body constitution of the patient), change in lifestyle (to include good sleep patterns, less mental stimulation and reduced stress) and change in activity (if the patient is lethargic, prescribe physical exercise; if they are hyperactive, prescribe meditation; in both cases, prescribe daily massages).

Add to this the care that the first hospitals for the mentally ill (which were also set up in India, around the third century BCE) provided, away from the hustle and bustle of the patients' daily lives, and you can see why, even 2,000 years later, this seems like a fundamentally sound and quite 'modern' treatment regimen, especially for conditions like depression and anxiety.

Islamic psychology, which was influenced both by Greek and Indian philosophy, believed that disturbances in the *nafs* (the 'soul' or the 'psyche') were the cause of mental illness. The nafs included the *qaib* ('heart'), *ruh* ('spirit'), *aqi* ('intellect') and *irada* ('will'). The study of it, therefore, was variously referred to as *a-'ilaj al-nafs* ('the treatment of the soul'), *al-tibb al-ruhani* ('the curing of the spirit') or *tibb al-qaib* ('the healing of the heart'). What a compassionate, beautiful way of looking at mental illness, right? As can be expected, treatments were similar to Ayurvedic ones – baths, music, occupational therapy (sewing, farming, cooking).

Across ancient Greece and Rome, psychotic disorders – disorders in which the sufferer is unable to differentiate between fantasy and reality – were attributed to supernatural beings, and religious leaders often prescribed exorcism (ridding the body of the evil spirit) as a remedy. Exorcisms weren't particularly calming – the one 'possessed' was often whipped, beaten and even – wait! – trepanned (Remember what that was? If you don't, look it up on page ix)!

The main contributors to Islamic psychology were the ninth century Persian physician and philosopher Muhammad ibn Zakariya al-Razi (in the West, he is called Rhazes), who was the chief of the Baghdad *bimaristan* (cool word for a hospital, what?), and the tenth-century all-rounder Avicenna, who provided descriptions and treatments for conditions like insomnia, mania, vertigo, paralysis, epilepsy and depression. The ancient Greeks had their own theories about what caused mental illness. Hippocrates, for instance, believed firmly that it was due to an imbalance in the four humours, or fluids that the body was made of – yellow bile, black bile, blood and phlegm. The Greeks also believed that the proportions of the humours in the body made you a certain kind of person. If you had an excess of yellow bile, you were of a 'choleric' temperament – extroverted, ambitious, decisive and irritable when you did not get your way. A surfeit of blood made you 'sanguine' – you were active, talkative, charismatic, optimistic by nature, happy in a crowd, and so unhappy when you had nothing to do that you often indulged in risky behaviour. Too much black bile made you 'melancholic' – introverted, deep-thinking, highly perceptive of other people's emotions, analytical and an anxious perfectionist inclined to depression. High levels of phlegm ensured that you had a – duh! – 'phlegmatic' temperament – you were the relaxed, peaceful, easy-going one who was also good at resolving conflicts. (Fun fact: This ancient humour–personality matrix is where the English words 'melancholic', 'sanguine', 'phlegmatic' and 'choleric' originally came from!)

But here's the really scary part – things didn't change very much in Europe until as recently as the eighteenth century. Even 300 years ago, the 'insane' were seen as equivalent to 'wild animals', creatures that had lost all sense of reason. Since 'madness' (which could range from depression to psychosis) was seen as incurable, there were no hospitals for treatment. The mentally ill were either thrown into prison, or sent to 'asylums' – where they could safely be put away for the rest of their lives. Most of the 'madhouses' were privately run and kept their occupants in the most appalling conditions. To make sure that the inmates were 'no trouble', treatments like bloodletting, skin-blistering (using corrosive acids), chaining naked (since they were like animals, it was reckoned they did not feel the cold), starving, and isolation from friends and family were the norm.

How was such a deep-rooted way of seeing the mentally ill overturned in the eighteenth century? Thanks to the other explosion of intellectual ideas that historians call Europe's Age of Enlightenment, or simply, the Enlightenment. According to experts, the Enlightenment began in 1687 with the publication of Isaac Newton's groundbreaking three-volume work *Principia Mathematica* and ended in 1789 with the French Revolution, when the French people, raising the rousing battle cry – '*Liberté! Fraternité! Egalité* – chopped royal heads off royal necks to create a more equal society.

One of the ideas that came out of the Enlightenment's intellectual churning was 'moral treatment'. It had its roots in a brand-new way of thinking, whose main points were: (1) societies had a responsibility to their poor, old and sick, and (2) every individual in a society had rights. (Seems like a no-brainer today? Thank your stars you didn't live back in the seventeenth century!)

Moral treatment had a very simple, straightforward premise: treat the mentally ill with kindness. But it went so against the thinking of the time – you may as well have said that one should treat a venomous snake with kindness – that it was not the most popular idea when it was first proposed. There was severe opposition from religious leaders, utter derision from the public, and downright fury from medical professionals, but it eventually caught on and, when it did, changed how the world looked at, and looked after, its mentally ill.

***

One of the earliest evangelists of the idea that kindness was as good a treatment as any was English physician William Battie, who, after practising for many years as a psychiatrist, was appointed chief physician at St Luke's Hospital for Lunatics in London.

St Luke's was a spanking new hospital, set up in 1751 as only the second public institution in London for the care of mentally ill people, and Battie saw it as the perfect setting for trying out his new ideas on the care of the insane. The only other such institution in London was the Bethlem Royal Hospital, for long the oldest (it was founded in 1246) and only asylum for the mentally ill in Britain. With no other asylum or physician to challenge its methods, Bethlem did pretty much what it liked with and to its inmates, including opening the asylum up to the public as a monstrous viewing gallery. For a fee, the public could come in and point and jeer at the inmates, who were usually chained or restrained in some way.

In 1758, Battie put all his 'modern' ideas on treating mental disorders into a fat book called *A Treatise on Madness*, the first modern text on mental illness. Most of its content was a scathing takedown of Bethlem's methods, with Battie arguing that what was needed in an asylum was cleanliness, good food, fresh air and distractions for the inmates, including access to friends and family, with the public being firmly kept out. He also proposed that mental illness could have something to do with the physical body and the brain, and could, therefore, perhaps be treated (expectedly, most people guffawed at that).

But Battie's ideas did get a lot of interest from the archbishop of York. In 1777, under his leadership, the York

Lunatic Asylum was set up, with a promise of better and more humane treatment of the mentally ill. Unfortunately, that promise did not last long. In 1791, a young widow called Hannah Mills, admitted to the asylum for suffering from 'melancholy' (today, we'd call it clinical depression), mysteriously died just six weeks later. During her time inside, she had not been allowed visitors, so no one could be sure if she had been mistreated, but no one could explain either how a healthy young woman had died in just six weeks.

One of the people most affected by Hannah's death was the philanthropist William Tuke, a prominent member of a Christian community called the Quakers. Hannah had been a Quaker herself, and to ensure that this kind of thing did not happen again in his own community, Tuke and his son, Henry, opened their own institution for the mentally ill, where all Quakers, and any others from the larger community who needed that kind of care, would be accommodated.

William Tuke

Tuke's baby, the York Retreat, opened its doors in 1796. Everything about it was fresh, avant-garde and based on compassion. Set in a large, eleven-acre park stocked with small domestic animals, the not-for-profit Retreat encouraged its patients to walk around the gardens, wear their own clothes and take up activities like sewing, knitting and farm work. The design of the building included long corridors with large, open windows for patients who were not allowed to enjoy outdoor walks, window bars and door locks encased in leather to camouflage them so that patients did not feel like prisoners, and a sunken wall around the park that, while it prevented patients from leaving the grounds, was barely visible. Physical punishments, chaining and handcuffing were banned, warm baths were recommended in place of bloodletting, the food was fresh and nutritious and the whole vibe among the patients and staff was that of a large family.

This kind of treatment of the mentally ill was so unheard of that Tuke had very few supporters apart from his own children – once, in his despair, he lamented, 'All men seem to desert me.' It was only in 1813, when his grandson Samuel Tuke wrote his famous book, *Description of the Retreat near York*, that physicians across the world became acquainted with, and began to adopt, William Tuke's methods to restore self-esteem and self-control in the mentally ill.

***

It was personal tragedy that brought Frenchman Philippe Pinel to the study of mental illness. When he first arrived in

Paris in 1778, all eager beaver about beginning his medical practice, he realized that his small-town degree was not recognized in the capital. Frustrated, he spent fifteen years as an editor (of medical journals), translator (of medical works into French) and writer (about medicine and other subjects that interested him, including botany and mathematics). He considered emigrating to America in 1784 (the new country had just gained its independence from England, with French help), but then stayed on because he had recently made some powerful friends, who were, like him, against the oppressive regime of King Louis XVI and his 'Let them eat cake!' queen Marie Antoinette.

In his book *Description of the Retreat near York*, Samuel Tuke referred to the methods used to treat mental patients at the Retreat as moral treatment. But the term was not his – he had in fact, borrowed it from the French phrase *traitement moral* that was being used across the Channel to describe the benevolent methods used in his practice by the celebrated French physician and mental-health reformer Philippe Pinel. What Tuke did not know was that, in French, the phrase was used more in the sense of 'treatment that improves the morale' rather than 'treatment that is ethical, or morally right'. But it works both ways, don't you think?

Things were going swimmingly when tragedy struck. One of Pinel's good friends, who had developed a 'nervous melancholy' and was supposedly being treated for it, committed suicide. Haunted by the feeling that he might have lived had his condition been better managed, Pinel applied for a position at the best-known sanatorium for the treatment of the insane in Paris, determined to study madness at close range and get insight into its treatment. He stayed there for five years, recording his observations and formulating some original theories on how mental illness could be managed.

When the French Revolution broke out in 1789 and the regime was dismantled, Pinel found himself on the winning side. Suddenly, opportunities earlier denied to him opened up. By 1793, he was ensconced as top dog in the Bicêtre Hospital, which had 4,000 inmates, all locked up. Among them were criminals, the terminally ill, the very old and, yes, about 200 of the insane. Pinel asked for a report on those 200 patients. It was written by the superintendent of the mental ward, a Jean-Baptiste Pussin. The man was neither a doctor nor a scholar, but his report was brilliant in its detail, insights, empathy and its intimate knowledge of the condition of each patient.

Overcome by admiration, Pinel adopted the unlettered Pussin as his mentor. In his next four years at Bicêtre, Pinel's respect for both Pussin, who believed in having long conversations with patients to bring them out of their delusions, and his wife, Marguerite Jubline (Madame Pussin), whose cheerful manner with her charges served to jolly them out of their melancholy, only grew. When Pinel left Bicêtre in 1797 for his next assignment at the Salpêtrière Hospital,

Philippe Pinel

Pussin, buoyed by the good doctor's confidence in him, unchained all the mentally ill patients in his charge for good. Before long, Philippe Pinel had Pussin join him at Salpêtrière; and when he did, the first thing the two of them did was to unchain all the patients in the mental ward there as well.

In his landmark 1801 book, *Treatise on Insanity*, Pinel generously acknowledged the contributions of the Pussins. Somehow, though, that part of the story got buried in history. Today, it is Philippe Pinel who is credited with being the great and glorious 'unchainer of the insane'.

But that isn't Pinel's fault. And to his credit, he used his power as the physician-in-charge in different hospitals to make a hundred other lasting reforms to how the mentally ill were managed. He also closely observed, documented and named a number of different mental disorders, spending hours talking with patients, in keeping with his belief that while the sufferer may seem irrational or delusional in certain ways, they had seldom 'lost all sense of reason', and could therefore, often, be 'talked out' of their problems. Pinel also insisted that not every kind of mental illness was permanent – some were temporary, the result of stressful events in the person's life, and not the result, as was commonly believed, of cosmic events like, say, the phases of the moon.

No kidding, people actually believed – and some still do – that full moon nights could bring out the 'madness' in a person. Where do you think the 'luna' in 'lunatic' comes from?

Philippe Pinel may not have been the first, and he was certainly not the only, physician of his time to espouse moral treatment, but he was the most influential in changing society's perception of 'mad' people, turning them from 'wild, uncontrolled beasts with no control over their thoughts or emotions' to 'people in need of care, compassion and conversation'. For bringing the mentally ill out of the shadowy margins of society to the front and centre of public attention, and for working tirelessly to find the best ways of treating them, Pinel is credited with kick-starting the discipline called psychiatry and celebrated as its founding father.

The Madness of King George

Remember Pinel's assertion that some mental disorders were curable? Well, across the Channel, people had believed that for several years before him. How come? Simply because their king, George III, aka Mad King George, had been completely cured of his madness before their very eyes! (What kind of madness was it? No one is quite sure, but he is suspected to have been suffering from bipolar disorder. Look it up!)

When George fell ill in 1788, his chief symptom was 'incessant loquacity' – he hadn't stopped talking for six months straight! His worried queen, Charlotte, on the recommendation of a friend whose relative had been cured by a Dr Francis Willis, called in the good doctor. Dr Willis ran his own rural sanatorium for the 'wrongheads' with great success. His methods included encouraging his patients to get involved in activities like farm work and spend time in fresh air. Dr Willis also used some of the established methods of treatment on the king, including occasionally restraining him in a straitjacket and blistering his skin, but he was far kinder to him than any of the other doctors had been. When he pronounced King George 'completely cured' in 1789, he became an instant national celebrity.

Just as significant as curing King George was Willis's other achievement – he proved conclusively to the British people, and to the world at large, that some kinds of 'madness' were curable. In 1845, Britain passed the Lunacy Act, which changed the status of the mentally ill to 'patients' who would receive the same kind of treatment as the physically ill – and in hospitals, not prisons. Phewwwwww.

IDEA 11

MAKING A HEALTHY PERSON ILL IS THE BEST WAY TO . . . KEEP THEM HEALTHY!

The Long History of Vaccination

Imagine this. There is a disease – a deadly, disfiguring, painful disease that could leave you dead, blind or terribly disfigured for life. It has been around for thousands of years, and no one in the world knows how to cure it or stop it from spreading. In the beginning, it was confined to certain countries and geographies, but since the fifteenth century, when ships became seaworthy enough to move large numbers of people over long distances, it has made its sneaky way around the world, moseying into entire unsuspecting populations and felling hundreds of thousands of them, mostly children. This horror kills three of every ten people it infects, and in the twentieth century alone, it has killed some 300 *million people*!

And now . . . it's coming for you.

Snap! You can stop screaming and wake up now. That killer disease – smallpox – now exists only in nightmares; it was completely eradicated from the world in 1979. All because of one curious, keenly observant English physician and scientist who, some 183 years before that date, figured out how to protect every single human in the world against the scourge. His name was Edward Jenner, and his gift to the world, in 1796, was a procedure called vaccination.

***

Considering that smallpox had been endemic (when it refers to a disease, 'endemic' simply means it is regularly found among particular people or in a certain area) to so many populations for so long, how come no one before Jenner came up with any kind of prevention or cure for it? Oh, but they did! In societies and geographies where it was rampant, physicians and healers, simply by observing survivors over several years and through several outbreaks of the disease, had figured out one important thing – people who had got smallpox once (and survived it) *never got it again*. It seemed as if the best way to protect oneself against the disease was to suffer it once!

So how could you make sure that a healthy infant or adult contracted the disease? From at least as far back as the fifteenth century, the Chinese had used a method that we now call variolation or inoculation to achieve this. By the seventeenth century, it was being practised extensively in Africa, the Middle East and India as well.

In the days before the chicken pox vaccine was created, parents often threw a 'chicken pox party' when their child caught chicken pox, so that all their child's friends could catch it too! That was one way to ensure that those children would not contract the more serious – and more painful – form of chicken pox when they were older. Any excuse for a party, huh?

How did variolation work? To understand that we must first understand how smallpox developed, and how it spread. We now know that smallpox, also called variola (Latin for 'pustule' or 'boil') is caused by a virus called variola (named after the disease), but no one could have guessed this before 1892. That was the year that Russian botanist Dmitry Ivanovsky discovered viruses for the first time, while investigating a disease in tobacco plants. Surprising as it may sound, the vaccine for smallpox was discovered almost a hundred years before anyone had the foggiest about what caused it!

Smallpox spread through the air; when a healthy person inhaled the virus, expelled as tiny droplets from the nose, mouth or pharynx of an infected person, they caught the disease (which meant everyone in a sick person's vicinity was at risk). It also spread through direct contact with the fluid in the boils on the patient's skin, or by contact with things like sheets and cutlery that had been used by the infected person.

The disease started like a regular flu, but spots soon appeared on the tongue and inside the mouth (at this point, the disease became highly contagious). Over the next few days, the spots changed into sores and broke open, spilling the virus into the mouth and throat. Around the same time, a rash appeared on the skin, starting on the face and spreading all over the body in twenty-four to thirty-six hours. The skin rash then turned into pus-filled sores, which in turn became hard, raised pustules (feeling like 'peas under the skin') which scabbed over in the next few days. This whole process, from fever to scabbing, took around two weeks, after which the scabs began to fall off, leaving marks on the skin. When all the scabs had fallen off, the person was no longer contagious.

Got all that? Good. Now, back to our original question – how did variolation work? Well, it essentially involved infecting a healthy person with weak smallpox germs. How was that done? By collecting the scabs that had fallen off a patient's pustules, powdering them and then either (1) rubbing the powder into a cut in the skin of the healthy person (sometimes, pus from a pustule was rubbed directly into the cut), or (2) having a healthy person inhale the powder. Since 'scab fall' was the last stage of the disease, the viruses the scabs contained were pretty weak. The healthy person would still break out into sores and suffer from smallpox, but it would be a mild form, and rarely fatal (1–2 per cent of smallpox patients died even from the weak form of the disease, so, inoculation wasn't perfectly safe, but they had a 98 per cent chance of survival, which was much better than the 70 per cent chance they would have had otherwise).

Western Europe got its first whiff of this treatment only in the eighteenth century. That happened mainly through the efforts of Lady Mary Wortley Montagu, wife of the

Considering that smallpox has such a long history in India – it was already here when the Vedas, the most ancient Indian texts of all, were being composed – it stands to reason that there would be an Indian god/goddess of smallpox. And there is – Sheetala Devi! An incarnation of the primal goddess Durga, the goddess Sheetala (in south India, she is called Mariamman) is worshipped in many parts of India and the subcontinent. The goddess of poxes, sores, pustules and all kinds of skin diseases, she rides a donkey and carries, in her four hands, a broom (to clean the area around the sick person), a fan, a pot of cooling water (both to bring down the temperature of the sick person) and a bunch of neem leaves (neem is an effective antiseptic, and neem oil is used to this day to treat psoriasis and other skin conditions). She is believed to have the power to both cause smallpox (when she is angry) and cure it (if our prayers have been done right).

British ambassador to the Ottoman Empire, which had its headquarters in Constantinople. Lady Montagu, who had lost a brother to smallpox and had survived a disfiguring attack herself, discovered variolation during her time in Constantinople, where it was extensively practised. In 1718, despite the risks, this brave mom had her five-year-old son variolated in the presence of the embassy doctor, Charles Maitland, and wrote letters singing its praises to friends back

Lady Mary Wortley Montagu

home. When she returned to England in 1721, she had her four-year-old daughter variolated in the presence of physicians of the royal court. Both procedures proved successful.

But even this demonstration of an upper-class woman's faith in a 'native' (and therefore automatically deeply suspect) procedure did not inspire the English nobility or public to embrace it to their bosoms. The whole thing sounded so bizarre to them – 'What? You are actually going to infect my kids with the killer disease that the Lord has shielded them from all these years? And I'm supposed to be grateful, and believe that this Eastern mumbo-jumbo is going to keep them safe? You've got to be out of your blooming mind!' – that they may never have come around if it wasn't for the burning curiosity of the doctor from the Constantinople embassy.

When he was transferred back to England, Charles Maitland asked the royal family for permission to test the efficacy of variolation once more, in full public view this time, using condemned prisoners on death row as his guinea pigs. Intrigued, the royals agreed, offering six volunteers the freedom to walk should they survive the procedure. In August 1722, Maitland inoculated the six men, allowed them to go through the mild form of the disease and then exposed each to an infected person. None of the volunteers became infected again, and all left Newgate Prison as free – and healthy – men. Thrilled, the royal family, and many members of the public, became enthusiastic promoters of the procedure. Very quickly, England became the European authority on variolation, attracting physicians and healers eager to know more, from all over the world. Variolation became all the rage across Europe, with English doctors travelling as far as Russia to inoculate the royals there. (France was the last country to capitulate. They waited until 1752, when the heir to the throne nearly lost his life to smallpox, to finally give it a try.)

Slowly and steadily, however, across the world, this apparently bizarre, counterintuitive and upside-down idea became accepted. The ground had been laid for Edward Jenner to enter, stage right, and find a most significant link in a very long chain.

In America it was a Boston clergyman, Cotton Mather, who first heard about variolation from his North African slave, Onesimus, and found that many of his other slaves had also be variolated as children. In 1721, when Boston suffered an outbreak of smallpox, Mather got his chance to implement the miracle treatment, but against severe opposition – the religious-minded denounced it as ungodly as it was not mentioned in the Bible, while scientists thought the idea of infecting a person to protect them from disease illogical. Still, in 1775, the year of the American Declaration of Independence, Commander George Washington ordered that the entire Continental Army be variolated. By the time America got her freedom in 1781, variolation had become the norm there.

***

Edward Jenner was born in 1749, when variolation was already a well established practice in England. Naturally, he himself was variolated while still in school. At the tender age of fourteen, he was apprenticed to a surgeon, and gained enough experience in his seven years there to become a surgeon himself.

Jenner went on to become a successful family doctor back in his home county of Gloucestershire, operating on William Harvey's (yup, the circulation guy) advice to his students – 'Don't think, try.' His childhood years in the countryside had given him a keen appreciation of Nature and animals, and it was his watershed findings in zoology, not surgery, that got him elected to the Royal Society in 1788.

Jenner's familiarity with animals also meant that he knew a lot about cowpox, a disease similar to smallpox, but far less deadly, that affected cows. It was on the udders of cows that the cowpox lesions (pus-filled boils) developed, and milkmaids whose hands came in contact with infected udders caught the disease too. For a while, their hands became quite unsightly, but apart from that, there were no side effects of cowpox, and the milkmaids and other infected dairy hands quickly recovered. The fascinating thing Jenner noticed (as, indeed, other farmers in England already had) was that milkmaids who had once contracted cowpox never contracted smallpox. If he could find a way, Jenner reasoned, to infect humans with the milder cowpox, instead of variolating them against smallpox, they would still be protected against the latter, and it would be less risky all around.

Jenner decided to test his theory ('Don't think, try' – remember?). On 14 May 1796, he scraped pus off the cowpox blisters on the hands of the milkmaid Sarah Neimes, and inoculated an eight-year-old called James Phipps, the son of his gardener (i.e., he introduced the pus into James's bloodstream via tiny cuts on both arms). As expected, James got a mild fever, but he soon recovered. After a few days, Jenner variolated the boy, introducing smallpox into his bloodstream. James remained in the pink of health – he did not even experience uneasiness. Jenner had discovered the perfect solution to protect people against smallpox!

The English milkmaid Sarah Neimes, made famous by Edward Jenner's experiment, had caught cowpox from a cow called Blossom. Today, Blossom's hide hangs on the wall of St George's medical school library in London, and her horns occupy pride of place in Jenner's house in Gloucestershire, which has been converted into a museum.

What made Jenner's inoculation so much better than old-style variolation? Well, mainly because, as we discussed earlier, it was much safer. But there was another advantage with both kinds of inoculation – when a large enough number of people in a community were protected, it became very difficult for an infectious disease to find a foothold, thus guaranteeing 'herd immunity', which protected even those of the community who were not inoculated (like newborns).

Edward Jenner

Jenner's term for cowpox was *Variolae vaccinae*, or 'smallpox of the cow' (*vacca* is Latin for 'cow'). That was how his version of inoculation began to be called 'vaccination'. His smallpox vaccine was the world's first vaccine, and a giant leap for mankind in learning how to contain infectious diseases. It also opened the doors to an entire new field of research called immunology, which studied the human body's

> One of vaccination's early – and unlikely – fans was French emperor Napoleon Bonaparte, who had all his troops vaccinated, never mind that he was at war with Britain in the vaccination years! He gave Jenner a medal, and even released two British prisoners of war (both scientists) at his request, saying that he could not refuse 'one of the greatest benefactors of mankind'.

defence system (or immune system) and worked out how it could be 'taught', through 'mock tests' (i.e., weak versions of disease-causing germs), to identify, fight and overcome deadly bacteria and viruses.

Jenner's findings were not immediately accepted, however. It was only when he submitted a paper detailing not just the case of James Phipps, but twenty-three others, including his own eleven-month-old son, that the authorities and his fellow doctors were finally convinced. In 1840, seventeen years after Jenner's death, the British government banned the riskier variolation and made vaccination mandatory, providing the vaccine free of charge to its people.

Fun fact to round up the smallpox story: Even though the disease was eradicated forty years ago, a few smallpox pus samples are still stored in a laboratory each in the US and Russia. And this, even after the former Union of Soviet Socialist Republics (USSR), in the 1980s, developed variola as an aerosol biological weapon and produced tons of virus-laden material intended for release via intercontinental ballistic missiles! Now, who wants to use this info as the starting point for a bioterrorism thriller (fiction only, thank you very much)?

How One of the World's Deadliest Diseases Won an All-Expenses-Paid Trip Around the World

How, and how quickly, do infectious diseases – and the germs that cause them – travel around the world? Today, with hundreds of thousands of people flying across the world 24/7, a day is more than enough time for germs, hitch-hiking on a human's body or sitting pretty in their lungs or gut, to travel from one side of the globe to the other.

It didn't always use to be that way, though. Since we have been talking about smallpox, let's see how that killer disease got from where it first reared its ugly head to everywhere else in the world.

Let's begin by travelling to Egypt, from where we have the earliest evidence of smallpox, in the mummified remains of, as far as we know, its first celebrity victim, the pharaoh Rameses V. When Rameses's mummy was discovered in 1898, the 3,000-year-old scars of lesions still visible on the face were a dead giveaway to the cause of his death. It was from Egypt that smallpox travelled to India around 1000 BCE. Once it had arrived, it made itself at home, becoming an endemic disease there. It probably travelled to China next – the first description of a disease resembling smallpox comes to us from Chinese writings of the fourth century BCE.

In the sixth century CE, Japan began to trade more extensively with China and Korea, blissfully oblivious of the bioterror that trade would bring in its wake – in the eighth century, an outbreak of smallpox, lasting two years, eliminated one-third of Japan's entire population. Arab armies of the Islamic Empire took the disease to North Africa and south-western Europe (Spain and Portugal) during their conquest of those regions in the seventh century. The Crusades – which were a series of religious wars launched by the Catholic Church against the Islamic Empire, to liberate the Holy Land (Jerusalem, which is holy to Christians since it is where Jesus Christ is believed to have lived and preached) from Muslim rule – saw thousands of Europeans travelling to the vicinity of Arabia in the eleventh century. They returned not just with the spoils of war, but also with – that's right – smallpox.

Between the fifteenth and seventeenth centuries, smallpox, travelling out of Europe this time with explorers, traders and colonizers from Spain, Portugal, England, France and the Netherlands, encircled the world with its deadly tentacles. Spanish colonizers brought the disease with them first into the Caribbean islands and then into Mexico – decimating entire populations of Aztecs and Incas who had no immunity to the 'foreign' germs.

In 1633, the Pilgrim Fathers, fleeing religious persecution in their native country, England, dropped anchor in Plymouth Harbour in Massachusetts, and proceeded to devastate the Native American population with the smallpox germs they brought with them. In fact, part of that devastation was intentional; during the American-Indian wars ('Indian' as in Red Indian, the old – and now politically incorrect – name for Native Americans) fought between 1754 and 1767, the

Americans indulged in what we would today call bioterrorism – they distributed blankets infected with smallpox germs to the natives, as a 'gesture of goodwill'. You already knew that the Americans won those wars – now you also know one of the reasons why!

In 1770, Captain James Cook made landfall on the south-eastern coast of Australia, and became the first European to contact the native population of the continent, the Aborigines. Unfortunately for the Aborigines, he also brought with him deadly European germs. Between 1780 and 1870, smallpox was the leading cause of death among the Aboriginal population.

And that's how smallpox reached the last continent on earth, and completed its terrifying global takeover.

PS. Yup, the colonization of the world and its native populations by the Europeans were not achieved by guns or guts alone – germs, specifically the smallpox virus, helped things along mightily.

IDEA 12

HOW CAN YOU TELL IF SOMEONE IS WELL? LISTEN TO THEIR TELLTALE HEART!

How a Doctor's Shyness Led to the Invention of the Stethoscope

Several great anatomists, starting with Andreas Vesalius, had done wonderful work on figuring out how exactly the organs were laid out inside the human body. But it wasn't until Giovanni Battista Morgagni come along that anyone thought of connecting the disease a patient had died of with the way their organs looked during dissection.

Um, let's go over that again. In fact, let's start with some background info. In the eighteenth century, no one, not even the best physicians and scientists, had any clue as to what caused disease. They knew, by observation of patients, how disease progressed, and could make a diagnosis ('what you have is smallpox, not cowpox or measles') and a prognosis ('things don't look very good for you, I'm afraid – when smallpox progresses in this manner, it is usually fatal'), and they knew what medicines helped patients get better, but they had NO idea about the 'seat of disease', i.e., the place where disease originated in the body, or what caused it.

Anatomists knew that certain diseases caused the body's innards to change in quite radical ways, but none had thought to map specific changes to specific diseases. William Harvey (yup, the same guy who discovered that blood circulates; we seem to run into him a lot, eh?) was among the first to make the vital connection between the morbidity (a lovely medical word meaning 'a diseased state') of organs and the illness the person had died of. In a letter to a fellow anatomist, he wrote, 'I venture to say that the examination of a single body of one who has died of tabes [the old word for 'wasting away' for no apparent reason] or consumption [another word for tuberculosis] . . . is of more service to medicine than the dissection of the bodies of ten men who have been hanged.' What he meant was that there was more to be learnt from dissecting a diseased body than a healthy one. Unfortunately, he never got around to exploring that line of thought further.

The world had to wait for over a hundred years after Harvey's death for the first definitive study of anatomical pathology (pathology is the science of the causes and effects of disease) to be published. Its author was the brilliant and well-loved Italian professor of anatomy, Giovanni Morgagni, who had taught thousands of medical students from many countries during his fifty-six years at the University of Padua. His monumental five-volume work, *On the Seats and Causes of Diseases Investigated through Anatomy*, was published in 1761, when he was eighty years old.

Morgagni's 'book' was really a collection of seventy letters that the good doctor had written to a young friend over twenty years of correspondence, describing the details of some 646 dissections he had conducted during that time.

From the time it was first published, the book changed how physicians thought about disease – from seeing it as a set of symptoms, they began to see it as 'the cry of a suffering organ'. 'Listening' to organs, and listening particularly for their 'cries of pain', became an important method of detecting and diagnosing disease.

***

In the same year that Morgagni's famous book was published, an Austrian physician called Leopold Auenbrugger, who was working at the reputed Spanish Military Hospital in Vienna, brought out a little booklet about a new technique he was using to listen to the heart and lungs – percussion. (Want to know more about him and his technique? Check out the box on page 136.) The booklet was in Latin, and titled *Inventum Novum*. Unfortunately, most of his peers did not pay Auenbrugger's book – or technique – much attention.

From ancient times, healers had practised percussion of the abdomen to detect a build-up of gas or fluid inside. Strangely enough, however, no one before Auenbrugger had thought to try percussion of the thorax .

Inventum Novum is the short version of the title of Auenbrugger's book. In English, its full form reads 'A New Discovery that Enables the Physician to Detect Diseases Within the Chest from the Percussion of the Human Thorax'. Yup, those chaps really were into long book titles.

Luckily for Auenbrugger, there were a few who did. Among his fans was a hugely influential French doctor called Jean-Nicolas Corvisart, who was so taken by percussion as a diagnostic tool that he not only used it extensively in his practice but also insisted his students do the same. In 1808, a year before Auenbrugger's death, he even translated *Inventum Novum* from Latin into French, instantly making it far more accessible to the world.

Corvisart added so many of his own notes, experiences and learnings on percussion to the translation of *Inventum Novum* that his book was four times longer than the original! Given his stature, his methods were picked up and followed by hundreds of other doctors across France. He wielded even more influence on his own students. One of those students was a shy and sickly young man called René Laennec.

What made Jean-Nicolas Corvisart so influential? Well, the fact that he was the personal physician to the great French ruler Napoleon Bonaparte, that's what! There's more – it was Corvisart who mediated between Edward Jenner and Napoleon when Jenner requested the emperor, who was then at war with England, to please release two English prisoners of war (see page 124 for more details).

Laennec's mother had died of tuberculosis when he was only five, and his father had sent him away to live with a great-uncle who was a priest. At the age of twelve, he moved again, this time to the home of an uncle who was a physician at the University of Nantes. His natural curiosity and intelligence pleased his uncle, and René was soon apprenticed to him for his medical studies. At the age of eighteen, he went off to the University of Paris to continue his studies and get himself a proper medical degree. It was during his time here that he learnt the art and science of percussion from Corvisart.

In 1816, he was consulted by a young woman who clearly had a diseased heart. In most cases, Laennec would have diagnosed the problem using percussion, but this patient was grossly overweight, and percussion would not have helped in this case. The other method he could have used was immediate auscultation (auscultation means 'listening to the internal sounds of the body'; immediate auscultation was done by placing the ear on the body), but to our shy René, that method, considering the age and sex of the patient, felt completely inappropriate.

While he wondered what to do, a thought suddenly came to him. He remembered 'the great distinctness with which we hear the scratch of a pin on one end of a piece of wood on applying our ear to the other'. Quickly, he rolled up a sheet of thick paper into a cylinder and placed it on the woman's chest, hoping for the best, and froze in amazement. Not only was he hearing the sounds of the heart, but they were louder and clearer than ever before! He didn't know it just yet, but in that moment, René Laennec had invented the stethoscope!

The first proper *mediate* (an old French word for 'instrument') that he built (you didn't think he kept rolling up sheets of paper, did you?) was a hollow wooden cylinder – 25 centimetres long and 2.5 centimetres in diameter. He refined it as he went on, and the final version had three detachable parts – a brass cylinder and a wooden cylinder that could be screwed together, and a smaller funnel-shaped bit that fit inside and helped to amplify the sound further. He often called it, simply, 'the cylinder', but later gave it a proper name: stethoscope (from the Greek words *stethos*, 'chest', and 'scope' – oh, come on, you know by now what 'scope' means).

Laennec's stethoscope was monaural – it only required you to use one ear. The first binaural ('two-ear') stethoscope, like the ones we are more familiar with, was invented over thirty years later, in 1851, by an Arthur Leared.

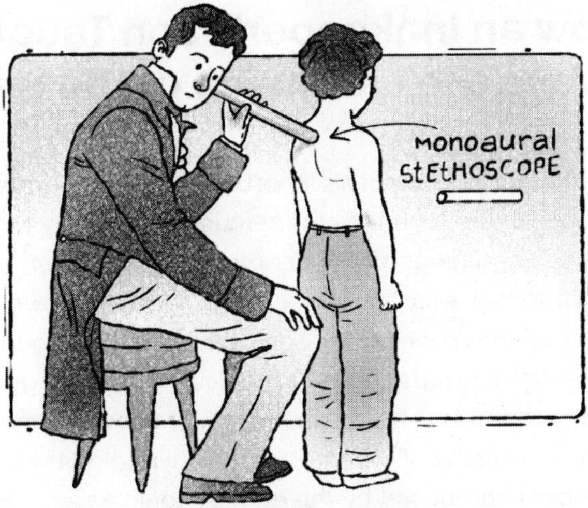

René Laennec at work

Three years later, in 1819, Laennec wrote his famous book *L'Auscultation Mediate* (Auscultation via an Instrument). As always in medical history, not many people took to the stethoscope immediately. But his own countrymen, and the hospital where he was working when he rolled up his paper cylinder, celebrated him, and continue to do so. Near the entrance of the Hôpital Necker in Paris is a marble tablet carved with a portrait of Laennec and the words 'In this hospital, Laennec discovered auscultation'.

Laennec died young, also of tuberculosis – he was only forty-five. But his invention is used every single day by grateful doctors everywhere, more than 200 years after his death, even in a time when there are so many other – and far more revealing – ways to listen to the telltale heart.

How an Innkeeper's Son Taught Doctors the Language of the Heart

Unlike many physicians of his time, Leopold Auenbrugger, who came up with the technique of percussion as a way to 'listen' to the heart and lungs, did not come from a family of medical men. His father was an innkeeper in his hometown, Graz, Austria, but very keen on his son getting the best education possible, both in music and in medicine. The youngster did well on both fronts – he graduated with honours in medicine from the University of Vienna, and also wrote a libretto for a comic opera composed by the great Antonio Salieri (Mozart's famous rival, and one of Beethoven's teachers) himself.

In the family inn, Auenbrugger had watched his father and the other staff using percussion (which means exactly what you think it means – striking something with the fingers or any other object to obtain different sounds) on wine barrels to detect the level of wine remaining inside. As a musician, he had a great ear for sounds. Putting the two together, Auenbrugger wondered if percussion could be used on a patient's thorax to detect the condition of the heart and the lungs, and began to experiment on patients in the Spanish Military Hospital in Vienna, where he worked. What he found amazed him. By applying his ear to a patient's chest, and lightly striking all over it with his fingers, he could draw a startling number of accurate conclusions about the condition of the organs and tissues that lay inside. In fact, he found he was able to plot the outlines of the heart simply by using this technique!

Equally, Auenbrugger experimented on cadavers, noting the difference in sounds between a live body and a dead one. By injecting fluid into the space between the two membranes covering each lung (in cadavers), he demonstrated how it was possible, through percussion, to tell where the fluid was present and, through that, figure out the best place from which to drain out any excess fluid. In later years, he focused on tuberculosis, and demonstrated how it was possible to detect the position and size of cavities in the lungs (one of the indications of tuberculosis is hollowed-out cavities in the lungs, caused by lung tissue getting destroyed by bacteria) simply through percussion.

Auenbrugger's marvellous technique went largely unappreciated by most of the medical fraternity for most of his lifetime. Today, the slim, ninety-five-page booklet he published in 1761 – *Inventum Novum* – is considered a landmark in the annals of medicine.

Dr Hahnemann, Homoeopath

If you have read this far, you know that the kind of medicine practised in the eighteenth century didn't inspire a lot of confidence. In fact, to a casual observer, it all looked pretty brutal.

But it wasn't just laypersons who suspected healing could be done better; even qualified doctors who themselves administered these 'treatments' were often not convinced of their efficacy. One doctor who was particularly perturbed was a German physician and polyglot (a lovely word for someone who speaks many languages; apart from his native German, this man spoke fluent English, French, Italian, Greek and Latin, and also taught himself Arabic, Syriac, Chaldaic and Hebrew) called Samuel Hahnemann. In 1784, at the age of twenty-nine, Dr Hahnemann gave up his medical practice in disgust, and became a translator of scientific and medical textbooks.

It was when he was translating *A Treatise on the Materia Medica* by the great Scottish physician Dr William Cullen that Hahnemann came across the claim that cinchona, the bitter bark of a Peruvian tree, was effective as a cure against malaria. Not quite convinced, he decided to experiment on himself.

When he chewed a piece or two of cinchona, he noticed that though he was perfectly healthy, he briefly developed malaria-like symptoms – fever, shivering, pain in the joints. 'Eureka!' cried Hahnemann (and we're paraphrasing here). 'What the ancient Greek healers said is true after all! *Similia similibus curentur*, people – like cures like!' (If you think about it, Jenner's vaccination was also somewhat posited on the theory that 'like cures like'.) Inspired, he began to develop a new system of medicine which he named homoeopathy, putting together the Greek words *homoios* – 'like' – and *pathos* – 'suffering'.

(Fun fact: It was also Hahnemann who first used the term allopathic medicine – allopathy, in Greek, means 'different suffering' – to disdainfully refer to the system of medicine that he believed merely suppressed the symptoms of the disease rather than healing the disease itself.)

Convinced that an effective drug to treat an illness was one that produced symptoms of that disease in patients, Hahnemann began to independently develop a range of medicines, by testing different substances on people. Realizing that the dose must be very mild, so as not to aggravate the disease, he invented a way of reducing a drug's potency. In 1810, he wrote his landmark work on the subject, *Materia Medica Pura*. It continues to be the handbook for homoeopathic doctors today.

To people suffering from all kinds of ailments in the nineteenth century, homoeopathy was such a gentle alternative to allopathy that it became hugely popular, both in Europe and America. Plus, with allopathy being in its infancy then, homoeopathy often had way better results with sick people. That began to change in the twentieth century, however, and homoeopathy gradually fell out of favour.

Be that as it may, this non-invasive, mostly harmless system of medicine continues to have its loyal fans to this day, especially in India.

IDEA 13

BREEEEEATHE! FINALLY, THERE'S PLENTY OF GAIN, WITH NOT A WHIT OF PAIN!

Hallelujah! Here Comes Anaesthesia!

Mention the word surgery, and most people will run for cover. Now mention – if you dare – 'surgery without anaesthesia', and you're likely to start a proper riot. But that fate worse than death was an actual reality for the world until a few good men – Humphry Davy, Hanaoka Seishu, Horace Wells, William Morton, James Simpson – came along and delivered us from that particular evil.

Why did it take until the nineteenth century for a 'proper' – read effective, safe and proven – anaesthetic to be employed during surgery? Simply because surgery was not a common procedure at all! Very often, understandably, patients chose certain death from an illness over a surgical procedure that was horrendously painful and not entirely foolproof. If it hadn't been for an unrelated parallel development – the sudden interest in the scientific community in different kinds of 'air' – anaesthetics, and therefore surgery, may have remained on the margins of medical science for much longer.

Different kinds of air? Yes! And it was Robert Boyle's experiments, which caused him to suspect that one kind of air was responsible both for sustaining life and helping things burn better (see 'The Breath of Life' on page 78), that helped kick-start the general interest in the components of 'common air' – i.e., the air around us. In 1754, British chemist Joseph Black isolated carbon dioxide, which he called 'fixed air'. In 1766, his fellow countryman Henry Cavendish discovered hydrogen or 'inflammable air'. In 1772, Black's student Daniel Rutherford removed (what we now know as) oxygen and carbon dioxide from common air, and discovered that the remaining air neither supported life (a mouse exposed to it died) nor combustion (a candle could not burn in it). He called this remaining air, which was nitrogen, 'noxious air'. In 1773, a Swedish chemist called Carl Wilhelm Scheele discovered oxygen, which he called 'fire air' (because it supported combustion – a candle burned brightly in the presence of this air), but he did not immediately publish his findings, allowing Joseph Priestley and Antoine Lavoisier to claim the credits for that particular discovery. Yup, there are various kinds of air (today, we call them gases) out there!

But it was Priestley's book *Experiments and Observations on Different Kinds of Air*, published in 1775, that really got everyone going. One of the people fascinated by the airs, particularly in terms of their possible applications in medicine (Could inhaling a particular air cure asthma? What about tuberculosis?) was English physician Thomas Beddoes. In 1798, he established the Pneumatic Institution for Relieving Diseases by Medical Airs in Bristol to investigate the effects of inhaling different airs. The first superintendent of the institute was a twenty-year-old called Humphry Davy.

The engineer who built the cool new inhalation machine – which included one part in which the gas was freshly generated and another through which it was inhaled – at the Pneumatic Institution was a chap called James Watt. Yes! The man who invented the steam engine!

One of Davy's jobs as superintendent at the Pneumatic Institution was to inhale different airs and record their effects on himself. When he inhaled nitrous oxide (which had been isolated by Joseph Priestley two years before oxygen), he was astonished to find that it made him laugh uncontrollably, and nicknamed it 'laughing gas'. In his book *Researches, Chemical and Philosophical, Chiefly Concerning* Nitrous Oxide *and* Its *Respiration*, published in 1800, he wrote that the gas appeared 'capable of destroying physical pain, and may probably be used with advantage during surgical operations'. As usual – you know the drill now – no one paid that throwaway line any attention, and the first surgical procedure using laughing gas, a dental extraction, wasn't performed until forty-four years later! Meanwhile, Davy made a habit of having his friends over at the institute for some laughing-gas tomfoolery, before he quit his post in 1801.

Three years later, half a world away, Japanese surgeon Hanaoka Seishu performed a major cancer tumour removal surgery on a sixty-year-old woman after having her drink a concoction of his own invention called *tsusensan*, made up of extracts of seven different plants. The tsusensan caused skeletal muscle paralysis, and the surgery went off painlessly and smoothly, becoming the first recorded surgery to be done under general anaesthesia.

Humphry Davy

Davy was so young and reckless and curious that he sometimes took that experimentation a bit too far. When he inhaled nitric oxide, it combined with air in his mouth to form nitric acid, which destroyed his mucous membranes. His attempt to inhale four quarts of carbon monoxide, as you can imagine, nearly killed him. As he was moved out of the lab into the open air, the inveterate scientist, while taking his own pulse – he recorded in his notes that it 'was thread-like and beating with excessive quickness' – whispered reassuringly to his fellows, 'I do not think I shall die.'

***

With news of the jolly times to be had with laughing gas spreading across the world, another similar gas, diethyl ether, whose pain-numbing effects had first been discovered in the sixteenth century by our old friend Paracelsus (see page 98; more about this in the box at the end of this chapter), made a comeback, especially across the Atlantic. In the 1830s, 'ether frolics' became a popular entertainment across America, with volunteers inhaling the gas and then staggering around the stage in a very cheerful mood indeed, much to the amusement of the audience. (It seems incredible, but even at this late stage, no one had thought to use either nitrous oxide or ether as an anaesthetic for surgery!)

One of the people who had participated enthusiastically in ether frolics, both as a volunteer and as an observer, was the physician Crawford Long. He noticed that when people were staggering around 'under the influence', many of them bumped into things or fell and hurt themselves but never seemed to notice the pain. This got Long thinking, and he decided to try an experiment. One of his friends, James Venable, had been told to get a couple of tumours removed from his neck, but had been consistently putting it off because he was terrified of the pain. Long suggested he get it done after inhaling ether, promising him that he wouldn't feel a thing. Venable agreed, and Long performed the surgery painlessly and successfully in 1842. This was the first time anyone had used ether as a general anaesthetic, but Long did not publicize his achievement until 1849, by which time another doctor had taken the credit.

In 1844, a dentist called Horace Wells was at a nitrous oxide demonstration conducted by American showman Gardner Quincy Colton, when he noticed that nitrous oxide seemed to make people oblivious to pain. He insisted that Colton administer laughing gas to him the very next day, and got a tooth extracted painlessly. He then himself proceeded to conduct several painless tooth extractions on his patients over the next few weeks.

Excited with the success Wells was having with using nitrous oxide as an anaesthetic, his business partner William Morton arranged for Wells to demonstrate the technique at the famous Massachusetts General Hospital (MGH) in 1845. Equally excited, Wells obliged, but the demo was a failure –

the patient cried out in pain in the middle of the extraction, and the watching audience rose in disdain, yelling, 'Humbug!'

A year and a half later, in September 1846, William Morton performed a painless dental extraction in his clinic, using ether (instead of nitrous oxide). On 16 October 1846, he was back at the MGH, his fingers tightly crossed, this time to himself publicly demonstrate the efficacy of ether as a general anaesthetic during a proper surgical procedure. After Morton had administered the gas to a patient, part of a tumour was removed from the patient's neck by John Collins Warren, the former dean of Harvard Medical College. The patient stayed unconscious through the entire procedure. When he came to, Warren asked him how he felt. 'Feels as if my neck has been scratched, sir!' said the patient. Warren turned to the watching crowd. 'Gentlemen,' he smiled, 'this is no humbug.'

The room erupted in cheers, and a brave new age of surgery was born. The operating room at the MGH was renamed the Ether Dome and, to this day, 16 October is celebrated annually as Ether Day, to commemorate the glorious occasion when humankind triumphed over pain.

***

Epilogue: Ether worked well as an anaesthetic, but it had side effects like excessive vomiting, and was itself explosively flammable. Looking for alternatives, English obstetrician (obstetrics is the branch of medicine concerned with childbirth) James Simpson stumbled upon chloroform, which was not only equally effective but also had fewer side effects. Chloroform was quickly adopted by doctors in England, but it wasn't until another physician, John Snow, administered it to Queen Victoria during the birth of her youngest child, Prince Leopold, on 7 April 1853, that it acquired celebrity status. Post-delivery, the queen declared that the experience had been 'delightful beyond measure', leading even American doctors to embrace the anaesthetic without ado. In the early twentieth century, however, chloroform fell out of favour after it was discovered that it could have grave negative effects on the heart and liver. Today, of the three famous anaesthetics of the nineteenth century – nitrous oxide, ether and chloroform – only the first is still in use as an anaesthetic.

Among the people who sent congratulatory notes to William Morton on his successful 'painless surgery' was the brilliant American physician, poet and polymath Oliver Wendell Holmes. 'Everybody wants to have a hand in a great discovery,' wrote Holmes. 'All I will do is to give a hint or two as to the name to be applied to the state of feeling no pain . . . It should, I think, be called "anaesthesia".' The unusual but apt name – constructed from the Greek words *an*, or 'without', and *aesthesis*, or sensation – stuck.

O Shaman, Give Me Something for the Pain!

The quest to find a painless way to perform surgery began in ancient times. Alcohol was commonly used in Mesopotamia as a sedative, and there were several herbal potions involving the juice of the opium poppy (Sumeria, Babylon, Persia), the mandrake fruit (Egypt) or the cannabis plant (India, China) that physicians used to make surgeries somewhat less agonizing for their patients. It was centuries later, during the Islamic Golden Age, that inhaled anaesthetics were probably used for the first time. Famous Arab physicians between the tenth and twelfth centuries, like Al-Zahrawi, Avicenna (of course!) and Ibn Zuhr, wrote about the 'sleep sponge' – a sponge soaked in a solution of various aromatics and narcotics (substances that induce sleep and prevent you from feeling pain) and placed under the patient's nose during surgery so that they may inhale the fumes and be knocked senseless for a few hours.

The idea of the *spongia soporifica* ('sleep sponge' in Latin) was picked up by surgeons in the Schola Medica Salernitana in Italy. (Remember we talked about it before? See page 39.) In England, between 1200 and 1500 CE, a herbal mixture called dwale – which contained a bunch of poisonous herbs like hemlock, henbane and bryony – was used extensively as an anaesthetic, not so much by physicians as by the wives of soldiers injured in wars, to ease their loved ones' pain. (And how many of those poor men who drank dwale woke up again? Given how many dangerous ingredients were in it, and that it was brewed at home to inexact recipes, not all.

In Cuzco, Peru, in the fifteenth and sixteenth centuries, Inca surgeons used coca leaves (coca is the plant from which the dangerous and highly addictive drug cocaine is extracted) as a local anaesthetic during surgeries. They chewed on coca leaves, spitting the juice on to incisions as they made them, to turn that part numb (no, seriously). While dwale and the sleep sponge were general anaesthetics, which made the patient unconscious, coca-leaf juice was a local one (it only worked on the part being cut into, while the patient was conscious).

Around 1525 CE, the temperamental Swiss physician Paracelsus experimented on chickens using a gas called diethyl ether and noted that inhaling the gas not only put the chickens to sleep but also protected them from pain. Strangely, it would be over 300 years before ether would be seriously investigated for human use, more's the pity!

Spongia soporifica

IDEA 14

HEY, SURGEONS! WASH YOUR HANDS SOMETIMES, MAYBE?

How a Simple, Non-surgical Technique Saved Thousands of Young Women's Lives

Sure, once anaesthetics became part of operating rooms, the agonizing screams of patients undergoing surgery were mercifully eliminated. But people still did not go smiling into surgery. How come? Well, because they knew they had only a 50 per cent chance of staying alive in the days after the surgery! No, seriously! Surgeries were usually followed by septicaemia (blood poisoning), gangrene (death of body tissue) and all kinds of post-operative infections. The story of how operating rooms became the clean, sterile and safe places they are today is a fascinating one, and we shall get to that soon.

Before that, though, we need to make a little detour to explore what people – both common people and doctors – believed to be the truth about infection.

We've talked about this before, but it is worth saying it again: 150 years ago, i.e., as recently as 1870, the idea that maybe, just mayyyy-be, it was germs – those itsy-bitsy teeny-weenies that Leeuwenhoek first saw under his microscope, or others very like them – that caused disease or infections was scoffed at, shot down or completely ignored. The general belief, at least in Europe and China, was that it was miasma – a stinky, noxious vapour that rose from rotting organic matter – that was responsible for all kinds of disease. Miasma, so the story went, contained tiny particles that were released when plant and animal bodies decomposed; anyone who inhaled those particles would sooner or later contract a disease. Wounds, surgical or otherwise, were also prone to getting infected by miasmic particles.

Because people thought that staying away from smelly fumes of rotting matter was good enough to prevent disease and infection, no one bothered to find any other way of doing it. Not even surgeons.

So how was a typical surgery conducted in the nineteenth century? Here's a visualization exercise for you – an operation theatre scenario from, say, 1850. Brace yourself and try to make it through without screaming.

You are lying on a raised flat surface in the centre of the room, waiting for your operation to begin. The surgeon walks straight in from the street, without even pausing to take off his work clothes. From a hook, he takes down his surgical apron, still stained and smudged with the blood and pus of a bunch of previous surgeries, and puts it on with a sense of great pride, joking about 'good old hospital stink'. As he gets ready to give you the anaesthetic, he apologizes for coming in late, saying he was held up at the mortuary, where he has just finished performing a dissection.

Operating rooms have traditionally been called theatres for a reason. The surgeon, who always worked alone, was the star of the play, the patient a mere prop. A high skylight ensured plenty of natural light. Operations were performed in the presence of an audience, who made themselves comfortable on the tiers of wooden benches running around the room, possibly even calling out, 'Hey, doc, break a leg!' in encouragement. Also, there were no sinks or basins or other facilities to wash up – this was an operation theatre, not a bedroom, for heaven's sake!

The anaesthetic takes over, and you pass out. When you come to, your friend, who has watched the surgery, tells you the surgeon did a great job. Sure, he dropped his scalpel a couple of times, but he just picked it up, wiped it on his apron and carried on like a trooper. When he had to use both his hands for something, he calmly held his scalpel between his teeth. And it was really cool to watch how he picked the suture threads straight off the little eyelets in his battle-scarred apron and used them to stitch you up. It was all a one-man operation, and your surgeon totally rocked it!

After the surgery, the windows are opened to let the fresh air in, so that the miasma from the wounds is carried away. All shipshape and Bristol fashion!

End of visualization exercise. Let's pause for a moment to let your breathing return to normal.

Right. Astoundingly, until very recently, this was exactly how things worked in the operating rooms of the best hospitals in the world. Surgeons were just as much at risk as patients, which is why even *they* recommended surgery only as a last resort. There was even a move to abolish surgery from hospitals altogether, so terrible and fatal and common were the infections that followed them.

***

Luckily for us, there were some physicians who questioned the status quo. One of them was a Hungarian obstetrician called Ignaz Semmelweis, who was losing his mind over the extraordinary number of young mothers who died during or soon after childbirth from a deadly infection called puerperal fever, or 'childbed fever'. In the Vienna General Hospital, where he worked, the rate of mortality from puerperal fever – i.e., the percentage of new mothers who died from the disease – was about 10 per cent. This in itself wasn't particularly worrying, because it was close to the average maternal mortality rate (MMR) across Europe. But there was one particular statistic at Vienna General that troubled Ignaz Semmelweis no end.

Ignaz Semmelweis

The hospital had two maternity clinics – the First Clinic, where Semmelweis worked with other doctors, and the Second Clinic, which was staffed mainly by midwives. Both were free clinics, and had been set up to take care of the babies of poor women who could not afford to do it themselves. In return, the women agreed to have their babies at the hospital, allowing doctors and midwives to get training and practice in obstetrics.

The statistic that so bothered Semmelweis was this: while the First Clinic's maternal mortality rate was 10 per cent, the Second Clinic's was less than 4 per cent! Expectant mothers begged to be admitted to the latter, even preferring to have 'street births' (having their babies right on the streets) over being admitted as patients of the First Clinic. The astounding thing was that the MMR even among street births was lower than that of the First Clinic. Feeling personally humiliated, Semmelweis grew determined to get to the bottom of the mystery. To begin with, he studied the workings of the Second Clinic closely, and replicated everything that was done there at the First. But the MMR did not change.

Semmelweis realized that the only thing that was different between the two clinics was the staff – it was doctors at the First, midwives at the Second. But he could not for the life of him figure out how that made a difference. Until 1847, when his fellow doctor Jakob Kolletschka died from an infected wound. The wound had been caused by a student accidentally poking him with a scalpel during the postmortem examination of a patient who had died of puerperal fever. When Kolletschka's own autopsy was done, the report showed Semmelweis that his infection was remarkably similar to puerperal fever.

The penny dropped. The fever had been transferred from the cadaver to Kolletschka via the scalpel! *That* was the difference between the staff of the two clinics – doctors who attended childbirths *also* worked on cadavers, while midwives did not! Clearly, doctors brought infectious 'cadaverous particles' from the mortuary to the labour room, *on their hands*!

There was no way Semmelweis could stop doctors from working on cadavers – it was part of their training – but what if they, say, washed their hands in between dissecting cadavers and attending on living, breathing mothers-to-be? Maybe washing with a solution of chlorinated lime (the main ingredient of bleaching powder) would do it – it certainly got the awful smell of rotting flesh off the hands, so perhaps it would also destroy the 'cadaverous particles'. It couldn't hurt to try.

Semmelweis worked feverishly to make the new routine of handwashing mandatory for doctors at the First Clinic. He introduced it in mid-May 1847, and then held his breath, hoping for the best. The results, when they came, were far more dramatic than he could have anticipated.

The First Clinic's MMR in April 1847 had been an unusually high 18.3 per cent. In June, the first full month of handwashing, it had dropped by 90 per cent, to 2.2 per cent! In July, it fell further to 1.2 per cent, and kept falling. In August 1847, the First Clinic at Vienna General reported an MMR of 0 per cent. For the first time in its history, not a single mother had died in childbirth for a whole month.

For making such an exceptional, outstanding discovery, Semmelweis should have been carried through streets of cheering crowds, given dozens of medals and had several monuments erected in his honour, but the wretched doctor only faced rejection and jeers in his lifetime. His peers either did not believe him, scoffing at his simple, one point formula – handwashing – for eliminating puerperal fever, or felt humiliated at his suggestion that their upper-class hands were unclean. Some doctors completely misunderstood the enormity of his findings, and since poor Semmelweis had no clue as to *why* handwashing was effective, he simply wasn't taken seriously.

There were more humiliations on the way. Political turmoil in Austria saw him being sidelined at Vienna General – Semmelweis was a Jew, a foreigner and a man who spoke his mind, all of which might have contributed to the way he was treated. By October 1850, just three years after his monumental discovery, he left Austria in anger and returned to his home country. Sadly, no warm welcome awaited him there either – the Hungarian independence movement was in full swing, and Semmelweis's sympathies lay with the rebels, which won him no friends among the rich and powerful.

Beginning in 1861, he began to suffer from severe depression and possibly what we now know as Alzheimer's disease. In 1865, he was forcibly admitted into an insane asylum. When he tried to escape, he was severely beaten, and died two weeks later from an infection in a wound that may have been caused by the beating.

In what is surely the most tragic irony of all, it was in the same year, 1865, that an English surgeon called Joseph Lister, following the ideas of a French chemist called Louis Pasteur about germs being the cause of infection (more on both gentlemen in Idea 17, page 188), tried a now famous experiment – he cleaned a wound with carbolic acid, which killed the germs in it and ensured that the patient recovered completely, with not a trace of infection. But because he could now explain why carbolic acid was able to prevent infection – it kills the germs, duh! – he was much feted during his own lifetime.

Sigh. Life isn't always fair, is it?

Across the Pond, Another Handwashing Evangelist

It was in 1843, a full four years before Semmelweis brought the maternal mortality rate at the First Clinic down to zero, that the American physician Oliver Wendell Holmes, the very man who came up with the word 'anaesthesia' (see page 147), published his now famous essay 'The Contagiousness of Puerperal Fever'. Like Semmelweis, Holmes had been aghast at the number of his young women patients who died from the disease, and in his bold essay, he argued that it was doctors, who were supposed to be lifesavers, who in fact passed on the infection to their women patients! As you can imagine, this theory did not go down well in the medical community, but Holmes had a lot of data to back his claim.

Six years earlier, at the age of twenty-eight, Holmes had been appointed to the Boston Dispensary, where he had been appalled by the poor standards of hygiene. It was common practice for doctors to go from patient to patient, performing surgeries and delivering babies, and he strongly suspected that they somehow 'carried' the infection from one patient to another. He had also mourned the death of fellow doctors who had themselves contracted puerperal fever after performing autopsies on women who had died from it. In his essay, Holmes insisted that any doctor who had had a patient die from the fever had a moral obligation to clean up nice – purify his instruments, burn the clothing he was wearing while

Oliver Wendell Holmes

conducting the ill-fated delivery and close his practice for at least six months, to ensure he did not infect any other patient.

Naturally, this seemed extreme, even deluded, to his fellow doctors, and some of them came down on him viciously. What made him even less credible was that he was not an obstetrician himself. But Holmes was not to be cowed. In 1855, he republished the same essay, including additional case studies, under a different title – 'Puerperal Fever as a Private Pestilence' – using an emotional tone this time. 'I had rather rescue one mother from being poisoned by her attendant,' he wrote, 'than claim to have saved forty out of fifty patients to whom I had carried the disease. I beg to be heard on behalf of the women whose lives are at stake, until some stronger voice shall plead for them.' Sadly, he was ignored again. Today, however, the essay is considered a landmark, and Holmes a visionary for seeing what so many others did not, could not or would not.

IDEA 15

IT MUST BE SOMETHING IN THE WATER

The Fascinating Story of London's Cholera Map, and How It Changed Cities Forever

Remember we talked about a novel 'air inhalation machine' constructed for the Pneumatic Institution in Bristol, where different kinds of airs could be tested for medical applications (see page 142)? We even talked of the engineer who built that machine, a certain James Watt. That engineer is far better known for his work on a very different machine – the steam engine. His steam engine, of which the first working models went into operation in 1776, was at the heart of a spectacular transformation of British manufacturing, British technology and British society called the Industrial Revolution.

The Industrial Revolution began in England towards the end of the eighteenth century and, in a few decades, changed the world forever. Hand tools, used to make every manner of product from cloth to cartwheels, were replaced with big, noisy, smoke-emitting and fearsomely efficient machines. A world in which animal or human effort had always been needed to crank levers or move things turned into a world where engines powered by water, steam, and fossil fuels like coal and petroleum (electricity came later) did all the work.

As age-old livelihoods evaporated, and poverty and squalor descended on entire communities of skilled craftsmen and weavers – not only in England but in all British colonies across the world, including India – people panicked, blaming the machines for stealing food from their children's mouths. But they soon saw all was not lost, for the machines needed people to operate them. And thus the workplace moved from the home to the factory, and the theatre of work from the village to the town, where the machines, and the jobs, were.

With thousands of people moving into towns, a whole new set of health issues arose. Because of overcrowding, infectious diseases spread rapidly, killing off hundreds of people at a time. With no drainage systems to speak of, no piped clean water and no garbage collection or disposal systems that could deal with so many humans eating, drinking, peeing and pooping in so limited a space, the new cities were islands of filth and ill health. Terrified that their precious machines would be forced to shut down if people did not come to work, and grappling with an unprecedented monster problem – urbanization – city administrators were often at a complete loss.

***

It was against this background that the brilliant English physician and pioneering medical scientist John Snow (remember him from page 147?) was born. His father was a labourer in a local coal yard, and the family lived in one of the poorest, most unsanitary neighbourhoods of his hometown, York. Young John, however, showed a great aptitude for mathematics and, by the age of fourteen, was apprenticed to a surgeon in a nearby town. In 1836, at the age of twenty-three, he enrolled in a medical school in London and began his medical education in right earnest. By 1844, he had completed his master's degree, had been admitted to both the Royal College of Physicians and the Royal College of Surgeons and had set up his own medical practice in London.

In those days, surgeon's apprentices in England were prohibited from drinking, gambling or marrying. Those disciplines stayed with John Snow – he remained a teetotaller and bachelor all his life. Along the way, for good measure, he turned vegetarian as well.

John Snow died tragically young, at forty-five, but what he contributed to medical science in that short period was formidable. His one major area of work was anaesthesia. If you remember, ether was introduced as a viable anaesthetic to the world by William Morton during a surgery at the Massachusetts General Hospital in September 1846. In England, Snow had been investigating respiratory diseases and the mechanism of breathing for a while, and when he heard about ether, he immediately began to test the effects of inhaling it on respiration.

The very next year, when chloroform was introduced in the UK, he worked on it as well, and became one of the first physicians to calculate safe dosages of both ether and chloroform for patients in surgery. Realizing that there was great danger to the patient's life if the right dose was not administered at the right time, he also recommended that the anaesthetic be administered by someone else who focused only on that part, and not by the surgeon himself.

Today, we take it for granted that every surgery requires a team of doctors and nurses assisting the main surgeon, but in Snow's time, and for decades after, the surgeon was a self-sufficient solo performer who carried everything they needed on their person. Remember the suture threads hanging from the eyelets of the surgeon's bloody, unwashed scrubs that we talked about on page 152?

Snow also advocated the use of anaesthetics for making childbirth less painful (believe it or not, the Church of England – and many of his fellow physicians – fought him over this, saying it was unethical to help a woman have painless labour!). It was only when Queen Victoria herself, charmed by the idea of painless childbirth, retained him to administer chloroform to her at the birth of her eighth child, Leopold, in 1853 and once again, at the birth of her daughter Beatrice in 1857, that the idea of obstetric anaesthesia slowly began to be accepted.

***

All this work was seriously wonderful. But it was his spectacular success in an entirely different area of medical research – cholera – that made John Snow such a celebrity in medical history and such a beloved folk hero in England. But before we go there, let's take a brief detour through the unholy terror called the cholera epidemic.

Cholera is a bacterial infection that affects the small intestines of humans (animals do not get cholera), causing severe diarrhoea that can lead to rapid dehydration, and even death. Since its origins in the nineteenth century, it has killed tens of millions of people worldwide – to this day, cholera annually affects between 3 and 5 million people, mostly in developing countries. The disease is believed to have originated in, the Indian subcontinent, specifically Bengal, and occurs as pandemic outbreaks (a pandemic is an epidemic, or infectious disease, that spreads quickly over a large geographical region, i.e., multiple continents, like COVID-19; an outbreak is a sudden occurrence of something unwelcome, like war or disease).

Since the first cholera pandemic, which lasted from 1817 to 1824 and spread from Bengal via trading routes (see how a good thing – a connected world – can be a terrible thing – a world in which infections can spread rapidly and widely – at the same time?) to Russia, and gradually to Europe, North America and the rest of the world, there have been six others. The last one originated in 1961 in Indonesia, and strains of that outbreak still persist in some parts of the world.

***

It was during the second cholera pandemic, which lasted from 1826 to 1837, that John Snow encountered the disease for the first time, in the coal-mining village of Killingworth. It was 1832, and he was only nineteen then, and a surgeon's apprentice, but he treated many sufferers and got to observe the progress and spread of the disease at close range. It led to his lifelong interest in epidemics – not just cholera but the plague as well. When the Epidemiological Society of London was founded in May 1850, no one was surprised to note that Snow was one of its founding members.

On 31 August 1854, cholera came to the Soho neighbourhood of London as part of the third cholera pandemic (it had already visited the city once in 1848 as part of the same pandemic and claimed over 14,000 victims). Over the next three days, well over a hundred people had died, causing three-quarters of the residents to flee the neighbourhood, away from the 'bad air'. By 10 September, over 500 Soho residents had fallen victim to the killer disease.

Well before that date, however, Dr Snow had rushed to the area, determined to track down the cause of the disease during its current outbreak. He had long been sceptical of the prevailing 'miasma theory of disease', which believed that people got sick by breathing in stinky, foggy air, and was determined to get to the bottom of the mystery this time. The 'germ theory of disease' would only be proposed by French microbiologist Louis Pasteur in 1861, so Snow wasn't sure what was causing cholera; he only felt strongly that it could not have come from the air. For some years, ever since the Industrial Revolution had reached its peak, the River Thames had become severely polluted, making the water supply to the city very suspect. Snow decided to investigate whether the disease had come from the water.

Many of the sick from Soho were taken to the nearby Middlesex Hospital, where their treatment was supervised by a thirty-four-year-old nurse called Florence Nightingale (Yesss! The famous one!). She was actually employed as superintendent in a different hospital, but had come over to Middlesex Hospital in early September to help out with the epidemic. You can read more about the Lady with the Lamp and her contributions to nursing in Idea 16 on page 174.

Like a detective, he began collecting data about the deaths, focusing specifically on where the victims had lived, and marked the homes of the dead on a map of Soho. He then overlaid this map on another that showed where the water pumps – pumps whose handles had to be worked to bring water gushing out of the spout and into buckets – in the neighbourhood were located. What he saw blew his mind – an incredible number of victims had lived around *one particular water pump on Broad Street*!

Only ten victims had lived significantly closer to a different water pump, but on investigating those deaths, Snow discovered that the families of five of the victims had always collected their water from the Broad Street pump, because they preferred the taste (different water supply companies drew their water from different sources and supplied different pumps). Of the other five victims, three had been children who attended school on Broad Street, and therefore usually drank from that pump. The case had been cracked – the 1854 cholera outbreak in Soho had originated not from miasma, but from the water of the Broad Street pump!

The only people who had not fallen ill, even though they worked right on Broad Street, were the employees of a brewery. That mystery was easily solved. Snow found out that the employees got free beer as part of their wages, and therefore never drank the water, whether from the Broad Street pump or elsewhere.

On 7 September – yup, he was a fast worker! – even as people continued to die around him, John Snow took his findings to the board of guardians of St James Parish, who served as the administrators of the area, and convinced them to have the handle of the pump removed the next day, so that no one else would be able to draw water from it for a while. The board agreed, and no more new cases of cholera were reported from the area.

John Snow, the Broad Street pump, and the disease-causing whatchamacallits

Only later did Snow discover how the water in the borewell under the Broad Street pump had got contaminated. With the help of Reverend Henry Whitehead – who had originally been a big believer of the miasma theory but had become convinced after seeing Snow's data that he may have a point – Snow set about investigating the pump further.

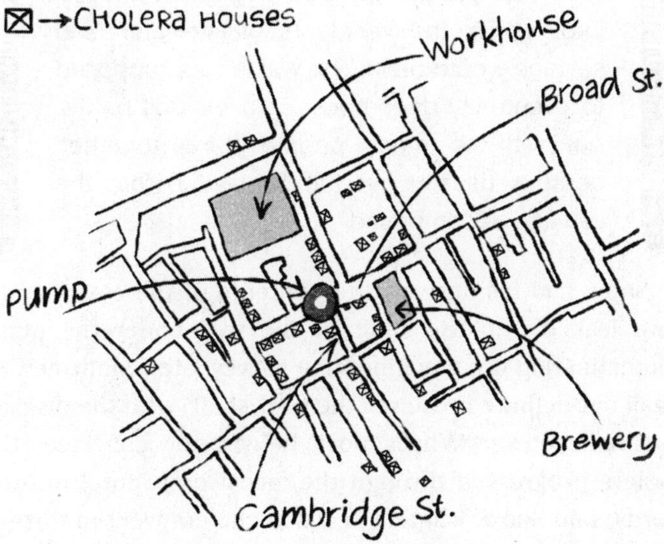

One of the first things he discovered was that the well under the contaminated pump had been dug only 3 feet away from a cesspit. The cesspit had originally been under a house but was now out in the open, and had been so since the house had been demolished for a road extension project. The next piece of the puzzle arrived via an interview Rev. Whitehead conducted with a woman who lived right opposite the pump –

she mentioned that she routinely emptied the water she used for washing her baby's nappies into the cesspit next to the Broad Street pump. The zinger – the last piece of the puzzle – was that her baby had died during the outbreak too, and quite possibly of cholera!

A cesspit was literally a pit dug under houses, into which the residents' wastewater and sewage would drain. The waste was supposed to eventually decompose into the soil below, but with so many people living together, cesspits usually got full up well before the sewage decomposed.

Snow had his answer: the contents of the cesspit must have leaked into the shaft of the well under the pump, contaminating it (an engineering survey later confirmed the small but definite breach in the well-shaft) with the disease-causing whatever! What's more, he was now convinced that cholera progressed through the faecal-oral route! In other words, said Snow, whatever caused cholera went in through the mouth (as water or contaminated food), travelled through the digestive system and came out on the other side (as watery poop). If, by some awful stroke of ill luck, that watery poop mixed with water or food, anyone who drank or ate of that contaminated food would become the next victim of cholera. Out of someone's back end, in short, and in through someone else's front end. Yup, simple enough to understand, but pretty darn yucky to contemplate.

So awful to contemplate, in fact, that the board of guardians of Soho, right after the cholera epidemic subsided, *reinstalled the handle on the Broad Street pump, scoffing at Snow's hypothesis*! Luckily, the outbreak had declined by then, but Snow's pleas that the leaky cesspit being so close to the pump made it ripe for another infection, if and when it should arise, found no takers. It was only in 1866 that it finally began to be accepted, mainly because one of the chief opponents to Snow's theory, a certain Dr William Farr, finally came around and ordered that all water should be boiled before drinking, when he was investigating another outbreak at a different location.

Today, John Snow is hailed as the Father of Epidemiology – a visionary and a prime mover in the improvement of public health and sanitation all over the world.

Since 1993, England's John Snow Society, which aims to promote the renowned anaesthetist and epidemiologist's life and works, has hosted the annual Pumphandle Lecture in his memory (fun fact: the 2015 lecture was delivered by the Indian American surgeon, writer, and public-health researcher Atul Gawande). The lecture is traditionally accompanied by the ceremony of removing and then replacing the pump-handle on the model of a pump, as a reminder that even in the twenty-first century, public health continues to be a real challenge, both for doctors and administrators

How a Reeking River Started a Civic Revolution

If you lived in 1850s London, you would have found it very easy to believe in the miasma theory of disease – there was illness everywhere, and the city stank something terrible.

And with good reason. Since the turn of the century, London had seen a huge increase in its population, from 1 to 3 million people, and the old brick sewer system was severely stretched. Not just human waste – most of which was being collected in the city's 2,00,000 cesspits – but a new menace, industrial effluents, was emptying into the River Thames, as well as blood and offal from slaughterhouses. Some of the stuff that belonged in the sewers often leaked into the city's drinking water system, which itself was in the process of being upgraded from wooden pipes to iron pipes, providing plenty of opportunity for material from different systems to mix.

In the summer of 1858, such an unbearable smell – a proper miasma – rose from the already malodorous Thames that the 'event' itself was given a name: the Great Stink (fortunately for him, John Snow missed the event – he had died a month before, in June). So much pressure was put on the local and national authorities that they hurriedly accepted a proposal from civil engineer Joseph Bazalgette to build an entirely new sewerage system for the city, which would ensure that the city's waste would be taken well beyond city limits, with pumping stations installed at regular intervals to move the sewage along a series of interconnecting sewers. The project, which was begun less than six months later, was completed in 1875, and brought an end to cholera outbreaks in the city. 150 years later, Bazalgette's sewerage system still serves London, a city now 8-million strong.

And that was how a completely erroneous belief (miasma causes disease) helped solve a very real problem conclusively, and brought about a revolution in public health and sanitation while it was at it. This focused, frenetic *swachhagraha* of nineteenth-century London, and the subsequent reduction in disease, gave doctors – even those who did not believe in the germ theory – valuable pointers about how to *prevent* disease – and turned cities into places where millions of people could live hygienically and well.

IDEA 16

YOU CAN TOTALLY 'NURSE' A SICK PERSON BACK TO GOOD HEALTH

Left, Right, Left, Right – Here Come the Ladies in White!

Here's a thirty-second exercise: think of a modern hospital and list out the important people on a typical medical team. Done? Chances are you put 'nurses' right after 'doctors'. And why not? Today, 'doctor' and 'nurse' are words that go together just as instinctively and seamlessly as salt and pepper or bread and butter!

It wasn't always this way, though. The image of the nurse as a woman (typically) in white (typically) who ministered to the sick, wounded and dying with a smile, a kind word and a brisk, efficient way about her is quite a recent one. Of course, there have been people – both men and women – who took care of the sick throughout history, but they were usually monks and nuns, who tended to the suffering out of a sense of religious duty, not as professionals who assisted a doctor. The one person who single-handedly changed all that, contributing more than anyone else to the modern idea of who a nurse is and what she (or he!) does, and creating a new and honourable profession called nursing, was the English gentlewoman Florence Nightingale.

Ever wonder why, in so many countries, nurses are still addressed as 'sister'? Because in the earliest days, female nurses were most often, that's right, nuns! Now you know.

That wasn't what Nightingale set out to do, however. In fact, she was many other things before she became a nurse: an outspoken feminist – she often referred to herself as a 'man of action' – who lived life on her own terms, rejecting the idea that marriage and children should be the main life goal of a young, affluent Englishwoman like herself; a traveller to exotic destinations like Greece and Egypt, who wrote well and prodigiously about her experiences there; a deeply spiritual person who believed that her true calling lay in the service of mankind; and an iconoclast who much preferred the company of intelligent men to that of educated women who willingly spent their lives doing nothing more than taking care of their homes and children.

As a young girl, Florence also showed a great aptitude for mathematics and statistics, which her delighted father encouraged, teaching her the subject himself. In 1850, at the age of thirty, she happened to be visiting a religious community in Dusseldorf, Germany, when she observed the deaconesses – female church officials – tending to the sick and poor. The experience made such a huge impact on her that she decided to stay back and work with them for a few weeks, learning a great deal about basic nursing skills, the importance of patient observation and the value of good hospital organization in the bargain.

Nightingale was born in 1820 in an Italian city. Can you guess which one? That's right – Florence! Her happy parents named their baby daughter after the city of her birth, because why not?

In 1853, using her social network, Florence managed to land her first job, as the superintendent at the Institution for the Care of Sick Gentlewomen in Distressed Circumstances (no, seriously) on Harley Street, London. It didn't pay much, but that didn't faze Florence – even though her mother and sister opposed her life choices furiously, her indulgent father settled on her an annual income of 500 pounds (equivalent to about 48 lakh rupees in today's terms), leaving her free to pursue any career of her choice.

While at the institute, Florence quickly demonstrated her excellent administrative skills, improving working conditions for the staff, training nurses in the importance of hospital and patient hygiene, and making the hospital far more efficient than it had ever been. She also helped out with caring for victims of the Soho cholera outbreak – yes, the same one John Snow investigated – at a different hospital the very next year, learning even more about the importance of clean water, food and agreeable surroundings for the prevention of infection and for quick patient recovery.

But the unrelenting hard work and the lack of sleep took a toll on her health. While she recuperated, she wondered if it might not be a good idea for her to quit nursing and move on to training nurses instead. She was beginning to seriously consider it when reports began to trickle in of the appalling conditions of the 18,000 or so English soldiers who had been injured in the Crimean War and were being treated in military hospitals there.

The Crimean War (1853–56) was fought between the armies of Russia on one side, and an alliance of Britain, France and the Ottoman Empire on the other. The main battlefield was the Crimean Peninsula on the northern coast of the Black Sea, but the British base hospitals were in Scutari, Turkey. Here's a side note: Crimea continues to be beleaguered to this day – in 2014, it lost its independent status as the Autonomous Republic of Crimea within the country of Ukraine when Russia invaded and annexed it.

Instantly, all thoughts of moving from nursing to training flew from Florence's head. Getting together a group of thirty-eight volunteer nurses, she petitioned her friend Sidney Herbert, who had just been appointed Britain's secretary at war, to arrange for permits for all of them to go out to Crimea and help with the war effort. It was a difficult pitch – the War Office had stopped sending nurses out to war zones. But Herbert knew and admired Florence and her work, and he championed her cause in the British parliament. In October 1854, Florence Nightingale sailed out to Turkey on the mission that would not only change public perceptions of nurses and nursing forever, but also turn her into an international celebrity.

Why in heaven's name would a war office not send nurses out to war zones? Well, because at that time, female 'nurses', who were usually put in charge of orphanages and workhouses, had quite a terrible reputation in England. Nurses were usually poor widows and destitute single women, and they were often corrupt, given to drink, spectacularly rude and neglectful of patients in their care. Remember Miss Hannigan from the movie *Annie*? Or Mrs Corney from *Oliver Twist*? Yeah, many nurses were like those fine ladies.

***

Florence had read all the reports about the terrible conditions at the British base hospital in Scutari (now called Uskudar, it is a municipality of Istanbul, Turkey), but what she saw when she got there stunned her beyond belief. The hospital, already bursting at its seams, sat on top of a large cesspool which regularly contaminated the hospital's water supply. Patients lay on stretchers in corridors, rooms and everywhere in between, in their own excrement, while rodents and bugs scurried around them. The hospital's most basic supplies – bandages, medicine and soap – were running out at an alarming rate as more and more soldiers were brought in. Most shockingly, ten times more soldiers were dying from typhoid, cholera and other infectious diseases than from the wounds they had sustained in battle. It was, in Florence's words, the 'Kingdom of Hell'.

Wasting no time, Florence sent the local staff out to procure hundreds of scrubbing brushes and dozens of litres of cleaning solution. Then she got to work. Along with her nurses and the strongest of the wounded soldiers, she scrubbed the inside of the hospital from floor to ceiling. Using her connection with Sidney Herbert, she ensured that fresh supplies of everything – along with donations of money – arrived from England for use at the hospital. She insisted the patients be bathed every day and enlisted the soldiers' wives to do the laundry, for the patients had to also have clean sheets and clean dressings.

She then set up an 'invalid's kitchen', where she made sure fresh, hot and tasty food was cooked for soldiers to suit their dietary requirements. And, of course, she insisted that all her staff wash their hands before and after they touched the patients.

Then Nightingale went further. For the mental and emotional wellbeing of recovering patients, she ensured that they got help with writing letters to near and dear ones back home in England, France or wherever in the Ottoman Empire they came from. She also set up a classroom and a library, where they could read and participate in educational and recreational activities. She wrote to *The Times* newspaper, asking for government help with the hospital, and to the Sanitary Commission for help with flushing out the sewers and improving ventilation. Six months after Florence went out to Scutari, in March 1855, the Sanitary Commission arrived and did as Florence instructed.

French surgeon Lucien Baudens celebrated Florence's impartial treatment of all her patients, writing, 'This frail young woman . . . embraced in her solicitude the sick of three armies.'

As for help with the hospital building itself, so taken was the government with Florence's efficiency and so high was the pressure from the British public that it commissioned the legendary civil and mechanical engineer Isambard Kingdom Brunel (he built Britain's Great Western Railway, as well as the first transatlantic steamship) to design a hospital that could be prefabricated in England and shipped to Turkey in a box, to be assembled there like a Lego project.

In October 1855, just five months after Brunel got his commission, the Renkioi Hospital went up in Renkioi (today called Erenköy), a suburb close to Scutari. Essentially, the hospital buildings – or 'those magnificent huts', as Florence called them – were made of wood and canvas, each large enough to accommodate fifty patients. Each building also incorporated ventilation, drainage, sanitation and even some basic temperature controls!

During Nightingale's first winter in Scutari, as many as 4,077 soldiers had died in the hospital. Six months later, with the sewers cleaned up and Florence in charge, the death rate had dropped drastically, from 42 per cent of all patients to – hold your breath – 2 per cent! And this was not from better surgical procedures or drugs, but simply from improving sanitation and hygiene, thus reducing infectious diseases!

Nightingale stayed in Scutari for a year and a half, working tirelessly not just during the day but at night as well, walking from patient to patient, checking on each of them one last time before she herself went to bed. A report in *The Times* described her little ritual in these words, '. . . as her slender form glides quietly along each corridor, every poor fellow's face softens with gratitude at the sight of her. When all the medical officers have retired for the night and silence and darkness have settled down upon those miles of prostrate sick, she may be observed alone, with a little lamp in her hand, making her solitary rounds . . .' – earning her the famous moniker 'Lady with the Lamp'.

***

When Florence returned to England at the end of the war, she was amazed – and more than a little embarrassed – to find that she had become a legend. The Nightingale Fund, set up by Sidney Herbert to collect donations for the training of nurses, had raised no less than 45,000 pounds from an admiring British public! Florence used the money to set up the Nightingale Training School at St Thomas' Hospital in London in July 1860. Five years later, the first Nightingale Nurses, or simply, Nightingales, began work, not in the posh hospitals but in the workhouses, where the poorest patients were.

Florence Nightingale's vast experience in the Crimean War had made her an expert at public health and sanitation, both military and civilian, and she brought those lessons to peacetime hospitals. Not only did she write two landmark books – *Notes on Nursing* (1859) and *Notes on Hospitals* (1863) – but she also used her expertise and interest in statistics to create a 'coxcomb chart', a marvellous graphic she developed to represent all the data she had meticulously collected on the deaths at the Scutari hospital between April 1854 (seven months before she got there) and March 1856. At a glance, the coxcombs revealed, month by month, how many deaths there were, how many were caused by battle wounds and how many by infectious diseases, and how the overall situation improved between 1854 and 1856.

She presented the coxcombs to British MPs and civil servants, demanding reform in military hospitals, and got it, for who could argue with hard data? There's a lovely ending to this story: in recognition of her contribution to statistics, Florence was elected the first female member of the Royal Statistical Society in 1859.

Florence Nightingale and her coxcomb

Unfortunately for Florence, while she was out in Scutari, she herself fell victim to a condition called Crimean fever, probably contracted through drinking contaminated milk. The lingering effects of the disease would confine her to bed with chronic aches and pains for long periods for the rest of her life. Undeterred, she continued to work tirelessly, and died peacefully in her sleep at the ripe old age of ninety.

Florence is immortalized in the Nightingale Pledge, an oath taken by all nursing students on their graduation. The Florence Nightingale Medal, awarded every two years to a distinguished nurse for outstanding service, is considered the nursing Nobel. Since 1965, Florence's birthday - 12 May - has been celebrated as International Nurses Day.

Imagine There's No Countries

One of Geneva, Switzerland's most famous sons was a man called Jean-Henri Dunant. Doesn't ring a bell? Never mind. The name of the organization Dunant founded will definitely send an entire carillon of bells chiming in your head. But *you* have to guess its name, and here are some clues that should help: the organization is an international one; it has some 17 million volunteers worldwide; its mission is to protect human life and health, to prevent and lessen human suffering, and to offer relief and nursing in wartime and peacetime to any human being in need of it, regardless of race, colour, creed or country. That's right, we're talking of the International Red Cross, and Jean Henri Dunant was its founder!

Like Florence Nightingale, Dunant had always been drawn to social work. At eighteen, he joined the Geneva Society for Alms Giving, and spent a lot of his time doing prison visits and tending to the poor. In 1856, at the age of twenty-eight, he turned entrepreneur, creating a corn-growing and trading company that he set up in the French colony of Algeria (at that time, Geneva was also part of France). But the colonial authorities were not very cooperative, and Dunant's business was struggling. That was when Dunant had his audacious idea: why not ask French emperor Napoleon III himself to intervene on his behalf with the authorities in Algeria?

Over the next few months, he wrote a flattering book about the emperor. Then, knowing that Napoleon III was in the middle of war with Austria, in Italy (there were a lot of wars being fought in those days, it seems), he decided to travel to Napoleon's headquarters in the small town of Solferino and make him a present of the book. Dunant arrived in Solferino in June 1859, on the very day that a big battle had taken place nearby. Thousands of wounded and dying people lay on the battlefield, and there was no organized attempt being made to help them. Shocked, Dunant bought materials and supplies needed to erect makeshift hospitals, got the local population together and convinced them to help every soldier, regardless of which side he had fought on.

When he returned to Geneva (he never did end up presenting his first book to the emperor), Dunant wrote another book – *A Memory of Solferino* – in which he described the Battle of Solferino, its costs, and the chaos that had reigned in its aftermath. He also suggested that each nation should develop a volunteer-based neutral relief organization to move in quickly after each conflict and take care of its wounded. He went on to add that, apart from such volunteers, doctors and (battle)field hospitals should be allowed to operate freely and securely, i.e., they should not be targeted by soldiers on either side. At his own cost, Dunant printed 1,600 copies of the book, and distributed them to influential political and military men in Europe.

A Memory of Solferino captured the imagination of several important people. The president of the Geneva Society for Public Welfare put together a committee of five, which included Dunant, to discuss how Dunant's ideas could be taken forward. The first meeting of the committee, on 17 February 1863, is considered the founding date of the International

Red Cross. Only one year later, the Swiss government invited the governments of all European countries, apart from those of the United States, Brazil and Mexico, to attend an official diplomatic conference. On 22 August 1864, the conference adopted the First Geneva Convention, which stated that wounded soldiers, doctors and institutions caring for wounded soldiers, and civilians helping with wounded soldiers – on both sides – would be protected in times of war.

For his vision and dedication in founding the 'supreme humanitarian achievement of the nineteenth century', Henri Dunant was awarded the very first Nobel Peace Prize in 1901. Both in his book, and in a speech he gave to an English audience in 1872, he acknowledged the huge impact Florence Nightingale's work had had on him. 'I would first remark,' he said, 'that I was inspired with the idea of this work by the admirable devotion rendered by Miss Nightingale to the English army in the Crimea.'

Take a bow, Florence!

IDEA 17

GOTCHA! IT'S DEM LITTLE CRITTERS THAT CAUSE DISEASE!

The Birth of Microbiology

By the beginning of 1860, against the pioneering work on cholera by Dr John Snow – it isn't foul air, but something in the water that causes cholera – the miasma theory of disease had begun to sound decidedly suspect to many in Europe's scientific and medical establishment. But it was the efforts of one French chemist – the towering thinker, observer and never-say-die experimenter Louis Pasteur – that sounded its death knell. By proving conclusively that it was often microbes, or microscopic germs (and 'non-germs' – we know them now as 'viruses') that caused disease in plants, animals or humans – and that applying heat (whether to milk, wine or beer) was one way to kill microbes, Pasteur deservedly won pride of place in the roll call of medical heroes.

But even this momentous achievement was only a small part of Pasteur's overall contribution to science and medicine. Let's quickly skim the list of his other breakthroughs – only skim, mind, because this book simply doesn't offer the space to explore them in more detail – to get some idea of the kind of mega-mind we are dealing with here.

As in the case of so many other great scientists, Pasteur's brilliance was nowhere in evidence in his childhood. He came from a poor family, and was a very average student, struggling to pass his degree in science and mathematics. At the age of twenty, he took the entrance test to a famous university in Paris but got such a low ranking that he decided not to take the seat he had been allotted, but to try the entrance again the next year instead. In that year, the year he devoted to exam prep, something changed for Pasteur – he developed a real interest in science, chemistry in particular. In 1843, at the age of twenty-one, he passed the entrance test to the same university with flying colours and entered the École Normale Supérieure. It was the beginning of a lifelong love affair with science.

It was at the University of Lille, where he had taken over as dean of the new faculty of sciences in 1854, that Pasteur began his studies in fermentation, the process by which milk turns into curd and grape juice turns into wine. But to understand what he discovered, we have to understand what fermentation is.

People had known, for thousands of years, that if you put fruit or grains into covered containers and let them be in a warm place for a longish while, they would turn into wine

Louis Pasteur

and beer respectively, but no one fully understood why or how it happened. The process was called fermentation.

The word 'ferment' comes from the Latin *fervere*, which means 'to boil'. Someone chose this name to describe how wine and beer are produced because they noticed that when they left grapes, for instance, in a covered container for a long time, they produced bubbles, which was also what happened when something was boiling! It is exactly what happens when we leave dosa batter in a warm place overnight – it begins to bubble and 'boil' .

We know that to make a fresh batch of curd, we need to add a little 'starter' curd from a previous batch into warm milk. Similarly, to make a fresh batch of wine or beer (or bread, even), people used to add a bit of 'ferment' from the previous batch (in the case of bread, people had mixtures of flour, sugar and water called 'bread starters', which they used a little of in every fresh batch of bread, so that it would 'rise', and be light and airy).

For thousands of years, no one knew what the 'ferment' was made of, they only knew that if they didn't put the ferment in, grape juice and milk would spoil instead of turning into wine and curd respectively. Antonie van Leeuwenhoek (Remember him from page 87? The first guy to observe microorganisms?) saw, through his superior, home-ground lenses, that 'ferment' was essentially globules floating in a liquid, but even he did not dream that those globules were living organisms.

By the 1840s, further investigations by scientists had shown that both wine and beer ferment and bread starters contained a living microbe called yeast, but they still did not understand what the yeast did. It was Louis Pasteur who was the first to figure out what actually happened during fermentation – the yeast, he discovered, broke down the natural sugars in a mixture into alcohol. He also discovered that yeast had to be alive and multiplying for the fermentation to happen.

In 1856, a local wine manufacturer, Monsieur Bigot, whose son was Pasteur's student, asked for his help to figure out why some barrels of his sugar beet wine had begun to taste like sour milk instead of wine. When Pasteur examined samples from different barrels, he found that in the samples where proper fermentation had occurred, there were plenty of yeast cells, but in the samples that tasted like sour milk, there were lots of other, tinier organisms. These tinier organisms, instead of breaking down sugars into alcohol, were breaking down sugars into acid, and making the grape juice bitter.

Once he knew what was causing wine to spoil, Pasteur set about trying to see how to ensure this did not happen. In 1864, he figured out that the way to do it was to heat (not boil) the wine, while it was still young, to about 50–60 degrees Celsius, for a short while.

Now, heating food to prevent spoilage was not entirely a novel idea, but it was Pasteur who first put down precise temperatures and heating durations, starting with wine.

More importantly, he was the first to understand *why* heating food helped it stay fresh longer – it was microbes that spoilt food, and heat killed microbes! This process – of heating something for a short while at a low temperature to destroy microbes and then cooling it – came to be called . . . that's right, pasteurization!

Win! Pasteur had rescued the French wine industry from certain destruction!

Wine and beer began to be pasteurized very quickly after Pasteur's discovery, but strangely enough, milk was not pasteurized on a large scale until decades later, even though Pasteur had shown that it was the same 'tinier organisms' which caused wine to taste bitter that also caused milk to spoil – the microbes were lactic acid bacteria, and they spoiled milk by converting lactose, the sugar in milk, into lactic acid.

The thing was, no one realized that raw, unprocessed milk was a great medium for not just lactic acid bacteria, but all kinds of other, far more dangerous, disease-causing bacteria to thrive. With milk having to travel from villages to cities without refrigeration, it was often a couple of days before it was consumed, by which time it was absolutely crawling with bacteria. For a very long time, though, no one connected a person's disease to his having drunk unprocessed milk. Right up to the 1930s, thousands of people died of tuberculosis they had contracted through this route! It was only around that time that the problem was flagged, and cities and countries began to make the pasteurization of milk mandatory.

Here's an interesting problem. The lactic acid bacteria, which spoil milk, are the very same that convert milk to curd, and by doing exactly the same thing – converting lactose into lactic acid. What makes curd so yummy and spoiled milk yucky, then? Well, curd-making is 'controlled fermentation' – you add lactic acid bacteria from yesterday's curd into today's milk, cover the vessel so that no other bacteria can get in and then put it in the refrigerator after the curd is set. Milk spoilage, on the other hand, is 'uncontrolled fermentation' – it happens when naturally occurring bacteria in the air (some of which may be lactic acid bacteria) begin to work on milk that has been left out too long.

***

The discovery that microbes caused spoilage in wine led Pasteur to a new thought – maybe it was microbes that caused disease in animals as well. (It also gave a British surgeon the same idea. See what he did with it in the box on page 202.) In 1865, he travelled to southern France, where a mysterious disease was attacking healthy silkworm eggs and devastating the French silk industry. Pasteur worked on the problem for five years, becoming a silkworm breeder himself. By the end of it, he had not only discovered that it was indeed microbes that were attacking the eggs, but also worked out how to prevent them from doing so.

Win! Pasteur had now saved the French silk industry from going extinct!

By this time, Pasteur was highly regarded in France, but the medical establishment still did not buy his theory that germs cause disease (yes, they still believed in miasma!), because they saw him as 'only a chemist', and not really one of them. Unconcerned, he turned his attention to the problem of chicken cholera. Inspired by Edward Jenner's smallpox vaccine, he figured that if there could be a vaccine for smallpox, the same method – injecting small amounts of cholera germs into healthy chickens – could be used as an inoculation against cholera. He began making cultures of the cholera-causing bacteria, and inoculating healthy chickens with it. Unfortunately, all the chickens he infected caught the virulent form of the disease (instead of the mild form) and died.

At the time when Pasteur was trying to find a way to protect chickens against cholera, only the inoculation for smallpox was called vaccination (Why was it called vaccination? Go back and read page 124). But once Pasteur began to create inoculations for different diseases, he decided to call them vaccines too, in honour of his idol Jenner .

While he continued to look for a safer inoculation method, Pasteur had to go away on vacation. In the summer of 1879, he instructed his assistant, Charles Chamberland, to inject the chickens with a fresh culture of cholera germs before Charles himself went away on holiday. Chamberland forgot to do it, but inoculated the chickens with the same culture when he came back a few days later. None of the chickens caught the disease. Assuming that the culture was 'spoilt', Chamberland was going to throw it away, when Pasteur was struck by a sudden epiphany. He instructed Chamberland to lay the spoilt culture aside, prepare a fresh culture and inject two groups of chickens with it – Group One would comprise chickens that had already been inoculated with the spoilt culture, and Group Two those that hadn't. Then he held his breath and waited to see what would happen.

A few days later, as expected, all the Group Two chickens developed a virulent form of cholera and died. But the Group One chickens *remained perfectly healthy, developing no cholera symptoms at all*! Pasteur's hunch that their exposure to oxygen may have weakened (or 'attenuated') the cholera germs, making them perfect for a chicken cholera inoculation, had been right!

Win! Pasteur had invented a vaccine for cholera!

It was a great moment in the history of immunization. Later, Pasteur would talk of that moment with pride, attributing his 'lucky' discovery to all his years of disciplined, focused work in the field, saying, '*Le hasard ne favorise que les esprits préparés* – Fortune only favours the prepared mind.' Today it is one of his most famous quotes.

***

In 1876, German physician and microbiologist Robert Koch (more about him and his rivalry with Pasteur in Idea 18, page 204) had shown that it was a microbe called *Bacillus anthracis* that caused anthrax, a sheep-infecting disease that had suddenly begun to kill large numbers of cattle. In 1879, after his success with preparing a chicken cholera vaccine, Pasteur decided to try making a vaccine for anthrax. First, he drew blood from infected animals and allowed the bacteria in them to grow. The problem now was to figure out how to weaken the bacilli and turn them into a vaccine (unfortunately, unlike the ones that caused cholera, not all bacteria were weakened by exposure to oxygen).

Simply put, immunization is a method of teaching an animal's or human's own defence systems to recognize and fight a particular disease-causing germ. One way to do it is to introduce weakened germs into the body so that the body's immune system can learn how to fight them (each kind of germ, or pathogen, is subdued using a different 'weapon', or antibody) and win. This practice (of introducing weak disease-causing germs deliberately) is what we know as inoculation or vaccination. How does this help? Well, the next time the same germ attacks, the body recognizes it instantly, draws the correct antibody from its arsenal, and subdues the strong version before it is too late.

Finally, in 1881, Pasteur figured out that a combination of heat and the addition of a chemical worked to weaken the anthrax germ. *Win!* An anthrax vaccine had been created!

Actually, Pasteur's deadly combo of heat and chemical not only weakened but killed the anthrax bacilli, but as he discovered, even dead germs apparently worked as a vaccine! The body's immune system learnt to recognize the *shape* of the germ, and that was enough for it to be ready with all its defences the next time it was attacked by the live, virulent form of the same germ.

Pasteur was on a roll. He decided to attack the dreaded disease rabies – which affected the brain and nervous system of animals – next. Rabies was passed on to humans through the saliva of infected animals when they (humans) were bitten. Collecting blood and saliva samples from diseased dogs, Pasteur examined them under his microscope, but saw nothing suspicious. (We know now that rabies is caused by a virus, but since viruses are so much smaller than bacteria, they were not visible to Pasteur.) Still, firmly believing it was caused by a 'germ', he set about investigating how it could be weakened.

Other research in the field had shown that one way of weakening germs to make them suitable as a vaccine for one species was to pass them through another species a few times.

Pasteur and his colleague Pierre Paul Émile Roux passed the 'invisible' rabies germs harvested from dogs through rabbits, then dried out the spinal cords of those rabbits (remember, the rabies germ attacks the nervous system!) to weaken the germs. When they inoculated dogs with the weak germs, and then exposed them to a 'live' rabies virus a few weeks later, the dogs did not catch the disease at all – their immune systems had learnt to identify and fight the rabies 'germ'. After they had tested their vaccine on fifty dogs and obtained the same results, Pasteur, and Roux were pretty confident. Now it was time for the big leap of faith – testing the vaccine on humans.

In his 1929 memoir, *The Story of San Michele*, Swedish physician Axel Munthe, who had observed some of Pasteur's rabies research first-hand, writes, 'Pasteur himself was absolutely fearless. Anxious to secure a sample of saliva straight from the jaws of a rabid dog, I once saw him, with a glass tube held between his lips, draw a few drops of the deadly saliva from the mouth of a rabid bulldog, held on the table by two assistants . . .'

No one since Edward Jenner had made a vaccine for humans, so there was a lot at stake for Pasteur, mainly because he wasn't even a qualified doctor. Still, going ahead with the insatiable curiosity and the brash confidence of a scientist who simply had to test his hypothesis, he inoculated nine-year-old Joseph

Meister, who had been badly mauled by a rabid dog. This was almost always a death sentence, so any treatment that might help, however experimental, was welcome.

Knowing that rabies took between ten and twenty days to develop in humans, Pasteur gave Meister thirteen inoculations over eleven days, using successively stronger and stronger rabies germs, teaching his immune system to recognize and fight the germ before it actually developed in his body from the bite. Three months after the first inoculation, which had been given on 6 July 1885, Pasteur examined Meister and found him to be perfectly healthy!

As a gesture of goodwill, the French government took no legal action against Pasteur for treating a sick person without a medical licence. The next year, Pasteur vaccinated 350 people, of whom only one died. No more proof was needed for the efficacy of the rabies vaccine. *Win!* Louis Pasteur was now an international hero.

In 1887, fundraising began for the Pasteur Institute, whose twin missions were the treatment of rabies and the study of virulent and contagious diseases. The institute was inaugurated in Paris in November 1888, with Charles Chamberland (the former assistant who went away on vacation without inoculating the chickens) and Émile Roux (who helped develop the rabies vaccine) as two of the co-founders. One year later, Roux set up, at the Pasteur institute, the first course of microbiology ever taught anywhere in the world.

Louis Pasteur died in 1895 at the age of seventy-two. The Father of Microbiology was laid to rest, and with him, at long last, was buried the centuries-old miasma theory of disease. Finally, *finally*, as a result of his sterling work, the world accepted the germ theory of disease, and readied itself for a full-scale attack on disease-causing critters. *Win!*

A small but important side note: Pasteur's vaccines were different from Jenner's in one significant way – while Jenner had used a milder virus which caused a different disease (cowpox) to protect people from the 'main' disease, smallpox, Pasteur had managed to artificially weaken the very microbes that caused the main disease (cholera and anthrax), in the laboratory. There would never be any need now to look for a similar, milder bacterium or virus to be able to create a vaccine! See why Pasteur's discovery, which came almost a hundred years after Jenner's, was the one that truly revolutionized work on infectious diseases?

Scrub Floors with Phenol? Nah, Scrub Wounds with Phenol!

In 1865, Joseph Lister, a thirty-eight-year-old surgeon at the Glasgow Royal Infirmary, was reading a medical journal when a paragraph fairly leapt out at him from the page. A French chemist called Louis Pasteur had proved that it was microbes that caused food to spoil. He advocated three ways of eliminating the microbes: filter them out, apply heat, or kill them with a chemical. A thought struck Lister: what if it was similar little devils that caused infections in wounds as well? And if yes, how could they be eliminated?

Well, he couldn't filter them out of wounds, and couldn't apply great heat either, but he could wash the wounds with a chemical and see what happened. About twenty years before, a chemical called phenol, or carbolic acid, had been discovered. It seemed a safe bet – it had been used to remove the stink in fields irrigated with sewage, and animals that grazed there later had not been adversely affected. The very next day, Lister began testing his theory, swabbing and spraying surgical wounds with phenol. That one simple step remarkably reduced the incidence of infection.

In August the same year, a seven-year-old boy was brought into the Glasgow Royal Infirmary with a gaping fracture on his leg where a cart had passed over it. Usually, that would have meant death from infection. Lister dipped a large pad of lint in phenol, laid it on the wound and bandaged the leg. When he opened the bandage four days later, no infection had developed! Six weeks later, he was amazed to see that the boy's bones had fused back together, without any pus forming! He instantly instructed his surgeons to wash their hands – and all their instruments – before and after surgery in a dilute solution of carbolic acid, and dramatically brought down incidences of infection at his hospital.

At first, his contemporaries mocked his methods, and the medical journal *Lancet* even warned against his madcap 'progressive ideas'. But Lister had the last laugh – phenol quickly became the most widely used antiseptic in surgery. In the years that followed, he was decorated by the king and queen of England several times, raised to the peerage – he was first made a baronet, and later, a full-fledged baron – and hailed as a pioneer in antiseptic surgery.

A surgical antiseptic was even named after him. Today, it is used as a mouthwash. Its name? That's right – Listerine!

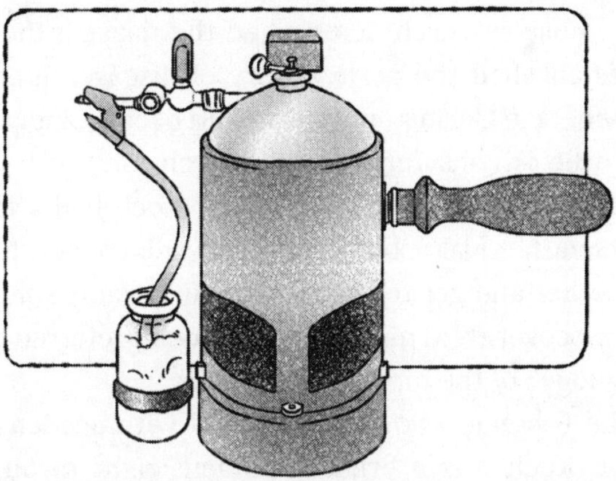

Joseph Lister's carbolic acid steam sprayer

IDEA 18

THERE'S BACTERIA, AND THEN THERE'S SOMETHING SMALLER, WEIRDER AND FAR MORE DANGEROUS

The Point at Which Things First Began to Go Viral

As we know from Idea 17, Louis Pasteur is often hailed as the person whose research demolished the miasma theory and firmly established the germ theory of disease. But there is one other – the German physician and bacteriologist Robert Koch – who is considered, by most scholars, to be equally responsible. Pasteur and the younger Koch had a long and bitter scientific rivalry, but out of their need to get the better of each other and get to the answers first came some of the biggest discoveries in microbiology (Koch preferred to call it 'bacteriology') of the nineteenth century.

Unlike Pasteur, who had struggled with academics as a teenager, Koch was a brilliant student right through high school and college, completing his medical degree in 1866 from the University of Göttingen with the highest honours, at the age of twenty-three. In 1870, he worked as a surgeon in the short but game-changing Franco-Prussian War.

A short but necessary side note on the war: The Franco-Prussian War lasted just six months, and ended with a disciplined Prussia, at the head of a coalition of German states, routing an overconfident France. After the war, all the German states united under Prussia to become one country. France lost its status as the most dominant political force in continental Europe, and 'unified Germany' took on the mantle. Germany would continue to dominate until the end of the Second World War in 1945. Moral of the story: the reasons why the Frenchman Pasteur and the German Koch didn't like each other quite possibly went beyond the boundaries of science.

In the University of Göttingen, Koch had studied under Friedrich Henle, who, way back in 1840, had published a theory that infectious diseases were caused by living microscopic organisms. Without experimental proof, however, the theory had remained just that – a theory. In 1850, the French parasitologist Casimir Davaine had observed organisms in the blood of diseased animals, and conducted experiments. He had inoculated healthy sheep with the blood of sheep suffering from anthrax, and noticed that (1) the healthy sheep developed the same disease, anthrax, soon after, and (2) when the blood of the newly diseased sheep was examined, the very same organisms that had been in the blood of the diseased animal were found (they hadn't been there earlier). Davaine published a report in 1863 with his findings – there was probably a connection, he said, between the presence of the rod-shaped microbes and the disease anthrax. But once again, the proof wasn't conclusive enough.

It was on this foundation that Koch began his research on the rod-shaped microbe. Pasteur had already demonstrated by this time that bacteria could be grown outside of an animal body, in the laboratory. The challenge for scientists now was to find the perfect medium on which the microbe could feed and grow and multiply, so that a 'pure culture' – a culture in which only one microbe was present (because, if there were more than one kind, how could you be sure which one caused a particular disease when the culture was injected into a healthy animal?) – could be created. This quest became Koch's big passion.

Koch first tried growing microbes on solid mediums like potato slices, bread, meat and coagulated egg whites, but found none of them worked for all microbes. He then tried semi-solid gelatine as a medium, but gelatine did not remain solid at 37 degrees Celsius. (Why 37 degrees Celsius? Well, because that is the normal human body temperature, and the point was to investigate how disease-causing microbes developed in the human body, at that temperature.) When

Robert Koch

he was casting about for another medium, his laboratory assistants, Walther and Fanny Hesse, suggested he use a material called agar, derived from red algae. Fanny was an American who had moved to Germany after her marriage, and she knew that agar held its shape even at warm temperatures from using it in puddings back home. Even better, it was a transparent medium.

Agar turned out to be the perfect medium for growing a microbe pure culture. But even before he zeroed in on agar in the early 1880s and became very famous for his pure-culture techniques, Koch had grown the anthrax microbe and observed its entire life cycle on a different medium. He had seen within each microbe oval, translucent bodies, and guessed that they were spores (think of them as seed-like entities, capable of growing into new organisms). To test his theory, Koch injected just the spores into healthy animals; as he had hoped, those animals developed the disease too. He also discovered that the spores could remain dormant, or inactive, for years, and then, when conditions were right, once again come alive and grow into dangerous anthrax bacteria – that was how, when sheep grazed in a once-infectious pasture that had been unused for years, the disease returned! The last niggling mystery had been cracked!

Koch named the microbe *Bacillus anthracis* and presented a report on his findings in 1876. For the first time, a scientist had offered definite proof connecting a particular microbe to a particular disease. Naturally, the world stood up to applaud – after watching the presentation, eminent pathologist Julius Cohnheim said, prophetically, 'I regard it as the greatest discovery ever made with bacteria, and I believe that this is not the last time that this young Robert Koch will surprise and shame us by the brilliance of his investigations.' More importantly, Pasteur himself called it a 'remarkable achievement', and undertook his own research on the bacillus, coming up with the anthrax vaccine some years later.

***

Years later, Cohnheim and Koch would work together on tuberculosis, resulting in Koch's celebrated breakthrough. More details later in this section.

After he had started using agar and become an expert at growing pure cultures, Koch declared that bacterial traits remained constant – bacteria did not, could not, become more or less 'virulent' (capable of causing disease) than they already were. This was true in pure cultures, but as Pasteur discovered when he was working on a vaccine for chicken cholera, some bacteria could be made less virulent artificially, by exposing them to air. Pasteur denounced Koch's theory, claiming victory in this round of the Great Microbe-Hunters Contest.

It was in 1882 that Koch made the breakthrough that he is best remembered for – finding out the cause of tuberculosis (TB). In Koch's time, TB was thought to be a hereditary disease, but Koch was convinced it was an infectious disease caused by a bacterium, and he tested his theory using his four 'postulates' – a checklist he had developed to prove that a particular disease was caused by a particular microbe – on guinea pigs. All four postulates turned out to be true! Koch published his findings, revealing that the cause of TB was the slow-growing *Mycobacterium tuberculosis*. For the first time, someone had offered proof connecting a specific microbe to a specific HUMAN disease. In one fell swoop, the germ theory of disease became king.

In 1883, there was a cholera epidemic in Alexandria, Egypt. Both Koch and Pasteur sent their crews out, hoping to become the first ones to isolate the cholera germ. But the epidemic ended almost as soon as they got there, and Pasteur's crew returned empty-handed. Determined to get to the bottom of cholera, Koch proceeded to India, where you could always be sure of catching a cholera epidemic. For some months in 1884, he lived and worked at Grant Medical College in the former Bombay Presidency, until – eureka! – he isolated the cholera germ, which he named *Vibrio cholerae*. Round Two of the Great Microbe-Hunters Contest, boys and girls, goes to Germany's Roberrrrrt . . . Koch!

A logical question you may have at this point is this: According to Idea 17, Pasteur already created a cholera vaccine by 1879. How could he do that when the cholera germ wasn't isolated by Koch till 1884? Well, hadn't Jenner invented a vaccine for smallpox too, almost a hundred years before, without ever having isolated the smallpox 'germ'? Pasteur used the blood of a diseased person, which contained the cholera germ (along with other germs, presumably), to make his vaccine – he never got around to working with the pure culture of the cholera germ.

In 1890, Koch developed a drug called tuberculin, which he claimed was a cure for TB. He kept the contents of the drug a closely guarded secret, but it failed spectacularly when it was tested on humans, causing many deaths. The scandal destroyed Koch's credibility for a time, and he was forced to agree to work for the German government under severe constraints, instead of working independently, in exchange for no action being brought against him.

All was not lost, however. Tuberculin was found to be an excellent way to diagnose the disease, if not treat it, and is still being used today, in the tuberculin skin test for TB. Also, so path-breaking was Koch's work on TB that it won him the Nobel Prize in Physiology or Medicine in 1905.

***

As we know, both Edward Jenner and Louis Pasteur developed vaccines to protect humans – against smallpox and rabies respectively. But here's the fun part: neither of them knew, or guessed, that those diseases were not caused by bacteria at all, but by a completely different class of 'micro-non-organisms' called viruses. Because viruses are way smaller than bacteria, no one could see them even under the most powerful microscopes of that time.

In 1876, a German agricultural chemist called Adolf Mayer showed that tobacco mosaic disease, which affected tobacco plants, was infectious. By now, it was known that infectious diseases were spread by microbes, but try as he might, Mayer wasn't able to see the germs, and concluded that the disease was caused by a very small bacterium.

In 1892, the Russian biologist Dmitry Ivanovsky began to investigate tobacco mosaic disease. The advantage he had over Mayer was the Chamberland filter (invented by Charles Chamberland – here he comes again! – Pasteur's lab assistant who forgot to inoculate the chickens), which had pores small enough to be able to filter bacteria out of liquids. Ivanovsky filtered an extract of diseased tobacco leaves, and then applied the filtrate (filtered liquid) on to healthy tobacco plants. They got infected again! But he could see no 'germs' in the filtrate. Ivanovsky proposed that the disease was caused by a poison secreted by bacteria, but he didn't pursue it further.

In 1898, the Dutch microbiologist Martinus Beijerinck repeated experiments by Adolf Mayer and became convinced that the filtrate in fact contained an entirely different kind of infection-causing 'thing'. He discovered that the 'thing' was not a microbe; in fact, it wasn't a living thing at all! Instead, it was a soluble non-living particle – he called it a 'virus' – that became 'active' only when it was part of a living plant or

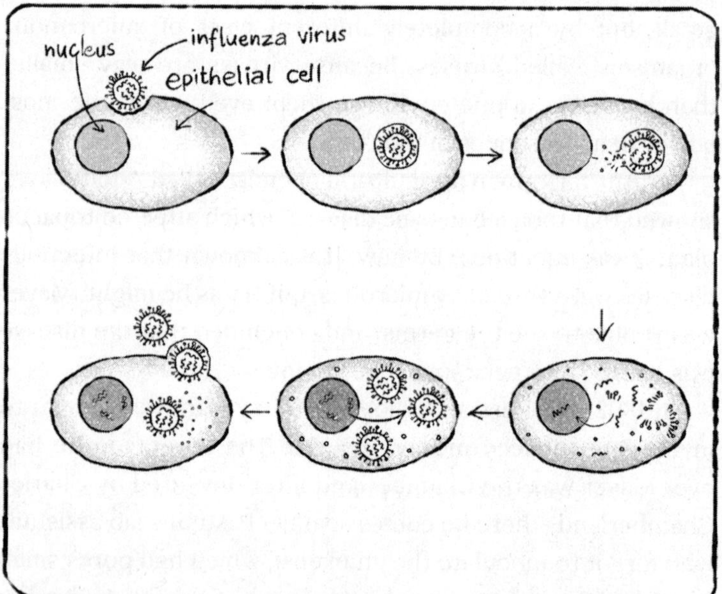

How a 'virus' turns into 'viruses'

animal cell. Since it could not 'reproduce' like a living thing, the virus cunningly took control of the cell's intelligence, and instructed it to make more and more copies of itself. Before you knew it – bam! – it had infected the entire tobacco plant!

This concept of a tiny, highly dangerous, but technically 'non-living' pathogen (disease-causing agent) sounded straight out of science fiction, and it was a long time before viruses were fully accepted and understood. And it wasn't until the electron microscope was invented in 1931 that the structure of viruses was observed for the first time. The very next year, South African-American physician and virologist Max Theiler isolated the yellow fever virus, and developed a vaccine for it – the first time a vaccine had been invented specifically against an identified virus. For that achievement, he was awarded the Nobel Prize in Physiology or Medicine in 1951.

Although viruses like the yellow fever virus, the influenza virus and the polio virus (against which American virologist Jonas Salk invented a vaccine) had been identified by 1950, it was the second half of the twentieth century that was the Golden Age of Virology – most of the 2,000 recognized species of plant, animal and bacterial viruses, including the ones that cause chicken pox, measles and, yes, the common cold, were discovered during this time. But with new viruses appearing all the time – like, most recently, the COVID-19 virus – they are a big challenge to doctors and scientists. But considering how quickly the COVID-19 vaccine was developed, it is clear that human ingenuity remains a force to be reckoned with. Onward!

Germ Theory? Miasma Theory? Or Both?

There is an interesting sequel to the whole germ theory vs miasma theory of disease – both Koch's work and Pasteur's work, while proving the germ theory of disease, also proved, in a sense, the miasma theory! How?

Well, for instance, by discovering that anthrax spores could remain dormant for years, Koch proved that one way to eliminate anthrax was to 'clean up' infectious fields (with chemical sprays or whatever). By discovering that the germs in milk not only spoilt milk but could also make humans sick, Pasteur proved that one way to prevent those diseases was to 'clean up' the milk, by heating it. In both cases, the two scientists showed that while it was true that germs caused disease, another, equally important cause of disease was the filthiness of our surroundings, our water, our air and our food (remember Florence Nightingale and John Snow proved this too!).

And isn't that what the miasma theory was really all about, in the sense that miasma smelt bad because of all the filthy, rotting stuff that was lying around or mixing with water and food?

IDEA 19

THE LITTLE DISEASE-CAUSING CRITTERS COME TO US VIA . . . OTHER CRITTERS!

How the Mosquito–Malaria Theory Was Proved

By the early 1880s, owing to the efforts of Louis Pasteur and Robert Koch, doctors knew of some of the ways in which germs travelled to us: they came from drinking contaminated water (as proved by John Snow during the cholera outbreak); through contact, either with an infected person (Remember how variolation worked? Idea 11?) or with the unwashed hands of doctors (as demonstrated exceptionally by Ignaz Semmelweis); through unhygienic surroundings (as Florence Nightingale proved); and through the air.

Of course, people also knew germs came to us through animals. In 1885, when he successfully inoculated Joseph Meister against rabies, Pasteur proved that human beings were infected with the rabies virus when they were bitten by rabid dogs. But since it was the animal that got the disease first, rabies was not considered a 'human disease'.

The great mystery that doctors and scientists were looking to crack in the last quarter of the nineteenth century was this – through which routes did the germs that caused uniquely human diseases travel to us, and how then did they spread from person to person? The diseases they were most concerned about were the truly deadly ones, like:

- the bubonic plague, aka the Black Death, which finished off – hold your breath – 25 million people in Europe between 1346 and 1353, and about 2.2 million between 1866 and the 1960s;
- malaria, which is still alive and kicking; according to a 2017 World Health Organization (WHO) report, there were an estimated 219 million cases of malaria worldwide and an estimated 4,35,000 deaths, more than 17,000 of them in India, in 2017 alone; and
- filariasis, or elephantiasis, which causes a person's limbs to swell in a most unseemly manner, so that the sufferer begins to look 'like an elephant'.

The first big – actually, BIG does it more justice – breakthrough in this case came in 1876, through the research of Scottish doctor Sir Patrick Manson.

As a boy, Manson was known in his family for having an excellent memory – at the tender age of five, he could repeat entire church sermons verbatim. He was also very much a fan of the outdoors, with a great interest in natural history, fishing, shooting, carpentry and cricket. At the age of sixteen, he enrolled in the University of Aberdeen for a medical degree.

By early 1865, at the age of only nineteen, the brilliant Manson had completed his studies, but since he could not graduate until he had turned twenty in October of the same year, he spent his time hanging out at museums, hospitals and other medical schools. Less than a year later, after he had been awarded not only a master's degree in surgery, but also a PhD equivalent in medicine and law, he sailed to the East, like his older brother had before him, to take up a job as medical officer in the maritime customs office at the port of Formosa (today called Taiwan).

In the nineteenth century, a very large part of the world was part of the British Empire. British doctors, botanists, geologists, mapmakers, anthropologists and manufacturers literally had the run of the place, and needed no permissions except from their own government to go exploring. So off they went!

For the next twenty-three years, Manson lived and practised in different locations in South-East Asia – Taiwan, China, Hong Kong – and had a grand time, learning a lot about all kinds of 'tropical' diseases (which occur in the warm and humid regions between the Tropic of Cancer and the Tropic of Capricorn) that he had never encountered in Europe. He taught himself Mandarin, and became very friendly with his Chinese patients, whether they were locals or belonged to the crews of the ships that docked at the ports he was at. Not much research on these diseases had been published in the West, so Manson had to figure out his own way, but he did marvellously well, with the help of only a microscope, his clinical skills and some excellent record-keeping.

From his early days in the East, Manson had become interested in a disease that later came to be called filariasis, which was pretty common in those parts. Filariasis was not fatal, but was an awful condition to have, because the victims' appearance became so repulsive that other people shunned them. They found it difficult to find employment, and their swollen limbs were often painful.

In the early 1870s, a Welsh doctor called Timothy Lewis figured out that filariasis was caused by a nematode (or roundworm) of the filarioidea type (see why he called it filariasis?). He had been studying cholera in Calcutta (Kolkata) when he made this discovery.

Lewis worked in India for fourteen years, returning to England in 1883, where he served on a committee to examine Robert Koch's findings about the cholera bacillus. Everyone's connected!

Manson's challenge was to detect how the roundworms, which were macroparasites – parasites large enough to be seen by the naked eye once they were full-grown – got into humans in the first place. As he examined many, many samples of blood under his microscope, Manson noticed one highly interesting thing – the microfilariae (the larval stage of the roundworm) could only be seen in blood samples that had been collected at night! Given the large number of mosquitoes in the tropics, and the fact that mosquitoes themselves were more active at night, Manson wondered if mosquitoes could have something to do with the transmission of the disease.

Luckily for Manson, his own gardener, Hin Lo, had filariasis, so Manson got mosquitoes to bite Hin Lo at night (no, seriously) and then captured the mosquitoes while they were still woozy after their hearty blood-meal. But let's allow Manson to describe the experience in his own words: 'I shall not easily forget the first mosquito I dissected. I tore off its abdomen and succeeded in expressing the blood the stomach contained. Placing this under the microscope, I was gratified to find that, so far from killing the filaria [roundworm], the digestive juices of the mosquito seemed to have stimulated it to fresh activity . . .'

'Aha!' said Manson to himself when he noticed how frisky the little microfilariae were. 'The roundworm does not grow from larva to adult inside the human body alone – it needs the mosquito as its "intermediate host"!' Over the course of the next few years (poor Hin Lo), he continued to study the worm's life cycle. Finally, in 1877, he had it!

This is what Manson worked out. First, the adult roundworm inside the infected human releases its offspring, the microfilariae, into their bloodstream. These are picked up by a mosquito when it sucks said human's blood. The microfilariae grow inside the mosquito's body for a couple of weeks until they are almost adult worms, passing through several larval stages and migrating at last to the mosquito's salivary glands. When the mosquito bites another human on another night, the worm, now at its last larval stage, enters the new host and infects them – i.e., actually gives them the disease. It then completes its growth to adulthood inside their body, and when it is ready, releases microfilariae into *their* bloodstream, beginning the whole sorry cycle again!

Patrick Manson didn't realize it then, but in the process of discovering that it wasn't air or water or human contact or infected secretions but an external agent, or 'vector' – the mosquito – that was responsible for the transmission of filariasis, he had single-handedly created a brand-new discipline of medical study called tropical medicine.

***

When Manson's results were published and conveyed to England in 1878, there was great excitement in the medical community worldwide. A few prescient doctors, like the American Albert Africanus King, became convinced that mosquitoes also transmitted malaria, and proposed that malaria-ridden Washington DC be surrounded by a fine wire mesh as high as the Washington Monument.

The idea caught on. Malaria became the buzzword (haha!) of the day, especially among doctors working in the tropics. It

The idea that malaria was spread by mosquitoes was revolutionary. It had been so firmly believed that it was caused by inhaling miasma that even its name, it is said, was coined as a combination of the Italian words *mal* ('bad') and *aria* ('air').

got an extra boost in 1880, when the French physician Charles Louis Alphonse Laveran, who was working in a military hospital in the French colony of Algeria at the time, made the stunning discovery that malaria was caused by a protozoan (a single-celled organism that is neither bacterium nor virus, and which, until then, no one had ever suspected of causing disease in humans) when he observed the crescent-shaped parasite in a blood sample he took from a soldier who had just died of malaria. He named the protozoan plasmodium.

> Some years later, Laveran would also show that trypanosoma, a different kind of protozoan, was responsible for causing the disease called sleeping sickness.

Years later, in 1894, in an article he published in the *British Medical Journal*, Patrick Manson also put forth what became known as the 'mosquito-malaria theory', saying that he suspected that plasmodium, like the filaria parasite, also spent part of its life cycle in a mosquito's body.

He regretted that he could not do research on it himself, since he was then back in England for good, but he urged doctors working in places like India, where both malaria and mosquitoes abounded, to proceed 'with confidence' on this line of research.

On 10 April of the same year, soon after the article had been published, a doctor called Ronald Ross, who had been working in the Indian Medical Service for over a decade but was now in England on a brief sabbatical, came to meet Patrick Manson. That meeting was to change Ross's life, and the history of medicine, forever.

***

Now let's rewind a little and find out a little more about this Ronald Ross. He was almost a desi, this Ross. Born in Almora to Scottish parents just three days after the First War of Indian Independence broke out in 1857, he had been sent off to England at the age of eight to get himself an education. Ross was a dreamy child and teenager, interested in drawing (at which he was pretty good), writing poems and plays (at which he wasn't bad but didn't have much success) and mathematics. At seventeen, he grandly declared his intention of becoming a writer, but his dad quashed such foolishness quickly, and made him enrol for a medical degree. Poor Ross did badly at college, and once he had scraped through the course, flunked the entrance examination to the Indian Medical Service. The next year, he took the exam again, and this time made it through by the skin of his teeth. In 1881, as per his father's dearest wish, he entered the Indian Medical Service.

Ross's first appointment as a surgeon was in the Madras Presidency (the least prestigious of three possible appointments – a place in the Bengal and Bombay Presidencies was far more coveted). Like other doctors in the tropics, Ross was also curious about malaria, but his personal interest came from having seen his own father suffer through a particularly severe bout of the disease. Plus, he was constantly treating soldiers for malaria, whether he was stationed at Mysore (Mysuru), Bangalore (Bengaluru) or Madras (Chennai).

Expectedly, since this was India, mosquitoes were also a big part of Ross's life. He got to know of Laveran's discovery of plasmodium well after the fact, and then spent years pricking the fingers of anyone who came to him with a fever, staining a slide with the blood and observing it under the microscope. He never, ever found anything that looked like plasmodium, however, and had come to the conclusion that Laveran had made a Himalayan error. When he returned to England for a break in 1894 and told his friends what he believed; they pointed him to Manson's article in the *British Medical Journal*, and packed him off to meet the senior doctor, who was considered the authority on tropical diseases in London.

Off Ross went, then, to visit Manson at his laboratory. Soon after, Manson showed him Laveran's slides, with the plasmodium crescents, under his microscope. Ross was stunned – he knew for a fact that no such crescents were naturally present in human blood. He requested Manson's permission to shadow him while he went about his work, and spent the next few months doing just that.

On a cold afternoon in November, Manson, impressed with the younger doctor's mind, shared his mosquito-malaria theory with him in great detail. Manson believed that while the plasmodium completed its life cycle inside the mosquito, it was transmitted to humans when they drank the water in which the mosquito had laid her eggs. Ross was unreasonably excited by Manson's hypothesis. By this time, he completely trusted the Father of Tropical Medicine and now, with sudden clarity, he saw himself as Manson's true successor, the knight in shining armour whose destiny lay in proving his mentor right.

When he was acting garrison surgeon in Bangalore, annoyed by them always buzzing around, and seeing that his bungalow somehow had more mosquitoes than anyone else's, Ross undertook an investigation, and found a particularly large swarm of the menace around a barrel of water outside his window. Noticing that the water was literally crawling with mosquito larvae, he emptied the barrel; by the next day, the number of mosquitoes had dropped drastically. It got Ross thinking – if all such stagnant pools of water were eliminated, maybe the mosquitoes could be too! But few took his advice seriously, much to his chagrin, and fewer still, including Ross himself, connected the mosquitoes to malaria.

Laveran's slides had been smeared with the blood of a malaria patient. The only way to prove Manson's theory that mosquitoes were the carriers (or vectors) of malaria was to find the same crescents in the blood of a mosquito that had feasted on a malaria patient. All that remained after that was to wait until the mosquito laid its eggs, have someone drink that water and then wait to see if they developed malaria. It was that simple!

Ronald Ross now had an overwhelming mission in life. On 20 March 1895, he ended his sabbatical and sailed back to India, impatient to get on with his life's work.

So eager was Ross to begin his mosquito-malaria investigations that he got to work on the ship bringing him to India itself! He used to rush about on deck and below stairs, pricking the fingers of anyone who would let him, to collect blood samples. He even spent time dissecting the ship's cockroaches, as essential prep for dissecting mosquitoes. When he reached Secunderabad, he was racing to the Bombay Civil Hospital, where he had been posted, before customs could even clear his bags.

Thus began three years of an overwhelming and often frustrating obsession for Ross. The trouble was that he could only do his malaria research in his spare time, and he had very little of it, given his job as a surgeon major in the army. He was also constantly being transferred, and often to places where malaria was not as prevalent as he would have liked. Through his darkest days, what kept him going was his correspondence with Manson, who gave him advice, pointed him in new directions when he seemed to come up against a wall and encouraged him at every turn – 'Above everything, don't give it up. Look upon it as a Holy Grail and yourself as Galahad and never give up the search.'

The 173 letters Ross and Manson exchanged between 1895 and 1899 – at a time when letters took three weeks to travel between England and India – are today considered one of the great scientific correspondences.

In the beginning, things went spectacularly well for Ross. As early as May 1895, he bred mosquitoes in captivity from larvae collected from water. He then put a malaria patient under a mosquito net and released the mosquitoes inside it, so that they would bite him, before he captured the mosquitoes and examined the blood in their stomachs. The crescent-shaped filaments of plasmodium were there, clear as day! To test the next part – transmission – he let four other mosquitoes bite the malaria patient again and put them in a bottle with a little water in it. Once the mosquitoes had laid their eggs, he got three people, including his servant Lutchman, to drink the water (he had to pay a decent sum of money to each to persuade them, of course!). None of them developed malaria.

It was a setback, but it was still early days, and Ross was about to start his next round of investigations when he was transferred to Bangalore. He spent a frustrating eighteen months there – despite the many mosquitoes in Bangalore, there was no malaria – but continued his research when he could. It was during this time, after several more trials of drinking contaminated water had failed to transmit the disease, that he began to suspect that malaria was transmitted by the *bite* of the mosquito. When he got mosquitoes that had bitten a malaria patient to bite a healthy person, however, once again, the person remained disease-free!

Ross didn't know it then, but this last failure was because he was using grey Culex mosquitoes, which are not malaria vectors. Once again, it was Manson who urged him to re-try the experiment using different species of mosquitoes.

In May 1896, Ross made good use of a short leave he had been granted to visit Sigur Ghat in Ooty, known to be a malaria-endemic region. Despite all his precautions, however – he slept under a net, with his windows closed, and had even taken a preventive dose of quinine, which was then the only sort of treatment for malaria – he caught the disease within three days of setting foot in Sigur. While he rested, physically weakened by the disease but with his senses still on high alert, he observed, on the wall by his bed, a mosquito that looked different from any he had seen before. This one was a 'brown' mosquito with dappled wings, and it was perched there in a peculiar posture. He filed the image away for the future, and when he was transferred back to Secunderabad in June 1897, he began the search for the brown mosquito, sending out his assistants to bring him mosquito larvae from every drain and stagnant pool in the city.

On 15 August 1897, an assistant brought him a bottle of water with several about-to-hatch mosquito larvae. The next day, many of them hatched, and Ross, to his great delight, saw that they were the brown mosquitoes (today we know it as the Anopheles mosquito). He immediately let them feast on his malaria patient Husein Khan (whom he paid 1 anna per mosquito bite) and recaptured them, looking to dissect them the next day.

By now, Ross had reached a stage where he wasn't dissecting mosquitoes only to observe infected human blood in their stomachs. He was examining every last bit of tissue – the gut, the head, the legs – to see where the plasmodium lodged itself and how it grew inside the mosquito's body.

On 17 August, he dissected two mosquitoes but found nothing unusual. On 19 August, he dissected one more and found some peculiar circular cells inside the stomach wall, about 10 microns (1 micron is one-thousandth of a millimetre) in diameter. Could these be plasmodium larvae? On 20 August, a very muggy day in Begumpet, he found that one of the mosquitoes had died. Bummer! There were now only two left, and he sacrificed the penultimate one at around 1 p.m. When he looked at the stomach wall of this mosquito, he saw the circular cells again, about twenty-one of them, except this time they had grown to about 12 microns. The plasmodium was growing in the mosquito's gut! If the circles were even larger in the last mosquito, which he had put aside to dissect the next day, it would prove his hypothesis!

Ross spent that night in a fever of anxiety, worried that the last mosquito would escape or die during the night, worried that he would find that the cells hadn't grown when he opened it up. His hands barely steady, he dissected the last specimen the next day and put its stomach wall under his microscope. There they were, the circular cells, bigger than they had been in the previous mosquito's gut.

This only proved that whatever was growing in the mosquito's gut was a parasite – it was almost certainly the malarial parasite, but there was no proof yet. Nevertheless, it was a huge win. There was still a lot of work to be done to figure out the entire transmission cycle, but the first door had been opened.

Ecstatic, Ross poured out his joy and triumph in the only way he knew – in a poem, giving all credit to divine grace:

Ronald Ross

This day relenting God
Hath placed within my hand
A wondrous thing; and God
Be praised. At His command,
Seeking His secret deeds
With tears and toiling breath,
I find thy cunning seeds,
O million-murdering Death.
I know this little thing
A myriad men will save.
O Death, where is thy sting?
Thy victory, O Grave?

But Ross's woes were not done. In September, he was transferred to Kherwara in Rajasthan, which had no malaria at all. He threw an almighty tantrum, threatened to quit the service and was only mollified when Manson used his connections in England to get him transferred to Calcutta's Presidency General Hospital on special duty in January 1898. There was hardly any malaria among humans in Calcutta either, but Manson persuaded Ross to research the transmission of malaria in birds instead, since bird malaria was plentiful, and was likely to be transmitted the same way as in humans.

With the help of his assistants, the unlettered Mohammed Bux and the science graduate Kishori Mohan Bandopadhyay, Ross began to dissect mosquitoes that had bitten infected birds, discovering that in bird malaria, the mosquitoes in which the parasite grew were his old friends, the Culex mosquitoes. On 2 July 1898, he discovered the typical circular malarial cells in the thorax of a mosquito. On 4 July, when he dissected its head, he found the cells there as well, *in the mosquito's salivary gland*! By 8 July, he was completely convinced that what he had long suspected was true – the plasmodium was transmitted through the saliva when a mosquito carrying it bit a healthy person. To complete the circle of proof, he sent Mohammed Bux to capture some healthy sparrows and then got mosquitoes that had already bitten an infected bird a few days before to bite them. All the sparrows developed malaria – the transmission route had been revealed beyond doubt.

***

For his outstanding work on the cycle of the malarial parasite, Ronald Ross was awarded the Nobel Prize in Medicine or Physiology in 1902. In his acceptance speech, Ross credited the work of several other scientists and doctors who had worked in the same field, including Charles Laveran, Robert Koch (both of whom would go on to win Nobels themselves), Albert Africanus King and, of course, Patrick Manson.

For all his wonderful dedication to his science, however, Ross was not a popular man. He was considered both eccentric and egocentric, and was constantly feuding with his employers, peers, assistants and students. In his 1923 book, *Memoirs, with a Full Account of the Great Malaria Problem and its Solution*, Ross did not mention his hardworking lab assistant Kishori Bandopadhyay at all. When Ross returned to

Calcutta's Presidency General Hospital in January 1927, for the unveiling of the Gate of Commemoration, where his statue and a plaque containing his poem still stands, Bandopadhyay registered his protest by not attending the ceremony.

Oh well, the greatest scientists are human too, right?

The moment he had cracked the malaria transmission route, Ross wrote off excitedly, to his mentor Manson. 'I think I may now say QED [*quad erat demonstrandum* – Latin for "that which was to be proved has been proved"],' he exulted, 'and congratulate you on the mosquito theory indeed. The door is unlocked, and I am walking in and collecting the treasures.' Fittingly, Manson received the letter during a meeting of the new 'tropical diseases' section of the British Medical Association. He immediately read it out to the assembled delegates, who greeted it with a standing ovation. 'I am sure you will agree with me,' Manson said, his chest visibly puffing, 'that the medical world, I might even say humanity, is extremely indebted to Surgeon Major Ross for what he has done.'

Dr Haffkine and the Great Bombay Plague of 1896

Remember how we talked of THREE killer diseases engaging medical researchers at the fag end of the nineteenth century? In Idea 19, you have read about how two of them – filariasis and malaria – were cracked. What of the third – bubonic plague? Was it also transmitted by mosquitoes? Here's the short answer.

In 1894, French bacteriologist Alexandre Yersin and Japanese bacteriologist Shibasaburo Kitasato independently isolated the bacterium that causes bubonic plague. Yersin also established that it was not mosquitoes but fleas that had feasted on the blood of rodents infected with the disease that carried the disease to humans. The bacterium was named *Yersinia pestis* after its own microbe hunter Alexandre Yersin.

Now the search was on for a plague vaccine, which was developed by a Russian bacteriologist, Waldemar Mordecai Wolff Haffkine, in 1897. And thereby hangs a fascinating tale.

Waldemar Haffkine, a Jew who had fled Russia to escape persecution, had been working at the Pasteur Institute in Paris for many years when he invented a cholera vaccine in 1892. While Pasteur had invented his vaccine in 1879, *before* Robert Koch had isolated the cholera bacterium in 1884, Haffkine created his vaccine well after, in accordance with Koch's postulates, using an attenuated form of the pure culture of cholera bacterium. On 18 July 1892, at great risk to his own life, he inoculated himself with his vaccine, and exposed himself to the virulent form of the cholera germ. Fortunately for him, the vaccine worked superbly and he remained hale and hearty.

Haffkine was thrilled, but no one in the fraternity, including Pasteur, was enthusiastic about the new vaccine. Convinced that it could save millions of people, Haffkine appealed to the British ambassador in Paris to organize his passage to India, where cholera epidemics were common. Haffkine travelled to Calcutta in 1893, where a cholera epidemic was raging. After initial resistance, his vaccine was widely accepted and hundreds of thousands of people inoculated.

In 1896, a plague epidemic hit Bombay (Mumbai) and its governor invited Haffkine to help tackle it. Haffkine set up a laboratory in Byculla on the grounds of the Sir J.J. Group of Hospitals, and began work on a vaccine. By January 1897, he had one! On 10 January, in his usual style, he inoculated himself with a culture of weakened *Yersinia pestis* in broth (he had earlier tested it successfully on rabbits) and exposed himself to the virulent form of the bacterium. He did not develop the disease. The first vaccine against bubonic plague had been invented, and began to be administered almost immediately.

In India and across the world, Haffkine was hailed as a saviour. In 1899, he was appointed director of the government's Plague Research Laboratory in Parel and worked there until he retired in 1914. In 1925, in honour of the brilliant bacteriologist who put his own life and career at risk, more than once, so that millions of people could live safer lives, the lab where he spent, in his own words, 'the best years of my [his] life' was renamed the Haffkine Institute. To this day, tit continues to be one of the country's premier biomedical research institutes.

SECTION 4: 1900 ONWARDS

THE GREAT CONVERGENCE: MEDICINE GOES MULTIDISCIPLINARY!

Is the science of medicine a 'physical science' (like physics, chemistry, geology, astronomy and metallurgy, which concern themselves mainly with inanimate objects), or is it a 'biological science' (like anthropology, botany, zoology, genetics and molecular biology, which concern themselves which living things)? In the nineteenth century, the answer would have been an emphatic 'A biological science, of course!' As the twentieth century dawned and progressed, though, the answer became more hesitant: 'We-ell, it's a bit of both, I suppose . . .'

And with good reason. Over the years, scientists and doctors began to realize that the human body was not only similar to a machine (see Idea 9), but also had a lot of physics and chemistry and metallurgy and electricity going on inside it. It was only when the learnings from different sciences were applied to the science of healing that the most significant breakthroughs were made; it was only through collaborations between scientists that the most intractable puzzles were cracked.

As specialization increased, and doctors and surgeons began to know more and more about less and less, it became vital for them to work in teams, leaning on others to fill in the gaps in their knowledge, while sharing their own expertise with those who needed it. Medical instrumentation – sophisticated machines that helped doctors look into, cut into (or *not* cut into) and monitor the human body – became an integral part of clinics and hospitals, requiring a separate set of experts who had nothing to do with medicine, to design, manufacture, operate and maintain them.

The age of the natural philosopher, who got his brilliant insights from having a broader education and outlook; the lone genius, who bent rules and didn't mind being a bit dodgy with ethics in the pursuit of a grand dream; and the alpha-doc, who was the only superstar in his operation theatre, faded, giving way to teams of people from across the world, connected by technology, working together to create a world free of pain and disease.

Which, as you can imagine, had both its good bits and its not-so-great bits. But hey, all progress and development comes with that caveat. The good news was that human curiosity in the twentieth century continued to be unbounded and, as a result, the wins never stopped coming.

IDEA 20

THERE'S A WAY TO LOOK INSIDE THE HUMAN BODY . . . WITHOUT CUTTING INTO IT!

The Magic of X-Ray Technology

Throughout this book, we have mainly focused on biology – as we should – when we've talked about medicine. But as we know from all the work that had happened in alchemy for millennia, and the exciting research that had been going on since the eighteenth century on the different kinds of air, chemistry was keeping well apace. Alongside, the new and exciting field of electricity, sparked by the investigations of people like Benjamin Franklin, Robert Boyle, Alessandro Volta, André-Marie Ampère, Michael Faraday, Georg Ohm and James Maxwell, had really begun to go places in the nineteenth century. In 1857, German physicist and glass-blower Heinrich Geissler invented a novelty item to demonstrate the 'cool' effects of electricity. Inside a sealed glass tube that had been filled with a gas and then 'partially

The scientists who made the big breakthroughs in the new field of electricity had, it seems, truly 'electric' surnames. Today, we know those surnames less as people and more as units of electrical measurement – ohm is a measure of resistance, volt of potential difference, ampere of current, and so on.

evacuated' (some of the air in the tube had been pumped out, creating a semi-vacuum), he placed two metal electrodes – a cathode and an anode – at either end of the tube, and applied a high voltage between them. Immediately, an electrical current began to flow through the tube, speeding up the 'free electrons' always present in a gas. These free electrons collided with the atoms of the gas, knocking electrons out of them and turning them into positively charged ions. When these electrons recombined with their ions (ions are always trying to become stable again), energy was released in the form of fluorescent light, and the gas in the tube glowed. Depending on which gas was inside – neon, argon, sodium, mercury vapour – the glow had a different colour. You can see why people who lived in an age without electric lights would want to have these wondrous tubes in their homes!

Fascinated by the Geissler tubes, English physicist William Crookes, among others, wondered what would happen if the tube was evacuated further. Using a better vacuum pump (which his assistant had invented), Crookes did exactly that and tried the experiment again. This time, the inside of the tube, between the two electrodes, went dark, but the glass wall of the tube itself glowed. What was happening was this: as more gas was taken out of the tube, there were fewer gas molecules for the free electrons to collide with. The electrons, therefore, sped straight from the cathode to the anode, and with no collisions and recombination happening, the inside of the tube went dark. However, now that they did not lose energy through collisions, the electrons were going so fast that some simply sped past the anode and hit the inside wall of the glass tube instead. The 'excited' atoms in the *glass* now gave off fluorescence, making the tube glow.

Amid the glow, researchers noticed the shadow of the anode form on the glass wall. You know how a shadow is formed in daily life – when light rays are stopped by a physical barrier, like your hand, the shadow of that barrier (your hand) is cast on the wall. Now, if the anode was casting a shadow, it meant that some kind of ray was being stopped by it. Clearly, these were not light rays, because the space between the electrodes was dark. In 1876, German physicist Eugen Goldstein proved that these invisible rays were coming from the cathode, and named them cathode rays. The tubes inside which these cathode rays were generated then began to be called cathode ray tubes (CRTs).

Let's move quickly now to a cold Friday afternoon in November 1895. That day, in his already-dark laboratory at the University of Würzburg in Bavaria, Germany, engineer and physicist Wilhelm Roentgen was investigating the effects of passing an electrical current through different kinds of cathode ray tubes. In the CRT he was using, a tiny aluminium window – small enough not to let outside air into the tube but large enough to allow the cathode rays to pass out of it – had been included at the anode end. To make sure that he would not be distracted by the glow of the CRT while he observed the cathode rays exiting it, Roentgen covered the tube with black cardboard, and applied a high voltage to get the electricity flowing between the electrodes.

That was when he noticed something strange – on a bench about a metre away from the CRT, something was shimmering softly by itself. Roentgen turned off the current to the CRT. The glow stopped too. He turned it on again, and the glow resumed. Striking a match, he investigated and found that the glow came from a piece of card that he had coated with a fluorescent material. He had prepared it beforehand, meaning to place it in front of the aluminium window and capture on it the pattern of the cathode rays leaving the tube.

But there was no way the cathode rays could have reached the fluorescent card on the bench – the window through which they were exiting was pointing in another direction entirely. Reasoning that the cathode rays were perhaps 'leaking' through the black cardboard covering the tube, because it wasn't quite 'light-tight', he inserted another thick piece of black cardboard between the fluorescent card and the CRT and repeated the experiment. The card on the bench glowed again. Casting about for another barrier, he picked up a 1,000-page book lying in his lab and placed that between the card and the CRT. It continued to glow. A wooden board about 2.5 centimetres thick was the next barrier to be inserted, this time in between the book and the fluorescent card. The card still glowed!

Clearly, these mystery rays – Roentgen called them X-rays – which were able to pass straight through so many different materials, weren't cathode rays at all! Was there any material that they could not pass through, though? Knowing that lead was a very dense material (the more electrons the atoms of an element have, the denser the element; and each lead atom is packed with eighty-two electrons), Roentgen fired up the CRT, picked up a lead disc he had lying around, held it up in front of the fluorescent card . . . and got the biggest shock of his life.

There on the card, clear as day, was the circular shadow of the lead disc – *and the bones of his hand!* In one fell swoop, he had found not one but two materials impenetrable by X-rays – lead, and his own bones! But he was more shaken than triumphant. To see through to a person's bones, past their skin and tissue, was impossible, surely! He would have to repeat the experiment several times to be sure.

Roentgen went home, had a quick dinner and returned immediately to his lab. He spent the rest of the weekend there, repeating his experiment using a number of different materials, sleeping on the floor when he was too exhausted to go on, fearful that if he announced his discovery about rays that could see past skin and tissue, he would be hounded out of his profession as a madman.

Two weeks later, finally caving to the demands of his wife, Anna Bertha, who was genuinely concerned about her husband's state, he told her what he had observed and enlisted her help for the experiment. Replacing the fluorescent card with photographic paper, he had her lay her hand on it, fingers splayed. Then, turning on the CRT, he took the world's very first X-ray picture. When she saw the bones of her fingers clearly revealed, along with her wedding ring, Anna Bertha completely freaked out, shrieking, 'I have seen my death!'

On 28 December 1895, Roentgen published his first paper – 'On a New Kind of Rays' – about his eye-popping findings. It became a worldwide sensation. In 1901, he was awarded the very first Nobel Prize in Physics, to which he responded by donating all the prize money to his university. He also refused to take out any patents on his discovery (a patent is a government license granted to an inventor to ensure that no one can make, use or sell his invention without his permission and/or paying him a fee), saying that he hoped that its practical applications would benefit everyone.

***

Once Roentgen himself realized the potential of what he had discovered, he turned into its biggest evangelist. On 1 January 1896, right after his paper was published, he wrote personal letters to physicians around Europe, urging them to experiment with the new technology. By 11 January, the first use of X-rays for 'medical imaging' under clinical conditions was recorded in the UK, when a British physician 'radiographed' a needle that had got embedded inside an associate's hand. On Valentine's Day, the same doctor was the first to use X-rays in a surgical operation. In May, the great American inventor Thomas Edison developed the vitascope, which allowed doctors to see a 'live' image of what the X-rays revealed, without having to wait for it to develop on a photographic plate; it became the standard device in medical X-ray examinations.

But the dangers of sustained exposure to X-rays were also discovered almost immediately. In early 1896, Russian physiologist Ivan Tarkhanov exposed frogs and insects to X-ray radiation and warned that X-rays not only photographed bones but also harmed the living tissue they passed through. In 1903, Edison's assistant, the glass-blower Clarence Dally, died of a severely malignant cancer in his hands and arms – he had been given to taking radiographs of his own hands as a fun pastime. In 1905, American X-ray pioneer Elizabeth Fleischman died from complications of her work with X-rays.

Yet, this very 'disadvantage' of X-rays was turned into a huge advantage in a different field called radiation therapy. If exposure to X-rays damaged or destroyed tissue, wouldn't it be a good idea to use that technique to destroy diseased tissue and malignant tumours? Today, radiation therapy is used extensively in cancer treatment.

There's more. While regular X-ray images are 2D images of the skeletal system, used extensively not only in medicine but also in dentistry and cosmetic surgery, X-rays can also be used to check for problems in soft tissue – like a swelling of the lungs or a blockage in the intestines. You've probably heard the words 'computed tomography' or 'CT scanning' –

CT uses X-ray technology as well, except it takes pictures of your organs slice by slice, and then combines them to form a fabulous 3D image that can show your doctor exactly where the problem lies! In fact, imaging technology based on X-rays is so ubiquitous today that it is impossible to think of a world without it.

Which is all fantastic, but what of the poor X-ray technicians at hospitals, who have to work in the presence of X-rays day in and day out? They have no need to worry – as Roentgen discovered way back in 1895, lead is one of the few materials that cannot be penetrated by X-rays. That's why, today, X-ray technicians stand behind a lead screen while working the machine, and stay safe.

Did you notice that apart from lead and human bone, the world's first X-ray photograph revealed another material that was mostly impenetrable by X-rays? That's right – Anna Bertha Roentgen's wedding ring, which we can presume was made of gold! A gold screen would certainly work as a safe barrier for X-ray technicians – for gold is very dense too, with seventy-nine electrons in each atom. The only reason we use a lead screen instead of a gold screen is that – duh! – the latter would cost a small fortune .

Marie Curie, Petite Fury

The great Polish-born French scientist Marie Curie, the first woman to win a Nobel Prize (in Physics, in 1903) and the only person in history to win two Nobel Prizes in two different scientific disciplines (she won again in 1911, in Chemistry), will need more than one chapter to herself if we are to do justice. In this book, however, we are only focusing on a tiny – but very significant – part of her achievements. This is a lovely story, because it says as much about her as a person as it does about her as a scientist.

By the time the First World War broke out in 1914, Marie Curie was already a double Nobel Prize winner. Earlier that year, she had been hard at work on the Radium Institute at the University of Paris, which was scheduled to open its doors in August 1914, on a street that was to be named Rue Pierre Curie after her beloved late husband. But war arrived, several researchers were drafted into the French army and the forty-seven-year-old Marie found herself at a loose end. Wasting no time, she threw herself into the war effort for her adopted country.

First, she tried to donate her gold Nobel Prize medals to the war fund, but the French National Bank sensibly refused to accept them. Disappointed, she used her prize money to buy war bonds instead. (In times of war, governments need a lot of money quickly. They raise it from their citizens, who 'loan' money to the government by buying war bonds.) Then, she began to cast about for a real problem that she could sink her teeth into, and found one when she realized that the lives of many more wounded soldiers could be saved if they could be X-rayed as quickly as possible after they fell, to help doctors decide on the best course of treatment. Unfortunately, very few (battle)field hospitals had radiography units (i.e., the equipment needed to take X-rays) and the ones that did were often too far away to be of much help to most of the wounded. If only there was a way to take the radiography unit to the soldiers, instead of the other way around!

Not one to let the grass grow under her feet, and definitely not one to be intimidated by a subject she knew nothing about, Marie read up everything she could about radiology, anatomy, and automobiles. She then procured X-ray equipment and portable generators for electricity, and fitted out twenty suitable vehicles to function as mobile radiography units. As the newly appointed director of the Red Cross Radiology Service, she also set up France's first military radiology centre, apart from radiography units at 200 field hospitals, all of which were in operation by late 1914. Then, recruiting her own seventeen-year-old daughter Irene as her assistant (Irene would go on to win her own Nobel Prize in Chemistry in 1935), she teamed up with a military doctor to start operations.

The sight of Marie Curie and her *petites* Curie ('little Curies') – the affectionate nickname given to the mobile radiology units – zigzagging across the battlefield in the aftermath of each battle, X-raying the wounded where they lay so that doctors could begin treating them immediately, cheered many a soldier, and won the hearts of all Frenchmen and women. It also saved scores of lives. Sadly, after the war

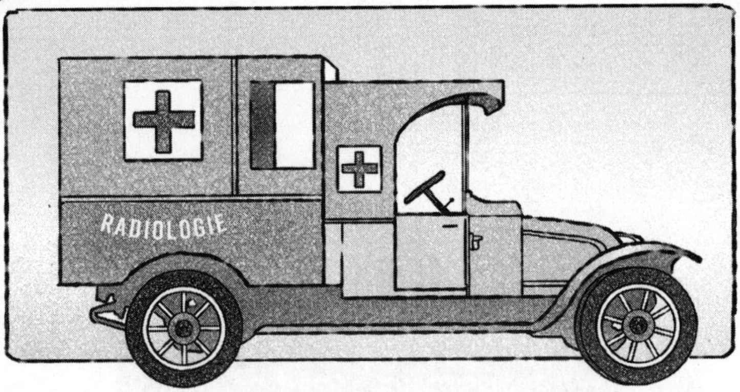

The Petite Curie

ended in 1918, the French government did not acknowledge her very significant contributions in this field.

An interesting endnote: Marie Curie is best known for her discovery of two radioactive elements, radium (which she named after the Latin word for 'ray') and polonium (which she named for her native country). She spent so much of her life exposed to the dangerous radiation from these two elements (apart from exposure to X-ray radiation during the war) that if you want to see her diaries – or even her cookbook – today, you have to put on protective gear to shield yourself from radiation contamination. When she died in 1934, she was buried in no ordinary coffin – it was lined with a very special material. Can you guess what it was? That's right, lead!

IDEA 21

ANIMAL BLOOD, CHEMICAL DYES, ARSENIC, MOULD – THEY ALL CURE DISEASE!

Antiserums, Antibiotics and Other Wonder Drugs

Even though microbes had been identified as the causes of some diseases by the last decade of the nineteenth century, there were not many effective *cures* against them. Sure, some vaccines had been developed, but they were meant to prevent disease, not treat it. As you can imagine, finding ways to treat and cure diseases was the big spur for researchers, doctors and microbiologists at the time. And the place where it was all happening was the Institute for Infectious Diseases in Berlin, which is today called the Robert Koch Institute. (Remember Koch? Not quite? Check out his achievements in Idea 18.)

In 1883, German bacteriologist Edwin Klebs identified the bacterium that caused the dreaded diphtheria, a disease that caused the respiratory passages to swell up and choked thousands of children to death each year. The very next year, Friedrich Loeffler, a bacteriologist working at the Koch Institute, cultivated (i.e., grew) the same bacterium in the laboratory (this is why, before it got its proper Latin name, the microbe was referred to as the Klebs-Loeffler bacterium). Loeffler also suggested it was a soluble poison the bacterium secreted that actually caused the tissue damage that diphtheria did, but did not pursue it further. Now the search was on to find a vaccine for the disease, as well as a cure for children who had already caught it.

In 1888, two French scientists, Émile Roux (the same one who had developed the rabies vaccine with Louis Pasteur) and Alexandre Yersin (after whom the bacterium that causes bubonic plague – *Yersinia pestis* – which he co-discovered, is named), who were working together at the Pasteur Institute, discovered, to their surprise, that even after they had filtered the diphtheria bacterium out of infected blood, the filtrate still had the power to infect animals like guinea pigs, rabbits and pigeons with the disease. Loeffler had been right, and now they had proof – it wasn't the bacterium itself, but some kind of poison that it released into the bloodstream that caused the disease! Roux and Yersin referred to this bacterial poison as a 'toxin'.

Researchers now began to wonder how it was that some of the children and animals infected with diphtheria survived. Could it be that animal and human 'immune systems' – our in-built disease-fighting armies – were capable of producing a corresponding 'antitoxin'? Perhaps the antitoxins were able to neutralize (or 'cancel out') the toxins when the bacteria producing them were weak! There was only one way to find out if the hypothesis was true: deliberately infect animals with small doses of weak diphtheria bacterium, examine samples of their blood, and see what came up.

Before we go on, do take a detour to the box 'The World's Best 24/7 Security System' on page 263 and get yourself a brief introduction to the human immune system. It will acquaint you with some fun words that you probably don't know the meanings of – hey, swotting up the jargon helps!

***

Done? Now back to our earlier discussion, about whether animal (and human) bodies naturally produced antitoxins to counter microbial toxins, specifically, the diphtheria toxin.

Among the scientists working feverishly on this project was a German military doctor called Emil Behring, who had joined the Koch Institute in 1888. Behring started by infecting guinea pigs with small doses of the diphtheria toxin, taken from the blood of a diphtheria sufferer, and discovered that guinea pigs did indeed produce antitoxins. When he drew a sample of antitoxin-laden blood from the guinea pig and put a few drops of a chemical into the sample to coagulate it, i.e., to make the blood cells clump together, a clear liquid called blood serum, which contained the antitoxins (and antitoxins are nothing but a kind of antibody), separated from the coagulated cells. When this serum, suitably processed and cleared of all microbes, was injected into a healthy guinea pig, the animal developed passive immunity, or temporary immunity, to diphtheria. What was even more exciting was that the guinea pigs that had diphtheria were cured when they received the 'antiserum' (antitoxin-laden serum).

'Blood-serum therapy', which offered only a temporary passive immunity, was not as effective as vaccine therapy, which offered lifelong immunity from a particular disease. How come? Well, unlike in the case of vaccination, no disease-causing germ or toxin was introduced into the healthy animal (in this case, the guinea pig) in serum therapy. That meant the animal's immune system would not be able to recognize the germ if and when it actually invaded in the future. However, since the diphtheria antibodies themselves had been introduced into its body, the guinea pig would at least be able to neutralize the diphtheria toxins if the bacteria came in, for a few weeks or months, until the antibodies died out. So yes, vaccines were better, but until a vaccine for diphtheria was developed (that happened over twenty-five years later, in 1923), antiserum was a great alternative.

In 1890, Emil Behring went public with his discovery of the diphtheria antiserum. He also published another paper, co-authored with Japanese microbiologist Shibasaburo Kitasato (who is also remembered for co-discovering the bacterium that causes bubonic plague – see page 233), on their discovery of an antiserum for another killer disease, tetanus.

In 1891, Behring treated a girl already suffering from diphtheria with antiserum. She recovered! Clearly, while vaccines could only prevent disease, antiserums could help your body fight the disease *after* you had got it!

The 'miracle' threw the whole medical and non-medical universe into a huge celebratory tizzy – for the very first time in human history, an effective way to treat a life-threatening infectious disease had been discovered.

***

Now to produce tons of antiserum to treat everyone with diphtheria! That was easier said than done, though, for guinea pigs simply would not be able to produce the amount of serum required for clinical trials, first on animals and then on humans (for more information on the heated debate around clinical trials, see the box 'Testing Times' on page 266). Behring decided to infect larger animals with the diphtheria toxin, to see if they could produce more antiserum, and began trying it on dogs and goats. It was then that another German physician called Paul Ehrlich, who had recently joined the Koch Institute, suggested that Behring try horses. Ehrlich's hunch turned out to be a mega-winner. Horses were not only able to produce loads of antiserum, but their antiserum also contained more antitoxins per millilitre than others! And since horses were believed to carry no diseases that could be transferred to humans, they were the ideal antiserum factories.

After its first stupendous success, however, serum therapy ran into problems. Not everyone who was administered the antiserum survived diphtheria, and treatment was suspended for a few years to work out the correct dosage and formulation. The man who worked out the ideal formulation of antiserum for humans was once again Paul Ehrlich. Dozens of life-saving 'serum horses', kept on large farms and kept well-fed, healthy and well-exercised, produced all the antiserum needed for the clinical trials. When the trials began in 1894, using Ehrlich's formulation, they were an unqualified success. Alongside, the historical human love for horses got a huge boost – horses were no longer just dependable, loving companions, they also produced stuff in their bodies that made human children well. Which other friend could do that for you?

Soon, antiserums were developed against rabies, tetanus and even snake venom. As for the Behring-Ehrlich Diphtheria Remedy, the German pharmaceutical company Hoechst took on the responsibility of maintaining the horses, and mass-producing and marketing it. Both scientists were supposed to get an equal share of the profits after Hoechst had taken its own share, but Behring managed to elbow Ehrlich out and keep the lion's share for himself. In 1901, Behring was also (alone, not jointly with Ehrlich) awarded the very first Nobel Prize in Physiology or Medicine for his discovery of the diphtheria antitoxin. He was hailed as the 'saviour of children', and became part of Prussian nobility, honoured with the title Emil 'von Behring'.

***

Shibasaburo Kitasato, Behring's collaborator on the antiserum project, was overlooked for the Nobel too – perhaps because no one realized how important the tetanus antiserum was until the First World War.

So Behring won that round hands down, but you can't keep a good scientist down, and Ehrlich was among the best of his breed. Both as student and physician, Ehrlich had been fascinated by chemical dyes, which he used to stain human, animal and plant tissue to be able to see it better under a microscope. In the process, he had noticed that not all cells were coloured to exactly the same extent when they were stained – certain dyes were 'taken up' better by certain kinds of cells. He also noticed that different microbes took up dyes to different extents, and wondered if chemical dyes could be used to target and kill harmful microbes.

Ehrlich was encouraged by his 1891 research on a dye called methylene blue, which, when used on the malaria parasite plasmodium, stained it darker and soon killed it, without doing any damage to the human host's own cells. This was exciting new territory in the treatment of disease. Vaccines and antiserums were all the rage at that time, but they both depended on living creatures – vaccines were made from weak versions of dangerous microbes, and antiserums from the blood of animals. What if, Ehrlich wondered, you could kill microbes and cure disease by using chemicals instead?

It may be a good idea to pause here for a moment and let that sink in. Today, so many pills that we pop so casually are made up entirely of chemicals. But the idea that consuming chemicals (which sounds terribly dire when put that way) could reduce pain and inflammation, stop allergic reactions, and target and kill microbes was a revolutionary, ridiculous-sounding one 120 years ago!

Back to Ehrlich. Behring's discovery of the diphtheria antitoxin had revealed to Ehrlich what he called the lock-and-key principle – each pathogen that attacked a human or animal body carried a particular antigen (lock) that could only be destroyed (unlocked) by a particular antibody (key). He made it his life's goal to find chemicals that would be the keys to the locks of only one pathogen, and destroy every instance of it in the body. He was, he said, looking for a 'magic bullet'.

In 1902, Ehrlich began experimenting on pathogens with dozens of different chemical compounds, which he carefully synthesized with his Japanese colleague Kiyoshi Shiga. A couple of years later, he began to focus on a chemical compound called Atoxyl (a compound of the very toxic arsenic acid) as a possible cure for sleeping sickness (he had heard that it was used in Africa as a treatment, with limited success), and synthesized hundreds of different compounds using Atoxyl as a base. When Sahachiro Hata, his new lab assistant, told Ehrlich that he had been successful in infecting rabbits with a deadly disease called syphilis, Ehrlich put him to work, asking Sata to test those hundreds of Atoxyl compounds on the diseased rabbits, to see if any of them made an effective cure – without causing horrible side effects.

Hata set to work, patiently testing the compounds one by one (and killing off hundreds of rabbits in the process through arsenic poisoning, no doubt). One day in 1907, a wild whoop from Hata brought Ehrlich running to where his assistant was (this probably did not happen in this exact way, but what's life without a little poetic licence?). A beaming Hata gave Ehrlich the good news – a rabbit had been cured of syphilis, with no apparent side effects, by Compound No. 606! (Yup, that means the first 605 compounds had not worked. Now think again about whether you want to be a pure science researcher.) Ehrlich had found his magic bullet, and the world was introduced to the very first 'antibiotic' – a drug that combated a particular infectious disease by destroying only a particular pathogen. A whole new science of healing using chemicals, called chemotherapy, had been unveiled.

If you have read this book carefully so far, you will know that the idea of healing using chemicals was not entirely new. The old, old science of Ayurveda used heavy metals like lead and mercury, suitably processed, in its healing preparations, not to mention arsenic itself.

Paul Ehrlich often said that to achieve success, one needed the four (German) G's – *Geld* (money), *Geduld* (patience), *Geschick* (intelligence) and *Glück* (luck). In 1907, after 'seven years of misfortune' that he had borne with geduld, he had his one moment of glück.

From that moment on, the accolades never stopped coming. In 1908, he won his own well-deserved Nobel Prize in Physiology or Medicine for his 'work on immunity'. In 1910, after years of clinical trials, Ehrlich and Sata announced the discovery of a treatment for syphilis in humans. Once again, the pharmaceutical company Hoechst stepped in to produce and market the drug, under the name Salvarsan, and this time, no one cheated Ehrlich out of the share of profits due to him. He did not become part of Prussian nobility, but was honoured by the Prussian government many times – with the Great Golden Medal of Science, the country's highest scientific distinction in 1903, and Prussia's highest civilian award, Privy Councillor – which meant he was to be addressed as 'Your Excellency' – in 1911.

***

Although Salvarsan was the first drug that may be considered an antibiotic, it would be another twenty years before the antibiotic revolution truly exploded. The drug that was responsible was named Prontosil by Bayer AG, the German pharmaceutical company in whose research labs it was discovered in 1933.

The researchers at Bayer, inspired by Paul Ehrlich's experiments with dyes and stains, continued to work in that area, trying to find a dye that would prove to be another magic bullet against one – or several – disease-causing bacteria. Their area of interest was coal-tar dyes, which seemed to love attaching themselves to bacteria and other parasites. Surely, one of those dyes would also have the ability to destroy the microbes they attached themselves to?

For several years, research teams at Bayer experimented with hundreds of different dyes, until, in 1932, a team led by the director of Bayer's Institute of Pathology and Bacteriology, Gerhard Domagk, finally made a breakthrough – a red dye that had been synthesized by a Bayer chemist was excellent at stopping a range of bacterial infections in mice, particularly those caused by a type of bacteria called streptococcus.

Streptococci (plural of streptococcus) are responsible for a whole range of diseases and conditions, from simple ones like dental caries (tooth decay) and pharyngitis (sore throat) to deadly ones like pneumonia and meningitis.

Bayer was ecstatic. They did not announce the breakthrough of the life-saving drug, Prontosil, for another two years, to give them time to apply for and receive a patent for it. That way, no other pharma company could manufacture it, and Bayer would be able to make a ton of money from it. With large companies – who understandably had a beady eye on the bottom-line – getting involved in medical research, the age of scientists like Marie Curie and Wilhelm Roentgen, who did not take out patents on any of their discoveries and gifted them instead to humanity, was clearly a thing of the past.

Unfortunately for Bayer, soon after they announced Prontosil in 1935, a team from the Pasteur Institute showed that it wasn't the red dye, on which Bayer had taken a patent, that was responsible for the cure – inside the human body, Prontosil was split into two components: the dye component, which was 'inactive', and a smaller, colourless, 'active' compound called sulphanilamide. It was this sulphanilamide, which had been patented in 1906, that was the real killer of bacteria. The patent on sulphanilamide had recently expired, so now anyone was free to make 'sulpha' drugs!

The news spread like wildfire. Hundreds of little pharma companies made thousands of versions of sulpha drugs. They were used extensively in the Second World War, particularly by American soldiers, to prevent infections in open wounds. Sulpha would continue to rule as the Giant Bacteria Killer until the next big deal – penicillin – made its appearance towards the end of the war.

In 1939, Gerhard Domagk won the Nobel Prize in Medicine for his breakthrough. But the Second World War had just begun, and the German establishment did not allow him to accept the award (because they were upset with the Nobel committee for having awarded the Nobel Peace Prize to a Nazi critic in 1935). He was finally able to collect it after the war, in 1947, although the poor man was never able to collect the cash part of the prize – it had lapsed by then. Yup, looks like the sulpha story was not only about a wonder drug, but also about a lot of people losing money!

***

'One sometimes finds what one is not looking for. When I woke up just after dawn on 28 September 1928, I certainly didn't plan

to revolutionize all medicine by discovering the world's first antibiotic, or bacteria killer. But I suppose that was exactly what I did.' – Alexander Fleming.

No, there's no mistake with the dates. Scottish physician and microbiologist Alexander Fleming did discover penicillin in 1928, four years before Gerhard Domagk discovered Prontosil! But penicillin only became available widely in 1944. Here's why.

On 28 September 1928, after a long summer vacation with his family, Alexander Fleming returned to his untidy laboratory in St Mary's Hospital, London. He had been working on a class of bacteria called staphylococci for some years, and had many cultures of them growing in his lab, all of which he had stacked up in a corner over a month before. When he examined the cultures, he discovered that one of them had become contaminated with a fungus, or mould. When he looked more closely, he saw that the area around the fungus had no staphylococci growing. 'That's funny,' said Fleming, realizing at the same time that it was probably something in the fungus that had killed off all the staphylococci in its vicinity.

Fleming studied the fungus, identifying it as belonging to the genus Penicillium. Then he conducted more experiments, using several different bacterial cultures, and discovered that the 'mould juice' was very effective against many kinds of bacteria deadly to humans (including our old friends, the streptococci). Finally naming the killer 'juice' penicillin, he wrote about his discovery in a medical journal in 1929, but not much attention was paid to it. In fact, Fleming himself soon lost interest – it was very difficult to grow the mould, and when you did, it was even more difficult to extract the bacteria-killing agent from it.

Twelve years after Fleming's accidental discovery, biochemists Ernst Chain and Edward Abraham, who were working on penicillin at Oxford, finally cracked the molecular structure of the antibiotic. By then, a way to grow the penicillin mould and harvest the antibiotic from it more efficiently had also been figured out. Clinical trials now began in right earnest. The results were so astounding – penicillin was such an effective antibiotic – that Chain and his head of department, Howard Florey, began to plan mass production and distribution of the drug, with financial support from the British and American governments.

Alexander Fleming

Sure, antibiotics are great and do their job — ridding the body of pathogens — swiftly and effectively. The trouble with them is that they also end up upsetting the delicate balance of our 'gut flora' — the millions and millions of microorganisms that live in our intestines and are vitally important to our well-being — by killing off many of them too. If you need to take antibiotics, make sure you follow all your doctor's instructions about them.

Their sense of urgency increased after the Japanese bombing of Pearl Harbour in December 1941, which prompted the Americans to enter the war. By D-Day – 6 June 1944, when the Allied Forces launched a massive seaborne invasion on Germany and her allies and effectively won the Second World War (although it would be several months before the official end of the war) – the Radcliffe Infirmary in Oxford had enough penicillin ready to treat all the Allied Forces.

Penicillin is still used widely today, and continues to save millions around the world. However, many kinds of bacteria that it once used to destroy have now become 'resistant' to it, something that Fleming had warned might happen. For their great work on penicillin, Fleming, Florey and Chain received the Nobel Prize in Medicine in 1945.

The World's Best 24/7 Security System

Our immune system, to put it simply, is our body's defence against infectious organisms and other invaders. The attacks our bodies launch against these invaders is what is called the body's 'immune response'. Typically, the immune response comprises three supercool lines of defence.

The first line of defence is made up of physical and chemical barriers to invasion, and includes the skin, the largest organ in the body and a virtually impenetrable fortress; the hair on our bodies, which traps dust and other more dangerous things; the cilia, or the hair that lines our nasal passages, which filter microbes, dust and pollutants; and our urine, sweat, snot and vomit (no, seriously) – all of which work to *eject* harmful microbes from our systems. This first line of defence is part of our 'innate immunity' – immunity that we are born with.

The body's second line of defence, which is also part of innate immunity, is made up of (1) phagocytes, little Bakasura cells that calmly and impartially gobble up everything that is alien, (2) inflammation (or swelling), which includes redness, swelling and pain, and happens at the site where something harmful – the stinger of a wasp, a bunch of bacteria – has entered your body (usually, inflammation is just an indication that the soldiers of your immune system have arrived at the breach, and are fighting the good fight), and (3) fever, which by raising the temperature of the entire body, creates a most inhospitable environment for bacteria to grow (yup, fever is a good thing – it tells your doctor that there is an infection somewhere in your body).

The last and third line of defence mounts a 'specific resistance' (unlike the non-specific resistance of the second line of defence) to the invader. The moment bacteria, viruses or other disease-causing germs (aka pathogens) enter our bodies, our white knights, the lymphocytes, launch a full blown attack against the antigens, or harmful proteins, that microbes carry on their bodies. (Extra info: both lymphocytes and phagocytes are types of leucocytes, or white blood cells.) The lymphocytes do this by releasing 'antibodies', which neutralize the antigens. These three lines of defence work very hard each day to deflect all kinds of attacks, and keep us healthy and functioning.

Now, the lymphocytes have to produce specific antibodies to take down specific antigens, and they don't always have the entire roster of germ antigens memorized. When they come across invaders they have never encountered before, they are sometimes at a loss to know exactly what antibody to

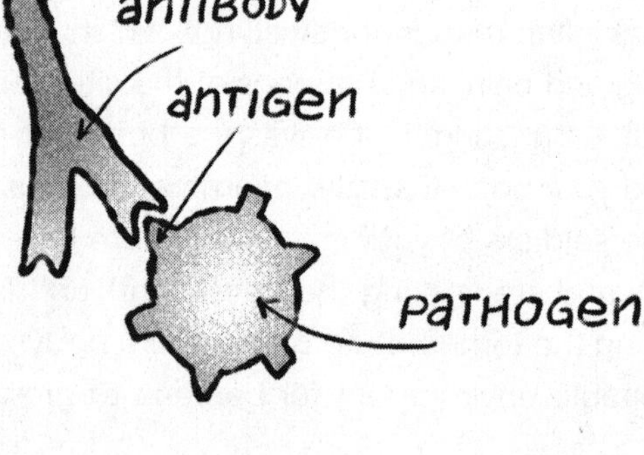

produce, and by the time they have figured it out by trial and error, it is sometimes too late – the infection has struck! One way to 'train' the lymphocytes to recognize different antigens is to introduce weak or dead (read: almost entirely harmless) versions of the pathogens that produce them into the body. That way, the lymphocytes have plenty of time to figure out which antibody works against that particular antigen. The next time, when a stronger version of the pathogen carrying the same antigen comes in, the lymphocytes scan their memories, recognize the intruder for what it is and quickly produce the correct antibody to take it down.

Each time our bodies are exposed to new pathogens, our immune system learns how to fight them. This is why children catch colds and throat infections so much more often than adults – adult bodies, simply because they have been around longer, are intimately acquainted with many more germs and know how to fight them. This 'learned immunity' is called 'acquired immunity'. A great shortcut to acquired immunity is – yes, vaccination! All the vaccinations that we receive as kids introduce our lymphocytes to a whole rogues' gallery of pathogens and their antigens, and help them get smarter quicker.

Right. Now that you have been suitably enlightened, you may send up a prayer of thanks to your fabulous immune system. Stay safe!

Testing Times

What are clinical trials? Simply put, they are investigations conducted by pharmaceutical companies (who are in the business of researching and developing new medicines for different diseases and medical conditions) and scientific institutes (which may have come up with some breakthrough medical technology or method of treatment) to make sure that the drugs and technologies are safe, effective, and do not have some horrible side effects. People who are suffering from diseases or conditions that do not yet have a cure – or at least a very effective cure – volunteer to test these new treatments, because they have a lot to gain if the treatment works.

Even before drugs or technologies are tested on humans, though, they are tested on animals. The focus of drug testing on animals is to observe the drug's 'pharmacology' – how the drug works, how it reacts with everything else in the animal's body and its effects on different organs and tissues – and its 'toxicology' – if and how it damages the body in any way. If a new device is being tested, on the other hand, the focus is to check the device's biocompatibility, i.e., to see if it can function with living tissue without damaging it. Only when it is considered safe for animals is a drug or device tested on humans. Only after several trials have proven that it is safe and effective for humans as well does the drug or treatment become available in the market, for doctors to prescribe and use.

While clinical trials are very, very important, there has been a sustained pushback against animal testing in recent years, both by animal rights activists and scientists themselves. While it is easy to see why activists would be upset, some scientists oppose it because there is enough data to show that a drug that has been proven safe for animals is not necessarily safe for humans. Which means hundreds of thousands of animals die unnecessarily, in the name of science, every year.

Needless to say, there is also enough data to prove the exact opposite – as you have already seen or will see in the following chapters, many life-saving antibiotics, hormones like insulin (which can manage diabetes), vaccines against deadly diseases, and procedures like organ transplantation have been developed and made safe for humans only through prior experimentation on animals.

Because this is such a fraught topic, governments now have stringent laws in place when it comes to experimenting on animals. The laws are meant to ensure that as few animals as possible are used for testing, that lab animals are treated well and that there is enough information-sharing between labs across the world for experiments not to be repeated. Unfortunately, while laws certainly indicate that governments take these matters seriously, they are not always enough.

Sigh – whichever side of the debate you are on, this is a good time to give thanks that you were born human.

IDEA 22

HAVE A PROBLEM WITH YOUR KIDNEYS? WELL, JUST USE SOMEONE ELSE'S!

Announcing the Age of Organ Transplants

> 'Two-year-old's heart, organ donation saves life of six others' – *New Indian Express*, 24 April 2019

> 'A hundred patients from Odisha undergo liver transplant' – *Odisha Diary*, 20 April 2019

> 'Researchers use 3D ice printing to create artificial blood vessels for organ transplants' - msn.com, 12 February 2024

Although it still makes newspaper headlines, organ transplantation is no longer such a novelty in medical therapy today. You probably know someone who has received an organ transplant, or at least know of someone who carries an organ donor card, declaring that they would like to have their organs donated on their death to someone who needs them. A century ago, however, although surgeons talked about it as a dream they would like to see come true in their lifetimes, organ transplantation was still only a theoretical concept.

Of course, certain kinds of transplantation, like autografts – transplanting tissue, mostly skin tissue, from one part of a person's body to another – had been practised even as far back as two millennia before. The ancient Indian surgical text, *Sushruta Samhita*, has a detailed description of rhinoplasty – reconstruction of a wrecked nose – using skin from the inside of that person's thigh. In the sixteenth century, Gaspare Tagliacozzi, the Italian pioneer of reconstructive surgery – which we call cosmetic surgery or plastic surgery today – also had reasonable success with skin autografts. What he couldn't crack, though, were allografts – transplanting skin from someone else's body to the body of his patient.

To this day, even with all the progress in transplantation surgery, it is allotransplants – you can guess what that means – that pose the biggest challenge to surgeons. How come? Well, remember our fabulous immune system, which we talked about in Idea 21? It is precisely because our immune system is so good, and so focused on protecting our bodies from intruders and invasions, that it attacks the 'foreign' organ or tissue with deathly intent, completely 'rejecting' it. While many surgeons wanted to have a go at transplants, very few understood or even anticipated the concept of 'rejection'.

It was the Swiss surgeon Theodor Kocher who performed what may be considered among the world's first successful transplant surgeries. In 1883, he implanted thyroid tissue back into people whose thyroid glands he had previously removed (Why? See box on page 294). The procedure reversed the mental and physical retardation his patients had experienced when their thyroid glands had been removed. Kocher's findings gave the first inkling that the thyroid gland – and perhaps others like it in the body – produced something vital to human wellbeing and functioning. Many years later, they would call the set of these 'somethings' hormones, and an entire field of medicine called endocrinology would come into being. But for now, back to the (hi)story of organ transplantation.

***

By the early 1900s, because of Kocher's pioneering work, the idea that some human diseases could be treated by replacing part of a failed organ had become accepted. Surgical techniques had to step up and keep pace if surgeons hoped to perform entire organ transplantations, and they did, spearheaded by the advanced suturing techniques (a suture is a surgical stitch that holds together the edges of a cut or surgical incision) developed by French surgeon Alexis Carrel.

In 1894, when Carrel was only twenty-one, the French President Sadi Carnot was attacked by a disgruntled man with a knife. One of the president's vital veins was severed, and Carnot bled to death, even as surgeons struggled to reconnect it. The incident made a deep impression on Carrel, and he began to focus on improving suturing techniques.

Between 1902 and 1910, he also performed a number of transplant surgeries on animals, successfully transplanting kidneys, livers and spleens in dogs. But the animals died soon after, leading Carrel to recognize and identify the problem of organ rejection before anyone else had done so. With his friend Charles Lindbergh (the famous American aviator who, in 1927, flew solo, and non-stop, across the Atlantic from New York to Paris, becoming the first man to do so), Carrel also developed a 'perfusion pump', which kept blood flowing through an organ removed from a human body while it waited to be transplanted into another body. Of course, no successful organ transplants were performed during Carrel's lifetime, but he had certainly laid the ground for future transplants through his work.

The young Carrel's skill at suturing was based on sewing lessons he took, as an adult, from a seamstress who was an expert embroiderer. These helped him develop a most effective method, used to this day, of repairing and reattaching veins and arteries. See how multidisciplinary education can be a good thing?

In 1912, German surgeon Georg Schöne discovered, for the first time, that the body's *own immune system* was responsible for rejecting organs. This proved to be such an insurmountable problem for scientists that organ transplantation was actually abandoned after the First World War.

***

It wasn't until 1951, when the British biologist Peter Medawar published a paper on 'acquired immune tolerance' that things began to look up again. During the Second World War,

Medawar had begun work on the problem of improving skin grafts. War was often a spur for technological and medical innovation, and the Second World War was one of the biggest the world had seen. So many soldiers came back with missing limbs, terrible burn injuries and part of their faces blown off that a lot of research began to be done on reconstructive surgery, of which skin grafts were a major component.

In 1949, Medawar came across a scientific paper by Australian virologist Macfarlane Burnet. He had proposed the theory that a person's immune system learns to distinguish between their own cells and foreign cells during their final weeks inside their mother's womb and right after birth. To test that theory, Medawar extracted cells from a young mouse embryo (let's call him Mickey) and injected them into a different mouse embryo (let's call her Minnie).

When Minnie grew into an adult, he grafted skin from Mickey onto Minnie. There was no rejection! Because Minnie had been given Mickey's cells before her immune system had learnt to recognize her own cells as hers, her system now thought of Mickey's cells as hers too! Medawar published a paper on his findings in 1951, calling the phenomenon 'acquired immune tolerance'. Finally, there was one proven way to avoid organ rejection, but since no one could be sure at embryo stage if they might need an organ transplant later and who their donor might be if they did, this remained a theory. However, it was still a landmark finding, and Medawar also won the Nobel Prize in Physiology or Medicine, in 1960.

The decision to award Medawar the Nobel may have got a boost by something that happened in Boston, Massachusetts, six years earlier. In 1954, a pair of identical twins named Richard and Ronald Herrick came to Dr Joseph Murray, a plastic surgeon at the Peter Bent Brigham Hospital in Boston. They were only twenty-three, but Richard was dying of kidney failure. Could Dr Murray try a transplant? Ronald was ready to donate one of his kidneys to his twin.

Dr Murray considered it. A few organ transplants had continued to be done in the previous years, but no recipient of a donated organ had survived more than a couple of months. Was it worth it? It was then that Dr Murray remembered Peter Medawar's paper. Richard and Ronald Herrick had been embryos together and shared a womb – maybe Richard's cells would not see Ronald's as alien! It was worth a try.

To make doubly sure, Dr Murray first grafted a piece of skin from Ronald onto Richard. There was no rejection! Encouraged, he went ahead with the surgery. On 23 December 1954, in a surgery that lasted five and a half hours, Dr Murray removed one of Ronald's kidneys and implanted it in Richard. Once again, there were no post-surgical complications at all. Ten days later, Ronald walked out of the hospital and went back to college. Richard joined him a few weeks later. The world's very first successful organ transplant had been performed! For his pioneering work in organ transplant surgery, Dr Joseph Murray won the Nobel Prize in Physiology or Medicine in 1990. He passed away after a stroke in 2012, at the age of ninety-three, in the very hospital in which he had revolutionized medicine and surgery in December 1954.

***

Richard Herrick lived for eight long years after his kidney transplant. Ronald lived a full life with one kidney, succumbing to post-operative complications after heart surgery in 2010, at the age of seventy-nine.

The next big prize for transplant surgeons was a proper, full-fledged heart transplant. But there were two challenges. The first was that the problem of organ rejection between people who were not twins hadn't been solved. The second was that the heart, unlike the kidneys, deteriorated within minutes after death at room temperature, so the surgery had to be done at a very high speed. Plus, no one had a clue as to how to keep a person alive during a heart transplant, when their very heart had been taken out of their body. Only after the world's first heart lung machine had been invented in the early 1950s were the doors to treating and curing heart ailments through surgery flung wide open.

It took until 1967, fourteen years after the heart-lung machine was invented, for the first partially successful human-to-human heart transplant (chimpanzee-to-human had been attempted before, not even kidding) to be performed. It was South Africa's Dr Christiaan Barnard who led the surgery, on 3 December 1967, at the Groote Schuur Hospital in Cape Town. The six-hour procedure was a worldwide media sensation, making both Dr Barnard and his patient, fifty-four-year-old grocer Louis Washkansky, household names. Although Washkansky died eighteen days after the transplant,

In 1953, American surgeon Dr John Gibbon, who had invented the heart-lung machine, hooked up a young female patient to it and performed on her the world's first successful open-heart surgery (NOT heart transplant). The machine took over the functions of both her heart and lungs during the operation, taking in oxygen, pumping oxygenated blood around her body, removing carbon dioxide from the blood when it returned to her lungs. The whole process was nothing short of miraculous.

Dr Barnard considered it a success, since the patient had regained consciousness. This had never happened before – in a previous attempt by a different surgeon, the patient had never come to. What's more, Washkansky had survived for eighteen days without being connected to a machine!

Why didn't Washkansky's body instantly reject the alien heart? As far back as 1951, Peter Medawar had suggested that what might help to counter organ rejection were immunosuppressant drugs, which suppressed the immune system's response to an 'invasion', allowing the new organ to settle in without being attacked. One such drug, cortisone, had only just become commercially available when Medawar wrote his paper. By 1967, when Barnard performed his surgery, immunosuppressant drugs had become commonplace.

Why did Washkansky die then? Five days after the surgery, when the patient began to show signs of organ rejection, Barnard pumped him full of immunosuppressants. The downside of these drugs, as you can imagine, is that they make the body vulnerable to actual disease-causing germs (because the immune system doesn't fight them either), and those were what got Washkansky. He died not from organ rejection, but from pneumonia! But Barnard was to taste sweet success soon enough. Less than a month after his first cardiac transplant, he performed his second one, on dentist Philip Blaiberg, who survived for nineteen months after his operation.

The Philip Blaiberg cardiac transplant got a lot of attention from all quarters for quite another reason too. In apartheid-riven South Africa, the fact that Blaiberg, a white man, had been given a coloured man's heart, led to months of heated debate, anger and controversy .

Encouraged by Barnard's success, over a hundred other heart transplants were attempted between 1968 and 1969, but only a third of the recipients survived for more than three months. Many medical centres stopped doing cardiac transplants altogether. But Barnard persisted. In 1970, a new immunosuppressant drug called cyclosporine, which was far more effective than the previous ones, was discovered. In 1971, Dr Barnard performed a cardiac transplant on Dirk van Zyl, administering cyclosporine to prevent organ rejection. Dirk van Zyl not only survived the operation, but thrived, for no less than twenty-three years after.

Nope, this section is not going to end with the usual 'For his great achievement, Dr Christiaan Barnard won the

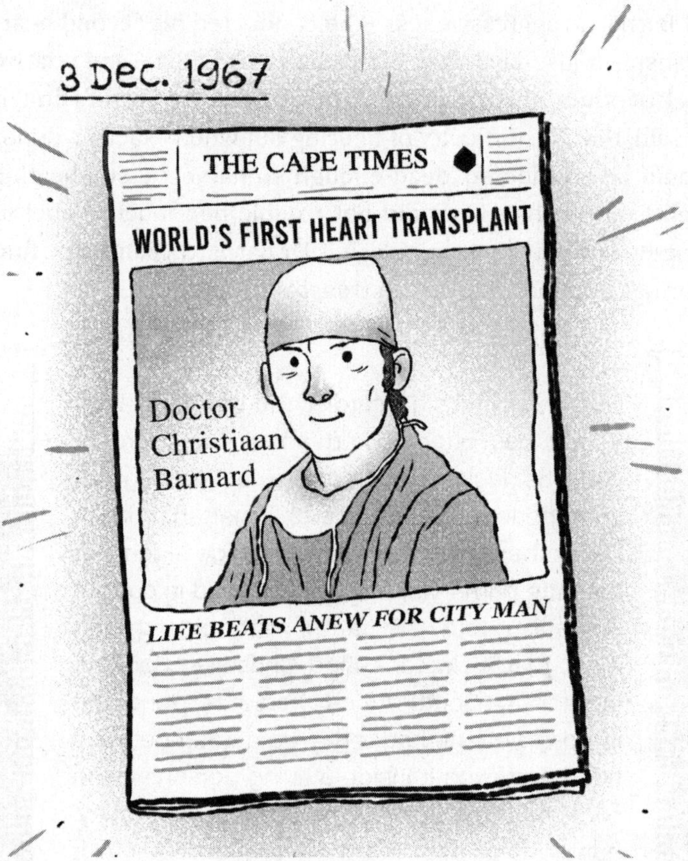

Nobel Prize in Medicine' because, stunningly, he did not. He himself maintained that the Nobel committee denied him the accolade only because he was a white South African who lived and worked at a time when his country practised apartheid (the terrible practice of treating white people as superior to coloureds and blacks). Others believe it was partly because of Barnard's aggressiveness – he conducted his second heart transplant just days after Washkansky had died – and relative lack of ethics – he was in such a hurry to be the 'world's first', it is said, that the difficulty of figuring out when exactly a donor could be considered 'dead enough' to harvest a still beating heart out of their body did not trouble him much. Nobel or not, however, to most people, it is Dr Barnard's name that first springs to mind when organ transplants are mentioned.

Our own rockstar cardiac surgeon Dr Devi Shetty has often talked about the moment when he decided to become a cardiac surgeon. It happened, he says, one unforgettable day in December 1967, when his fifth-grade teacher at the little primary school he attended in coastal Karnataka told the class, with big, shining eyes, that a doctor called Christiaan Barnard, in faraway South Africa, had just done the impossible – he had removed a dead person's heart and fixed it inside a living person whose own heart was sick, and helped him live! Today, hundreds of poor Indians – and others – with cardiac disease have had a new lease of life because of Dr Shetty's efforts to bring affordable cardiac surgery to them.

IDEA 23

ALL THE BODY NEEDS FOR GOOD HEALTH ARE CARBS, PROTEINS, FATS, SALTS – AND SOMETHING ELSE!

Clue: It Starts with a V

Let's leave the brave new world of miracle drugs and organ transplants of the twentieth century for a bit, and zip back in time to the Age of Exploration, when mighty sailing ships with doughty captains travelled great distances from European ports, discovering new lands and peoples, swapping horses and weird vegetables called potatoes and tomatoes for aromatic spices and deep-blue dyes, fighting mid-sea battles against enemy European ships, capturing booty-laden Spanish galleons, transporting Peruvian and Mexican silver . . . stuff like that. In the process, these ships also connected and mapped the world.

It all sounds terribly exciting and Pirates-of-the-Caribbean cool, but it wasn't really. If the 'discovered' peoples suffered as a result of the voyages of exploration and conquest, so did the crews of the conquering ships. Between the tail end of the fifteenth century – when Christopher Columbus sailed out of Spain – and the mid-nineteenth century, when steamships became commonplace – more than 2 million sailors lost their lives, not in pitched battles with pirates, enemy navies or native people of conquered lands, not from their ships being destroyed in storms and sinking full fathom five, but from contracting a deadly disease called scurvy.

The worst recorded scurvy disaster happened during the circumnavigation of the world by British navy officer Commodore George Anson. In 1740, Anson set out, with eight ships and 1,854 men, to disrupt and capture Spanish possessions in the Pacific. He returned in 1744, with one ship and 188 men. Nearly all the others had perished of scurvy.

We know today that it is a lack of vitamin C that causes scurvy, which causes teeth to come loose from gums, old wounds to reopen, mucous membranes to bleed, skin to bruise as capillaries break, and innards to bleed as arteries and veins come apart. But no one in the eighteenth century had heard of vitamins, or guessed that the lack of something in our diet could cause disease. We can't blame them too much for their ignorance either; they really did try to figure it out, but there were so many variables that they never knew which one was the key one.

Ouch! How does the scourge called scurvy make such terrible things happen to the body? Well, vitamin C is needed to keep our connective tissue – which, among other things, helps gums hold on to teeth – healthy. When you don't eat enough fresh fruits, particularly citrus fruits, and vegetables, which are rich in vitamin C, connective tissue is weakened, causing all the awful symptoms of scurvy.

It was mainly sailors who got scurvy, doctors reasoned, so it clearly had something to do with sailoring. But what, exactly? Was it sustained exposure to the sea breeze, lack of fresh water, bad hygiene in the ships' holds where the men slept, food contaminated by the bugs and rats that were permanent stowaways on ships, an imbalance in the humours, an excess of salted meat (ships carried salted, preserved meat as food for their crews because there was no way to get fresh meat out at sea), homesickness (no, seriously) or something else altogether? The sad thing was that although various people through the centuries had figured out cures to scurvy, simply through observation and experimentation, their findings somehow got neglected or forgotten. One possible remedy that kept popping up over and over again across the centuries was a regular intake of lemon and lime juice. (For exciting details, check out the box on page 289.)

But there was still plenty of confusion, for many reasons. One was that a diet of fresh meat, with no fruits or vegetables, or oranges or lemons, for that matter, also seemed to prevent scurvy. When British explorer Robert Scott led an expedition to the Antarctic in 1901, he found that putting fresh seal meat on his crew's menu immediately reversed the effects of scurvy and prevented all fatalities. Plus, the oranges-and lemons formula didn't always work – while fresh juice was great, juice that had been exposed to the atmosphere, left to stand for a long while, or boiled, was not an effective cure at all.

And so, we blundered into the early years of the twentieth century, with no real idea of what caused scurvy and no sure-fire way to prevent it.

***

As you can imagine, sailors on long voyages did not just suffer from a lack of vitamin C; a diet lacking in fresh fruits, meat and vegetables led to deficiencies of other vitamins as well. The trouble was that, in the nineteenth century, when miasma – bad air – was seen as the chief cause of disease, and the germ theory (the theory that diseases are caused by germs) itself was seen as new and revolutionary, it was incredibly hard to convince people that a simple 'nutritional deficiency' could cause such terrible diseases as scurvy, beriberi and night blindness, all of which afflicted sailors.

Between 1878 and 1881, Takaki Kanehiro, a British-trained Japanese doctor of the Imperial Japanese Navy, discovered that Japanese sailors fell ill at least four times a year, and some 35 per cent of them from a disease of the nerves called beriberi. Symptoms included numbness of hands and feet, an increased heart rate, digestive problems and severe fatigue. On further investigation, Kanehiro noticed that beriberi was far more common among the low-ranking local crew, who ate only polished white rice, and not among the higher officers, whose diet included meat and vegetables.

Albert Szent-Györgyi, the Hungarian biochemist who finally isolated vitamin C in 1930 and figured out how it worked, captured the difficulty of explaining the importance of vitamins to nineteenth-century people in these words: 'A vitamin is a substance that you get sick from if you don't eat it.'

With the permission of the Japanese navy, he conducted an experiment on the crews of two battleships: one crew was fed only polished white rice, the other a diet that included meat, barley, fish, beans and rice. At the end of their respective voyages, the crew that had eaten only rice reported 161 cases of beriberi, while the other crew reported just fourteen! It was clear that it was something in the diet – or more accurately, something that was *not* in the diet – that caused the disease. Kanehiro concluded, wrongly, that the missing element was protein. The fact that he was wrong didn't matter to the crews of the Japanese navy ships, though – from then on, they all received a more varied diet and stayed beriberi-free.

In 1887, a Dutch military physician called Christiaan Eijkman moved to the East Indies, a Dutch colony, to investigate beriberi, which was causing havoc among the people there. Ten years later, by complete chance, he discovered the problem with white polished rice – it was, erm, *polished.* This is how it happened.

Among the many animals and birds Eijkman experimented upon in his lab were chickens, and at some point, those chickens began to be fed leftover military rations, which was essentially polished white rice, instead of their usual feed. Very soon after, they began to show symptoms of beriberi. This went on until a new cook arrived, and took an executive decision that military food would not be fed to civilian animals, so there! He put the chickens back on their regular feed – unpolished rice – and the birds recovered completely in a few days. Eijkman realized that the 'polishings' – the stuff that had been scrubbed off the grain, turning it from brown to white – contained what he called the 'anti-beriberi factor'.

Years later, Eijkman's findings caught the imagination of a British biochemist called Frederick Gowland Hopkins. He began a series of experiments with mice and milk, noticing that when artificial milk – a liquid made up of the carbohydrates, proteins, fat and salts contained in real milk – was fed to mice, the mice did not grow very well. However, when a small portion of real cow's milk was added to the artificial milk, the mice grew rapidly. There was clearly something in milk, besides its four main constituents, that caused the mice to thrive. Hopkins didn't know exactly what those miracle ingredients were, so he referred to them simply as 'accessory food factors' in an article he published 1912 revealing his discovery. This was the first time anyone had ever proved, through a proper experimental study, that human diseases – or more correctly, disorders –

could be caused not just by germs but also by a diet that did not include certain vital ingredients.

***

Two years before Hopkins published his findings, a Japanese scientist called Umetaro Suzuki had extracted a set of nutrients from rice polishings, and discovered that feeding that extract to beriberi patients cured them fully. When his article, which was first published in a Japanese scientific journal, got translated to German, the translator did not mention that this was a newly discovered nutrient, and it therefore did not get the attention it deserved. (Yup, the road to scientific glory has claimed many victims, precisely through such random happenings.)

It was left to the Polish biochemist Casimir Funk, who was exploring the constituents of brown unpolished rice in his own bid to isolate the anti-beriberi factor, to garner this particular prize for himself (like Hopkins, he was also inspired by Eijkman's research). Funk was able to extract niacin (which we today call vitamin B3) from brown rice, and noticed that it had an amine group as part of its molecule (for now, don't worry about what an amine group is; all you need to know is that it is a particular set of atoms bonded together in a particular way). In a famous article he published in 1912, Funk suggested that there were at least three other 'vital amines' – life-sustaining amines – besides niacin that were responsible for overall good health: one that prevented scurvy, another that prevented the bone disorder rickets, and yet another that prevented pellagra, a terrible disease that caused the three D's – dementia, diarrhoea and dermatitis. He named the set of those amines 'vitamines'.

Niacin was not, as Funk had hoped, the anti-beriberi factor after all. However, it was the vitamin whose deficiency caused pellagra, so it was a very important amine indeed. The anti-beriberi factor was, in fact, thiamine, which we today call vitamin B1.

In the years that followed, more accessory food factors were discovered, and researchers began to realize that not all of them had an amine group. They protested that 'vitamine' was not an accurate name for those wonder nutrients. In 1920, British biochemist Jack Cecil Drummond proposed that, instead of changing the name entirely, the last 'e' be dropped from the word 'vitamine'. He also suggested that until we knew exactly what these 'vitamins' were, it was best that we gave them placeholder names, using letters of the alphabet, so that we had vitamins called, simply, A, B, C and D. Well, what do you know – even though so many more vitamins have been discovered since, those placeholder names have stuck!

For their pioneering work in establishing the existence of 'deficiency disorders', Eijkman and Hopkins shared the Nobel Prize in Physiology or Medicine in 1929. Several other scientists, including Albert Szent-Györgyi (we've mentioned him on page 283), who worked on vitamins, also received Nobel Prizes in later years, not just for medicine but also for chemistry. Research on vitamins also unleashed a whole

VITAMIN CHART

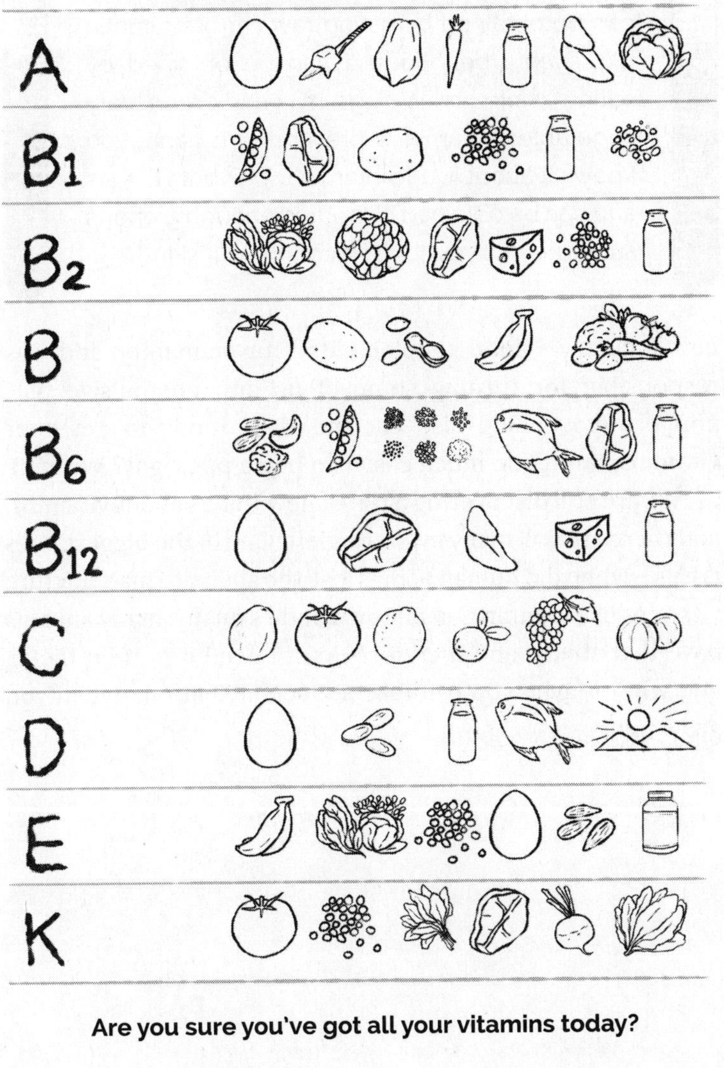

Are you sure you've got all your vitamins today?

FYI, vitamin A prevents night blindness and can be obtained by eating raw carrots, vitamin B prevents beriberi and can be obtained by eating whole grains, eggs, milk and green leafy vegetables, vitamin C prevents . . . aaah, you know all about it, and vitamin D prevents rickets and can be obtained by getting enough glorious sunshine into your body through your skin.

new industry – food supplements – on humanity, and was responsible for turning some of us into compulsive pill-poppers (you could also eat the right foods to get your vitamins, but it's so much easier to pop a pill, right? Wrong!).

We are still discovering a ton of new things about vitamins, and there are still many mysteries left. One of the biggest ones is this – when did human beings lose the ability to manufacture vitamins like vitamin C in our own bodies (many, many animals have that ability, and therefore do not need it in their diets), and why? Maybe you can take a crack at that one when you grow up!

Ahoy There, Matey! You Got a Cure for Scurvy Yet?

When Vasco da Gama set out on his now-famous expedition of 1497 – in the course of which he discovered the sea route from Europe to India – the search for a way to battle scurvy had been on for several years. Portuguese sailors, for one, had noticed that oranges and lemons helped significantly to keep the dreaded disease at bay.

But fresh fruits and veggies did not last long on ships in the days before refrigeration; crews had to wait until they stopped at a port to stock up, and those stops did not happen for weeks at a time. In 1579, the Spanish physician Agustin Farfán published a book recommending citrus fruits for sailors, and so did English admiral Sir Richard Dawkins in 1593. In 1614, John Woodall, surgeon general of the East India Company, published what sailors and mariners had discovered through experience – a diet of fresh fruits and vegetables, along with oranges, lemons, limes and tamarind, would prevent scurvy. But he could not explain why, and was not taken seriously.

After George Anson returned from his circumnavigation in 1744, having lost over a thousand men to scurvy, the problem came sharply back into the limelight. In 1747, James Lind, a naval surgeon on the English ship HMS *Salisbury*, conducted one of the first 'controlled clinical experiments' in the history of medicine. He picked twelve sailors on his ship who were sick with scurvy and divided them into six pairs. To each pair, he administered a daily dose of one of the six suggested scurvy cures, to see which was most effective: (1) a quart of cider (fermented apple juice), (2) twenty-five drops of vitriol (dilute sulphuric acid), (3) two spoonfuls of vinegar, (4) a half-pint of seawater, (5) a paste of garlic, mustard seeds, dried radish root and some other ingredients, pressed into a ball, and (6) two oranges and a lemon. The results were spectacular and convincing – the two men who had got Possible Cure No. 6 – were completely cured, even though the few oranges and lemons on the ship meant their 'medication' had to stop after five days. Lind recorded this result in a book but did not proclaim it as the single cure for the disease, and once again, the remedy was lost. Aaarrrgghhhh – so close and yet so far!

In 1764, Dr David McBride and Sir John Pringle (called the Father of Military Medicine) came up with the theory that it was a lack of fixed air (which we today know as carbon dioxide) in the digestive system that caused scurvy. They recommended drinking an infusion of malt and wort (which was a by-product of the beer-brewing process) to prevent scurvy – the wort would ferment inside the body and produce carbon dioxide, they said, which would open up blocked glands.

In 1768, the British explorer, navigator and cartographer Captain James Cook set out on his first voyage into the Pacific (during which he became the first European to touch Tahiti and the east coast of Australia, and to circumnavigate New Zealand), carrying a load of malt and wort. Cook did not lose a single man to scurvy during the four-year voyage, and malt and wort were hailed as the great scurvy remedies. No one realized that it was for entirely different reasons that Cook's men had not gone down to scurvy, chief among them that they stopped often at ports and replenished their stores of fresh fruit and veggies.

In May 1794, the HMS *Suffolk*, a sixty-four-gun ship, sailed out to India with two other battleships, escorting a convoy of merchant vessels. By now, English naval doctors had more influence with the so-called Sick and Hurt Board, which took decisions on rations for crews of navy ships. In the past, the board had been governed by physicians who had never been to sea and did not take the naval doctors' word too seriously. Now there were two naval doctors on the board, so they listened when an important naval officer, Rear Admiral Gardner, spurned malt and wort and asked for lemons instead.

The board agreed, and the HMS *Suffolk*'s hold was duly packed with lemons and sugar. The captain, as per the admiral's instructions, ensured that his men got a daily dose of lemonade on their twenty-three-week voyage. In November, when the *Suffolk* docked at Madras, every member of its crew was alive and thriving. The experiment had been successful! From that day on, most English ships did not leave port unless they were weighed down with lemons. Later, when Spain allied with England's enemy, France, in the Napoleonic Wars, and the supply of Mediterranean lemons to England dwindled; they were replaced with limes from the West Indies (that's how English sailors got their nickname – Limeys!) Yet, it would not be until over a hundred years later that someone would figure out exactly *why* the Limeys had always had it so good.

That's just one of the millions of good reasons to celebrate living in the twenty-first century. Let's toast it, then, with a tall, cold glass of . . . that's right, lemonade!

IDEA 24

ARE YOU DOPEY, SLEEPY, GRUMPY, BASHFUL OR HAPPY? IT DEPENDS ON YOUR . . .?

That's Right, Hormones!

Yeah, that's a fun title for this chapter, particularly because of the Snow White reference and all, but it is important to know that hormones, the tiny chemical messengers that we produce in our bodies, are responsible for far more than our moods. Among a whole load of other things, they control:

- how (and if!) we grow to our full height and weight,
- how well we digest our food and regulate the amount of sugar in our bodies,
- how much we sweat, pee and poop,
- how quickly – and effectively – we react to dangerous situations.

And so on. Hormones, in short, are the little guys who bring our bodies back to homeostasis (a complicated but cool word meaning 'balance' or 'equilibrium') whenever something is out of whack.

Are you sweating too much? The hormone vasopressin comes zipping out from the brain and travels straight to the kidneys, where it instructs the tissues to absorb water back into the body from the urine, so that you don't get dehydrated before you get yourself some water. Are you running a race and need that last burst of energy to win? Your adrenal glands, which sit on top of your kidneys, swing into action, releasing the hormone adrenaline into your bloodstream; adrenaline gets busy very quickly, increasing blood flow to your muscles, making the heart pump harder and stronger, ratcheting up your blood sugar levels – doing everything, in short, to give you the advantage you need.

The more important thing is that the adrenal glands know when to stop – if they didn't, you'd probably die of cardiac failure from an overworked heart. Once the race is over, they stop producing adrenalin, bringing the body back to . . . that's right, homeostasis!

One of the cool things about hormones, as you must have realized from reading the previous para, is that, while they are produced in one part of your body, they often have an impact on a different part altogether. They are also only produced in response to a specific situation (sweating too much, running a race, etc.). The set of all glands and tissues that produce hormones is part of what is called the body's endocrine system. Because ideas like 'I want to win this race!' or 'OMG, I need to get out of here quick!' come from the mind, the body's endocrine system often works in conjunction with the nervous system (i.e., the brain, the spinal cord and the nerves).

In the 1880s, Swiss physician Theodor Kocher expertly removed entire thyroid glands from patients suffering from goitre, a condition where the neck swells because of an enlarged thyroid. He had no idea that those glands produced hormones (that we today call T4 and T3), which contain iodine, and are responsible for something as basic as regulating the speed at which our cells work. With their cell activity slowed down, Kocher's patients suffered physical and mental retardation.

Until a little over a hundred years ago, however, no one in the world had a real clue about what the endocrine system was and how it worked. Some slivers of light had been filtering through, randomly, for half a century, but no one had put it all together yet.

***

Remarkably, as far back as 1849, a genius German zoologist called Arnold Adolph Berthold had worked out most of the stuff about the endocrine system. But the poor chap was so far ahead of his time that no one, least of all himself, considered taking his theories forward. (And let that be a lesson to you, boys and girls, not to abandon your world-beating ideas simply because everyone tells you they are too fantastical.)

Berthold had done most of his experiments on roosters. Choosing six roosters as his sample birds, he removed the testes – the pair of male reproductive organs which produce sperms – from four of them (this process is called castration). The two uncastrated roosters grew normally, each developing a fine comb (the crest on top of a rooster's head) and wattle (the fleshy fold of brightly coloured skin that hangs from the neck and throat of many male birds). Both had excellent crowing voices, chased the hens, and were aggressive with each other, all of which was typical rooster behaviour.

The castrated roosters, however, developed very differently – they had weak crows, they were not aggressive, they did not chase the hens, and their combs and wattles did not sprout and thrive with their usual flair. Clearly, the testes had something to do with producing the male characteristics!

But from where did the testes get their instructions? Berthold thought that it was the brain that stimulated the testes, through the nerves, to produce the male characteristics. To test his theory, he reimplanted one testis into a rooster, but in a different location – its abdomen. If it was indeed the nerves that brought messages to the testis, they should not be able to find it in its new location, and nothing would change. To Berthold's astonishment, however, the rooster with the testis in its abdomen quickly got its crow back, and grew a fine comb and wattle. When he opened up the bird, Berthold saw that the implanted testis had grown a network of blood vessels, which plugged into the body's circulatory system for nourishment but had grown no nerves at all. Clearly, then, it wasn't the nervous system that instructed the testes to produce whatever it did!

Was it perhaps a genetic factor, then? Some coded information that came to the rooster via its parents, and could work only in its own body? If that were so, the rooster should not be able to regain its male characteristics if its testes were swapped with another rooster's. Berthold tried that experiment, and once again, to his surprise, the rooster grew back its wattle and comb, and began chasing hens aggressively around the yard.

That meant the testes were independent, and went to work as soon as they were inside a rooster's body – any rooster's body – telling its head and voice box exactly what to do! But how did those chemical instructions travel to the rooster's head and voice box, if not via the nerves? The only reasonable answer, reasoned Berthold, was that they travelled via the bloodstream.

Today, we know that Berthold had all the answers right – the mystery chemical that the testes secrete into the bloodstream is a male hormone called testosterone. But like so many other lines of research, this one, so full of promise, was inexplicably abandoned.

***

Over forty years later, in 1891, a Russian physiologist called Ivan Pavlov was invited to head the brand-new department of physiology at the Imperial Institute of Experimental Medicine in St Petersburg. Pavlov had already done some groundbreaking work in physiology, and over the next forty-five years, under his direction, the institute was to become the world's foremost research centre in the field.

Physiology is the study of the functions of the different systems and organs of living organisms – the excretory system of dogs, for instance, or the nervous system of frogs, or the brains of birds . . .

Even people who have nothing to do with science are familiar with one of Pavlov's famous experiments on what he called 'conditioned reflex', but we shall come to that in a bit. What Pavlov was essentially interested in, however, was figuring out exactly how digestion progressed, and what happened to food in different parts of the digestive system (in other words, he wanted to know how and where French fries and *medu vada* were transformed into the carbohydrates and proteins and fats and salts that the body could use as fuel).

He did this by performing several experiments on the digestive systems of dogs (trigger warning: if you love dogs, you may not want to read further!). For instance, he would remove a dog's oesophagus, the part that connects the throat to the stomach, and surgically create a fistula, a channel that led straight from the throat to the outside of the dog's body. However much the dog ate, the food would never reach its stomach – it would simply fall out through the fistula. However, by this time, the salivary glands would have produced a lot of saliva to begin digestion of the food. That saliva would get collected outside the dog too, and could be analysed both in terms of quantity (how much saliva was secreted while chewing?) and chemical content (did saliva help in breaking down food? If yes, what was it in saliva that was responsible?).

In a different dog, Pavlov would let the oesophagus be, and take out the duodenum, the first part of the small intestine. He would then create a fistula in the stomach. Food would now fall out of the stomach when the dog ate, mixed up with the gastric juices secreted by the stomach to digest the food. Now the gastric juices would collect outside for Pavlov and his team to analyse. In a third dog, he would let the duodenum be, and remove the jejunum, the second part of the small intestine, to see what happened to food as it passed through the duodenum. And so on.

It was while performing this last experiment that Pavlov noticed that as soon as partially digested food from the stomach (the technical word for this food is 'chyme') entered the duodenum, the pancreas began to work, producing its own secretions of digestive enzymes and sending them into the duodenum.

Pavlov was completely fascinated. It was understandable that the stomach produced gastric juices when food entered it, but how did the pancreas, which was somewhere else, know that food had entered the duodenum? What triggered the pancreas to produce its digestive enzymes at exactly that moment? He concluded that it must be the nerves that carried messages from the duodenum to the pancreas.

While Pavlov was conducting these experiments, he noticed another remarkable thing. His dogs would begin to salivate as soon as they saw the white lab coats of the people who fed them, even before they saw or smelt their food! (He knew this, of course, from the sudden increase in saliva falling through the throat fistula. Oh dear.) He decided to investigate these inexplicable 'psychic secretions'.

For this, he devised a fascinating experiment. For several days, he would first play a particular sound and then give the dogs their food. In the beginning, the dogs salivated only when they saw the food. A few days into the experiment, however, the dogs began to associate the sound with a meal, so they would begin to salivate at the sound itself! Pavlov concluded that this was learned behaviour, or what he called a 'conditional reflex' – an involuntary reaction (production of saliva) to a neutral stimulus (a sound, object, person or situation that actually had nothing to do with food), which the dog had learnt to associate with a biological stimulus (food).

Clearly, the brain was involved in this process – first the ears heard the sound, then the brain processed the sound and associated it with food, then the nerves carried the message 'There's food coming!' from the brain to the salivary glands, sending them into overdrive – so Pavlov became even more convinced that the digestive system, particularly gastric secretions, was very closely linked with the nervous system.

For his work on the physiology of the digestive system, and specifically on the functioning of the digestive glands, Ivan Pavlov was nominated for the Nobel Prize for four successive years, starting in 1901. He finally won it in 1904.

Even though most stories about Pavlov's famous experiment have him ringing a bell before feeding his dogs, the truth is that he actually used a metronome, a device that musicians use to mark time (think of it as a clock that ticks quite loudly).

***

Now what does all this have to do with hormones? Well, although Pavlov's theory about the nerves bringing messages to the pancreas was a good one, because it certainly explained a bunch of things, not everyone was convinced. Two British scientists called Ernest Starling and William Bayliss, who worked together on many projects, were among the sceptics. Their early collaborations were on blood pressure in veins and capillaries, but in 1897, they suddenly changed direction and began studying how food moves through the digestive system.

By this time, it was well known that the pancreatic secretions began as soon as acidic chyme entered the duodenum (chyme was acidic because it had mixed with gastric acid in the stomach). One of the functions of these secretions was to neutralize the acid in the chyme, so that the mucosa (lining) of the intestines would not be destroyed by it. To test if it was indeed nerves that brought the message to the pancreas to begin secretion, Bayliss and Starling performed the vivisection of a dog on 16 January 1902 at the University College, London. They tied off a loop of the jejunum at both ends, and cut off all the nerves that connected it with the rest of the body. Now that loop was connected only to the blood vessels.

Now the two scientists introduced some weak hydrochloric acid (HCl) into the duodenum. As expected, the system was fooled into thinking this was food, and the pancreas began secreting its digestive enzymes. Once the acid was neutralized, the secretions stopped. Now Bayliss and Starling introduced some HCl into the loop of jejunum that had been disconnected from the nerves. To their surprise, the pancreatic secretions began again. The message could not have gone to the pancreas via the nerves, so it must have gone through the blood! But from where did these messengers go? Suddenly, Starling had an epiphany, an out-of-nowhere inspiration – could it be that the mucosa of the jejunum itself produced these messengers and sent them out to the pancreas through the blood?

Quickly, he cut open a flap of the jejunum and rubbed its inside lining – i.e., its mucosa – against some sand mixed with HCl (this was the closest approximation to chyme that he could think of at that moment). Then he filtered the sand and mucosa out of that mixture and injected the filtrate into one of the dog's veins. If it was indeed the intestinal mucosa that produced the messengers and sent them out to the pancreas, the filtrate should contain them too. As he and Bayliss counted the seconds off with bated breath, the pancreas began to work, producing even more secretions than it had the previous two times!

The experiment had been a grand success – Bayliss and Starling now had all the proof they needed that the pancreas got its signals from the lining of the intestine itself, through the blood, and not through the nerves. More importantly, they had proved, for the very first time, that it wasn't just the brain, but also chemical messengers, that controlled physiological processes.

Just one week later, Bayliss and Starling presented their findings at a meeting of the Royal Society. During the presentation, Starling referred to the chemical messengers as 'hormones', a word he had formulated from the Greek *horman*, meaning 'I arouse to activity'. They also named the hormone they had discovered – which was generated by the intestinal mucosa and was the very first hormone to be discovered – secretin.

***

By the end of the First World War in 1918, scientists had figured out that there was also a link between pancreatic secretions and diabetes, an ancient disease in which glucose levels are higher than normal in the blood. The pancreas, they found, was not only stimulated by a hormone – secretin – during digestion, it was itself a gland, producing a hormone that kept blood sugar levels in control (in other words, the pancreas was also part of the endocrine system). When too little of this hormone was produced, the blood sugar shot up to dangerous levels.

In May 1921, a Canadian physician called Frederick Banting, with the help of a medical student called Charles Best, succeeded in extracting that vital hormone from an area of the pancreas called the islets of Langerhans. This extract, when injected into animals with diabetes, helped them bring their blood sugar levels under control. Banting and Best named this hormone 'isletin' (because of where it was generated), but later changed its name to 'insulin', from the Latin word for 'island', *insula*.

Banting and Best's experiments were done at the University of Toronto, in the laboratory of a Scottish physiologist called John Macleod, who had lent the space to them while he was away on vacation. As you will see a little later in this story, Macleod's act of generosity was to bring him unexpected rewards.

Before insulin could be tested on humans, it had to be purified and made safe. This vital part of the operation was done by James Collip, who joined the team in December 1921. Just a month later, in January 1922, Leonard Thompson, a fourteen-year-old boy dying of diabetes in Toronto General Hospital, became the first human to receive an insulin injection. To the joy of the research team, his blood sugar levels, which were high enough to send him into diabetic coma, dropped dramatically. It took the team another two weeks to prepare his next injection, but when it was administered, it brought Thompson's blood sugar levels even lower. In May 1922, completely recovered, Thompson left the hospital.

In 1923, the Nobel Prize in Physiology or Medicine was awarded – not to Banting and Best, as one might have expected, but to Banting and Macleod. Banting felt very strongly that Best deserved the prize as much as he did, and shared his prize money with Best. Inspired, Macleod did the same with Collip.

The discovery of insulin, and its success with a human patient, took the world by storm, and began a revolution in the study of endocrinology. Many, many other hormones were discovered, including stress hormones like cortisol, and, on the other end of the scale, the so-called happiness hormones – serotonin, oxytocin, dopamine and the endorphins – which are released when you exercise, reward yourself for a job well done, spend time in Nature or with loved ones, help someone in need, or simply count your blessings.

Yup, you don't always need outside help to boost your hormones – sometimes, just thinking positive and being grateful for all that you have will do it!

The Brown Dog Affair

As you can tell from reading this chapter, a lot of medical research, particularly in physiology, was unbearably cruel to animals and birds. Even today, despite all kinds of animal cruelty laws, this kind of research continues, and is often seen as unavoidable, a necessary evil to advance our understanding of the human body and its workings. The general public doesn't get to hear of it much; there would be a huge outcry if they knew.

People in the nineteenth century weren't okay with it, either. There were so many protests during Queen Victoria's reign (1837–1901) against vivisection, and the queen herself was so strongly opposed to the practice, that very few vivisection licences were issued. They went to select researchers, stipulating certain conditions, including that (1) the animal should be properly anaesthetized, and (2) no animal should be used more than once.

Two of the researchers who had such a licence were our friends Bayliss and Starling. In February 1903, they performed a public vivisection on what they said was a fully anaesthetized brown mongrel. However, according to two young Swedish medical students in the audience, Lizzy Lind af Hageby and Leisa Schartau, founders of the Anti-Vivisection Society of Sweden, the dog struggled during the operation, which meant it was not properly anaesthetized. Also, because Lizzy and Leisa had been attending vivisections and keeping notes for over a year, they realized that the dog was being used for the second time.

Old Brown Dog memorial, Battersea, London, 1906–10

Shaken, the girls took their 200-page diary – *The Shambles of Science* ('shambles' being another word for slaughterhouse) – to the English barrister Stephen Coleridge, also secretary of the National Anti-Vivisection League. Instead of taking the case to court, where justice was not guaranteed, Coleridge spoke about the incident in a public meeting attended by close to 3,000 people, and supported by writers like Thomas Hardy, Rudyard Kipling and Jerome K Jerome.

The impassioned speech was published in the *Daily News* (a newspaper founded by Charles Dickens) the next morning, creating a huge public furore. Furious, Bayliss sued for libel. The celebrated trial, which took place in November 1903, ended in four days, with a verdict of 'not guilty' for Bayliss. However, in 1912, as a result of this trial, a new and more stringent set of rules on vivisection came into practice in England.

From what you know now about the cruelty of vivisection, and also about how much it has contributed to our understanding of the human body, where do you stand on it? Are you in favour of it, against it, or somewhere in between?

IDEA 25

IT'S TRUE – THERE'S NO ONE QUITE LIKE YOU!

It's All in the Genes

Since the dawn of humanity, families have gathered around cribs and cradles where newly minted humans lie, to ooh, coo and launch into heated discussions about which parent – or grandparent, or aunt, or distant cousin – the baby resembles the most. But always, first, comes the pause of wonder – how is it that its father's nose or mother's jaw has passed on so faithfully to the baby? How does life, or Nature, ensure that it replicates itself, not entirely, not precisely, but in such a fascinating, mind-boggling variety of forms and shapes and colours, each recognizable as the child of its parents, but so unique in itself?

Unlike the scientists of today, who consider observation and experimentation their gods, the ancients preferred to ponder this endlessly engaging mystery of life in their own minds, until an epiphany, an inspiration, a revelation came to them. Sometimes, their conclusions were spot on, and sometimes, just like it happens with science, they were not. For instance, the ancients saw a man's sperm as similar to a plant's seed: just as a plant similar to the parent plant grew out of a seed when it was nourished by fertile soil, so did a child that looked like its father grows from *his* seed when it was nourished in the 'soil' of the mother's womb. The mother, they believed, made no other contribution to the baby.

This story, as you can imagine, had several plot holes. For instance, the plant metaphor did not work in the case of daughters, who were hardly the same as their fathers, biologically speaking. Plus, a great many daughters – and sons! – looked uncannily like their mothers. The philosophers skirted around these thorny issues, as they always did, with obscure explanations that no one could understand, let alone contradict. As for regular folks, especially those who owned cows and sheep and horses, they didn't need philosophers to explain the fundamentals of life to them – they knew, through long experience, that both parents contributed characteristics to their offspring. In fact, they knew enough to put the strongest males, or the ones that provided the tastiest meat, together with females that were not only hardy but also produced the largest quantity of milk, so that they could breed calves or lambs or foals that would bring them the highest price in the marketplace.

But we shouldn't be too hard on the ancient scientist-philosophers. With no microscopes, they had no way of knowing about the existence of the eggs – or ova (singular: ovum) – that every female mammal produces in her body.

It was only in 1826, therefore, that the 'mammalian egg' was proposed, by the Estonian scientist Karl Ernst von Baer; in 1827, he became the first person to observe a human ovum, or egg cell (human sperms, on the other hand, had been observed as early as 1677, by our old friend Antonie van Leeuwenhoek from page 87). It would be another fifty years before German scientist Oskar Hertwig observed the fusion of the sperm with the ovum while experimenting with sea urchins, and proved that it was not just the mother's womb, but also her cells that were involved in the creation of a baby.

> Given that the human egg or ovum, with a diameter of 0.1 mm, is one of the largest cells in the body, you don't actually need a microscope to see it. The reason it hadn't been 'found' was because no one was looking for it!

***

While the mechanism of how a baby inherited characteristics from both its parents had been a mystery until the end of the nineteenth century, no one had ever been in any doubt that the making of a new life – human, animal, bird – required both a male parent and a female one. What came as a total and mind-blowing surprise was the discovery that even plants had male and female reproductive organs. That revolutionary finding was published in 1694, by German botanist Rudolf Jakob Camerarius.

Up until the eighteenth century, some truly strange beliefs persisted about how certain creatures were born. People thought that flies and grubs and mice and frogs (which no one believed were grown-up tadpoles, since the two looked so different from each other) 'spontaneously generated' from non-living matter. Maggots, they believed, were born from rotting meat, frogs from the muddy slush around ponds, and mice from pieces of bread and cheese wrapped in rags and kept in dark corners!

In flowering plants, said Camerarius, a seed (or 'plant embryo') is created only when pollen (produced by the anthers, which are perched on top of the stamens, which are the male part of the flower) is dropped down the opening (or stigma) of the pistil (the female part of the flower) and fuses with the egg inside the ovary (find a diagram to understand this better). The article attracted immediate attention; many scientists were so fascinated, they made it their life's work to study this aspect of plants further.

But Camerarius's work was not the only pioneering work on botany to come out in 1694. The other was by the French botanist Joseph Tournefort, who came up with a method of classifying plants that was neither very original nor very accurate but became very popular because of the amount of information it contained about a huge variety of plants. Thirty-five years later, a twenty-two-year-old botanical genius called Carl Linnaeus, who had already written his own brilliant thesis on plant reproduction as a student at Uppsala University in Sweden, began to doubt the accuracy of Tournefort's classification system, and decided to create one of his own. He classified plants according to the number of stamens and pistils their flowers had, and developed a system of naming each species of plant using two Latin words.

In 1735, he published *Systema Naturae*, a twelve-page booklet detailing a new way to classify and name plants using 'binomial nomenclature', or the two-word system. By the time it reached its tenth edition in 1758, *Systema Naturae* was a whopper, containing the classifications and names of 4,400 species of animals and 7,700 species of plants! Two hundred and fifty years later, Linnaeus's classification system is still in use among the mammals whose official Latin name, as per his system, is *Homo sapiens*.

***

In the Europe of Linnaeus's time, everyone believed that all the different kinds of plants and animals had been put on earth at the beginning of time by a creator, and that new species could not be created. But scientists who closely studied plants and animals, like Linnaeus, noticed that new kinds of 'hybrid' plants – or plants that looked a bit like one plant and a bit like another – were being created all the time. Linnaeus did not test his theory that 'cross-breeding' – getting two species to mix – would produce an entirely new hybrid species, but a German botanist called Joseph Gottlieb Kölreuter, who lived around the same time, did.

Kölreuter began his experiments around 1760, using two different species of tobacco plants, which he cross-pollinated artificially. What that means is that he physically transferred pollen (using a paintbrush, perhaps) from the stamens of one species of tobacco plant (the father plant) to the pistil of a different species of tobacco (the mother). When the flowers of the mother plant dried up, they left seeds behind, inside the tobacco fruit. Kölreuter planted the seeds and waited to see what kind of plant would grow. As he had hoped, what resulted was a new and different hybrid plant, which had some characteristics of the mother and some of the father. Kölreuter was ecstatic – it was now conclusively proven that new species could be created!

Kölreuter wasn't doing anything unnatural when he helped the pollen of one species come into contact with the egg of another. This kind of thing happens all the time in Nature – when a bee flies from flower to flower, feeding on nectar, it often picks up pollen by its feet from one flower and drops it down the pistil of quite another.

But the real test was to see if these hybrids could produce their own 'babies', i.e., their own fertile seeds. So, in the second round, Kölreuter artificially pollinated the *hybrid* plants with each other. This time, fewer seeds were produced, but Kölreuter dutifully planted them. When these plants grew, he was gobsmacked to see these 'grandchildren' plants showed characteristics not just of their parents (the hybrids) but also of their grandparents! By solving one mystery about whether or not new species could be created, Kölreuter had created another grand riddle for scientists to sink their eager teeth into – how the heck were characteristics of the original parents transmitted across generations, and how did Nature decide which characteristics to suppress and which to keep vibrantly alive in each generation?

***

Enter, stage right, the British naturalist Charles Darwin. Born in 1809, three years after Kölreuter had passed, Darwin was also hugely interested in the question of how new species evolved. In 1831, at the age of twenty-three, he was invited to travel as a naturalist on the survey ship HMS *Beagle*, whose chief mission over the next two years was to map the coastline of South America. Darwin would have to pay his passage, but he would then be free to disembark at ports and islands, and spend time observing, cataloguing, classifying and conducting experiments on all the flora and fauna there.

It was during this voyage that Darwin first started putting together his theories of evolution. Having observed over thirteen different species of finches during his time on the Galapagos Islands off the north-western coast of

South America, each with a beak adapted to a specific kind of food, Darwin began to wonder if species developed particular characteristics to help them survive in a particular environment. But his light-bulb moment came in 1838, two years after the voyage had ended, when he happened to read British priest Thomas Malthus's famous essay about population growth. In the essay, Malthus predicted gloomily that if it kept growing at the same rate, human population would soon exceed available resources, thus causing a 'Malthusian catastrophe', where all humans would be forced to go back to basic survival methods.

Darwin persuaded his wealthy doctor father to finance his journey, and sailed out of England in December. The proposed two-year mission ended up lasting almost five years, but by the time the *Beagle* returned to England in October 1836, young Darwin's regular despatches on geology, botany and zoology had made him the toast of the scientific world back home.

It suddenly struck Darwin that a similar catastrophe should have already happened in the natural world, many times over, given the fact that so many species were fighting for the same limited resources. Somehow, though, it had not. Somehow, Nature had kept each species to a manageable number!

Aha! said Darwin to himself. Just like animal breeders chose certain animals with the most desirable characteristics for breeding, and never bred the animals that did not have those characteristics, thus ending the bloodline of 'unprofitable' animals, Nature must also pick members of a species that had the most desirable adaptations!

The ones that did not have those adaptations lost out in the competition for resources. Only the fittest survived and reproduced, passing on their desirable adaptations to their offspring. Darwin called his theory 'natural selection', and polished and perfected it for almost twenty more years. It was only in November 1859 that his pioneering work, *On the Origin of Species*, was published.

Expectedly, it led to a huge furore, because it contradicted what the Church believed – that all species were designed and put on the earth by God, and could not evolve on their own into other species. It also caused a hue and cry among the general public, and even large sections of the scientific

Theory of Evolution by Charles Darwin

community, because Darwin's belief in 'common descent' – all life forms had evolved from a common ancestor (or ancestors) – seemed to suggest that human beings and apes had come from the same source. And that, surely, could never be.

***

While Darwin was confident in his theory that the adaptations that helped a species best survive in its environment were the ones that were passed on to their offspring, creating a new species in the bargain, he could not explain *how* the information about those adaptations was passed on to the father's sperm and the mother's egg and then appeared in their offspring. If only he had met the Austrian priest Gregor Mendel, or had even read his work, which Mendel published in 1866, we might have figured out a whole bunch of things about inherited traits, or heredity, at least half a century before we did.

Unfortunately for Mendel, no one in the scientific community took his revolutionary findings seriously until twenty years after his death in 1882. Given that Mendel himself was conducting his experiments a hundred years after Kölreuter – except he was working on pea plants instead of tobacco plants – this seems like an unforgivable delay; but in science, it seems, as in life, things only happen in their own good time. What Mendel discovered was this:

- When he cross-pollinated a yellow-pea plant with a green-pea plant, the first-generation offspring were all yellow-pea plants.

- When the first-generation plants were pollinated among themselves, their offspring, the second generation, were neither all yellow nor all green. Instead, yellow- and green-pea plants occurred in the ratio 3:1 (of every four pea plants of the second generation, three produced yellow peas and one produced green peas).

This happened over and over again. In the first generation, only one particular trait – whether we are talking seed colour, seed size, pod colour, pod size and so on – would be expressed, and in the next, the trait that had been suppressed in the first generation would return, but in a small way.

Mendel called the trait that appeared in the first generation the 'dominant trait', because it expressed itself so forcefully, and the one that reappeared only in the second generation the 'recessive trait'. This pattern was constant and predictable, said Mendel, and was determined by pairs of 'invisible factors'

Gregor Mendel

(one of the pair being from mum and one from dad). Today, we know those invisible factors as the building blocks of all biological inheritance, which we call – that's right – genes!

***

Meanwhile, with microscopes getting better and better, scientists were able to take a far closer look at plant and animal cells than ever before. In 1839, German scientist Theodor Schwann published his findings on cells, in which he noted that both plant and animal cells had a central structure called a nucleus. His research, he said, had shown clearly that (1) the cell was the basic building block of all living things, and (2) each cell was complete in itself, but it also worked with other cells to build larger elements like tissues and organs. Which were both true. The only thing that Schwann got horribly wrong was his contention that cells 'generated spontaneously' – in other words, they appeared out of nothing.

> In Schwann's time, as you read earlier, most people believed that even large creatures like mice and frogs generated spontaneously. To them, it made perfect sense that cells would do the same.

It was the great German polymath Rudolf Virchow – he was pathologist and physician, anthropologist and politician, writer and editor, and many other things besides – who, in 1858, declared famously, '*Omnis cellula e cellula* – all cells come from cells.' That was the beginning of the definitive 'cell theory' that stands to this day. Virchow was building on the work of the Polish-German embryologist Robert Remak, who had discovered that new cells are created when a pre-existing cell splits in two, creating an exact copy of itself. It was through this continuous multiplication of cells, said Remak, that plants and animals grew. He called this kind of cell division mitosis.

In fact, German scientists were making all the breakthroughs in cell biology at this time. They were not only using better lenses in their microscopes, but had also figured out that staining a tissue sample, i.e., colouring it with a suitable dye, helped them see a great many more things clearly, because different parts of a cell picked up colour in different amounts. When one of those scientists, Walther Flemming, used a particularly bright purple dye to stain his samples, he noticed thread-like shapes he had never seen before in the nucleus of the cell – the threads had eagerly lapped up the dye and stood out clearly against the background. Today, we know those threads as chromosomes.

Flemming's name for the brightly stained threads in the nucleus was originally 'chromatin'. The name was derived from the Greek word *chroma*, meaning colour.

Now that he could see chromosomes so clearly, Flemming also got to observe what happened to them during mitosis.

Just before a cell divided, the chromosomes suddenly became more visible, because they had 'doubled' themselves – i.e., each chromosome had made an exact copy of itself. Each chromosome then bonded with its twin at its centre. When the nucleus split in two, so did the chromosome twins; one twin went into the nucleus of one of the new daughter cells, the other into the nucleus of the other. Scientists who saw this wondrous sight were most excited – could it be that it was the *chromosomes* that carried the information about the parents' characteristics to the offspring, just as they carried every 'mother' cell's information to the two 'daughter' cells?

In the early 1900s, two scientists – the young American biologist Walter Sutton and the German Theodor Boveri – independently proved that this was indeed the case. It *was* chromosomes that carried hereditary information – whether it was about the mother's curly hair or the father's dark skin or a grandfather's prominent jawline – to a new baby, and built them out of it. This tremendous finding immediately brought Gregor Mendel's work on inherited traits out of the mothballs – and into the spotlight that he had been denied in his lifetime.

***

As scientists studied chromosomes further, they noticed that the cells of all animals did not have the same number of chromosomes. Human cells, for instance, had forty-six chromosomes, or twenty-three pairs, while dogs had thirty-nine pairs and rice plants twelve. Chimpanzees and potatoes both had forty-eight pairs (no, seriously). Which led scientists to one GIANT, brain-scrambling question: If the human father's sperm cell (with its twenty-three pairs of chromosomes) combined with the human mother's egg cell (with its own twenty-three pairs of chromosomes), wouldn't the very first cell of their baby have forty-six *pairs* of chromosomes? Which would then replicate, giving every cell of the growing baby the same forty-six pairs of chromosomes? But that didn't happen – the baby still had only twenty-three pairs of chromosomes in each cell. How come?

> If a baby actually had forty-six pairs of chromosomes in each cell, it wouldn't be a human baby anymore – it would turn into a creature called Pittier's crab-eating rat, which has ninety-two chromosomes in each of its cells!

Curious, scientists now began studying 'germ cells', or germination cells, i.e., the sperm cells and egg cells responsible for the birth of a baby, and discovered something remarkable. It was Theodor Boveri, in fact, who discovered that germ cells were the products of a different kind of cell division, with two stages, called meiosis. The first stage is regular mitosis – each of the mother cell's chromosomes makes a copy of itself, and when the cell splits into two daughter cells, each cell gets one copy of each chromosome. In the second stage, however, each daughter cell splits into two *without the chromosomes first making copies of themselves.* Second-stage daughter cells, therefore, only have twenty-three chromosomes each, not twenty-three pairs. These 'half-cells' become egg cells in the female body and sperm cells in the male. When the sperm and egg combine to form a baby, their nuclei fuse with each other, ensuring that there are, once again, twenty-three pairs of chromosomes in the baby's first cell, and, as it grows, in every other cell as well. Phew.

***

The next question, of course, was what chromosomes were made up of. That story takes us back to 1869, to the stinky lab of Swiss physician Friedrich Miescher. Keen to know what proteins were contained in white blood cells, Miescher brought home pus-laden bandages from his local hospital (now you know why his lab was stinky), washed them out in a basin of water and filtered white blood cells out of the water. When he ground the cells up and tested the extract, he expected to find only protein. (Until a hundred years ago, everyone believed that the building blocks of our body were nothing but proteins, whose own building blocks were chemicals called amino acids, which themselves were made up of carbon, hydrogen, oxygen and nitrogen atoms combined in different ways.)

To Miescher's surprise, he found another mysterious substance as well – it had nitrogen in it, but also a lot of phosphorus. He named this mysterious substance nuclein, because he suspected it came from the nucleus. This was a very important discovery – what Miescher had discovered was the material from which chromosomes were made, the stuff that contained the code of life itself! But – you know what's coming, don't you? – no one paid it much attention.

Although it looks and smells yucky, pus is actually made up of dead white blood cells, the brave soldiers of your immune system who have been martyred in their attempt to keep your body free of infection. The next time you see pus, show some respect .

No one, that is, except a few German biochemists at the University of Strassburg. One of them was Albrecht Kossel. In 1881, Kossel took a closer look at nuclein, and identified it as an acid, changing its name to the more accurate nucleic acid. By 1901, he had also identified the five chemical compounds, called nucleobases, in nucleic acid – adenine (A), guanine (G), cytosine (C), thymine (T) and uracil (U). For his outstanding work, Kossel was awarded the Nobel Prize in Physiology or Medicine in 1910. Around the same time, a Russian-American biochemist called Phoebus Levene worked out that nucleic acid was made up of a chain of repeating molecules called nucleotides, with each nucleotide made up of a phosphate, a sugar and a nucleobase.

By the 1920s, scientists had worked out that there were two kinds of nucleic acid in each cell. One kind – ribonucleic acid or RNA – was found mainly outside the nucleus, in the cytoplasm. It was made up of four nucleobases – A, G, C and

U. The other kind – called deoxyribonucleic acid (because it had one oxygen atom less than RNA) or DNA – was found only inside the nucleus. It was made up of four nucleobases too – A, G, C and T. Now, DNA is what chromosomes are made of – in fact, each chromosome is made up of a single, very long DNA molecule made up of some 3 BILLION nucleotides.

Jaw-dropping fact: if you uncoiled a single molecule of DNA, with its billions of nucleotides, and laid it out, it would stretch 6 metres! Imagine how tightly coiled it must be to fit inside the nucleus of a cell! And don't forget that there are forty-six of those in each of our cells (except the germ cells), with plenty of room left over for other stuff!

And it is in the forty-six DNA molecules – twenty-three of which you have inherited from your mum and twenty-three from your dad – which inhabit the nuclei of each of your cells, that you carry all your genes. The unique pattern in which the four DNA nucleobases are arranged in these forty-six molecules forms your 'genetic code' – the formulae and the recipes that tell your cells how to build the very special, one-and only person called you. The 3 billion nucleotides on each chromosome determine, among a whole bunch of other things, exactly how you looked, look, and will look, at the ages of two, ten, twenty-five, fifty and eighty; what diseases you will be prone to; what size shoes you will wear; whether your heart will be healthy; what your sex will be, and much more. Goosebumps, what?

> Actually, all our genes – the instructions our cells need to make our bodies and keep them running – are contained in just 1 per cent – or a mere 30 million nucleotides – of each DNA molecule. We still have no clue as to what the other 99 per cent of our DNA is responsible for, or why it is there.

***

On 25 April 1953, two scientists from Cambridge University called James Watson and Francis Crick published a short but momentous article about what they believed was the structure of the DNA molecule, in the scientific journal *Nature*. They hadn't done a single experiment themselves – instead, they had used data collected by several other researchers, mainly Maurice Wilkins and Rosalind Franklin, to come up with their revolutionary idea that the DNA molecule was made up of two strands of nucleotides twisted into a double helix. When untwisted, the two strands would look like a ladder, whose vertical sides, or 'backbones', were made of the sugar and phosphate part of the nucleotide. The rungs were formed of the nucleobases A, T, G and C, with A always pairing with T and G with C.

Watson and Crick's model of the double-helix DNA dazzled the world and gave a huge boost to the field of molecular

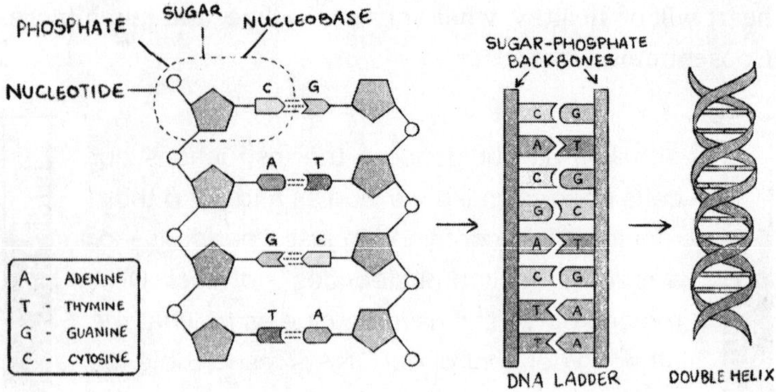

DNA Expanded DNA Twisted DNA Compressed

biology. For their work in cracking open one of the great mysteries of genetics, Watson and Crick won the Nobel Prize in Physiology or Medicine, jointly with Maurice Wilkins, in 1962. Tragically, Rosalind Franklin had died of cancer in 1958, at the age of thirty-seven, and missed out.

Today, science's big dream is to figure out how we can rewrite, or at least edit, our own particular genomes (the complete set of our genes), by learning to first recognize, and then eliminate, the most undesirable bits of them, like the genes that carry life-threatening inherited diseases. In other words, through the bravest, newest, terribly-exciting but also-pretty-scary frontiers of medicine – genetic engineering – we are dreaming of playing God.

So far, though, God seems to be winning. For even with all the spectacular progress we have made in understanding how life is created, we still have no idea, not even the foggiest, about how to do it ourselves.

Har Gobind Khorana – the Man Who Read the Gene

By the 1950s, it was clear that chromosomes were made of DNA, and that DNA was essentially two strands of nucleotides twisted together. However, the intertwining wasn't random; each nucleobase in one strand paired only with its partner – A pairing with T and G pairing with C – in the other strand. RNA, on the other hand, was just a single strand of nucleotides, which did not contain hereditary information. Instead, RNA copied the DNA's information onto itself, and took it outside the nucleus into the cytoplasm, where that information was interpreted and proteins manufactured for the body, according to the DNA recipe. This kind of RNA was called messenger RNA (or mRNA).

But how and where in the cytoplasm was this mRNA sequence read and interpreted? Which cell organelle performed the translation? And how did it decide which proteins were to be made? After all, to us, mRNA reads like an unintelligible series of letters – AUGCUGCGAAACUUCGGCUGA (the T's in a DNA molecule get copied as a U on an mRNA one), for example. What was the RNA translation code?

It was an Indian-American scientist, who won the Nobel Prize in Physiology or Medicine in 1968, who cracked this fundamental mystery. His name was Dr Har Gobind Khorana, and he brought his vast knowledge of chemistry and physics to cell biology, revolutionizing nucleic acid research. It was Khorana who figured out that mRNA's string of letters, which seemed like gobbledygook to us, was actually a series of three-letter 'words' called 'codons' and that each codon referred to a particular amino acid. Once mRNA left the nucleus and entered the cytoplasm of the cell, it made straight for an organelle called the ribosome. The ribosome 'read' the mRNA, translated it into codons and instructed the cell to make the appropriate amino acids, which then bonded with each other to form proteins. (There are twenty essential amino acids, so there are millions of ways in which these can combine to form specific proteins. You see why it is SO important that the sequence of genetic letters and words is in the right order?)

The next question was this – how did the ribosome know when and where to start reading the mRNA strand? Once again, it was Khorana's work which cracked this mystery – 'punctuation codons'! Yes, one particular codon (AUG, if you must know!) was the 'start' codon – as soon as the ribosome 'read' this particular combo of 'letters', it began to convert this and every codon that followed into amino acids. When it encountered a 'stop' codon – and there are three different kinds of those – the ribosome understood that a particular protein had now been synthesized and stopped turning codons into amino acids. It then went back to idly scanning the mRNA strand, until it encountered another AUG. Cool, huh?

Four years after he had won the Nobel Prize, Khorana also became the first to 'make' a gene in the laboratory. The method of synthesizing genes that he pioneered is still the one in use today.

What is most remarkable about this story is that Har Gobind Khorana had had his entire primary education under a tree (in the 1920s, that was the only 'school' in his tiny village of 100 families in that part of Punjab, which is now in Pakistan)! That probably explains why this incredible genius, who was only interested in tackling the 'big problems' of science, no matter how difficult they seemed, was so unassuming about his success, believing that if he had seen so far in science, anyone could. All it needed, as he put it, was extreme focus, curiosity, perseverance and hard work.

Har Gobind Khorana passed away in 2011, at the age of eighty-nine, but his trailblazing contributions laid the foundation for the emerging field of biotechnology, which continues to engage and fascinate students of science to this day.

PS. In 2009, two years before Khorana's death, the Nobel Prize in Chemistry was awarded to three scientists for their work in figuring out the exact structure and working of the ribosome. One of them was another Indian-born scientist, Dr Venkatraman 'Venki' Ramakrishnan.

WHY DO WE GO AWAY? SO THAT WE CAN COME BACK WISER

It's ironic, but very appropriate somehow, that the last idea we have explored in this book has so much in common with the most ancient ideas around health and healing that we discussed in the first few chapters. Let's explore a few of them.

Remember when we discussed Ayurveda, and discovered that it is based on the assumption that every individual has a unique balance of doshas or energies, and that it is an imbalance of these that causes illness? The kind of treatment that was administered to each sick person, therefore, was also unique to them – the same aspirin (or its equivalent), insisted Ayurveda, could not possibly heal five different people, even if each complained of the same symptom – a headache.

In the twenty-first century, a much deeper understanding of genomics, or the science of the human genome, has led modern medicine down the same path to a 'new' and increasingly popular concept of healing called 'personalized medicine' (because, of course, no two genomes are exactly the same). Personalized medicine believes treatments should be, umm, 'tailored to the individual'.

Or let's talk about the newfangled 'lifestyle diseases', like diabetes, heart disease, obesity, stroke, hypertension, various cancers and anxiety. With more and more evidence that they are inextricably linked to bad diets, smoking, excessive drinking, disturbed sleep patterns, stress and environmental pollution, ways to *prevent* disease are now taking precedence over ways to *manage* disease. Which – surprise, surprise! – takes us right back to Idea 2: Prevention is better than cure!

And that's why it seems that wherever we turn, people are talking of nothing but new and faddish diets, fitness regimens, the elusive thing called work-life balance, meditation, getting back in touch with Nature and her rhythms (epitomized in the mantras 'Early to bed, early to rise . . .' and 'Eat fresh, local, seasonal, *organic*') and, yes, going back to 'traditional' ways of living.

Inevitably, side by side, there has grown a deep – and unfortunate – mistrust of modern medicine.

Which is fine in its place, for a little scepticism about received wisdom is a good thing. The danger is that we humans, in our hurry to dissociate ourselves from the 'evils' of modern medicine, often behave like lemmings (the little rodents from the Arctic regions that get so desperate for food when their populations explode that they throw themselves into the ocean, in the hundreds, apparently in an attempt to get to the other side, but drown instead), and go overboard in the opposite direction! This isn't even futuristic fantasy – the World Health Organization identified 'vaccine hesitancy', a reluctance or refusal to be vaccinated, or to have one's children vaccinated, as one of the top ten global health threats of 2019, and we all saw it play out during the COVID-19 pandemic. (Remember when men's tennis World No. 1 Novak Djokovic was banned from the Australian Open 2022 because he refused to take the COVID vaccine?)

Adherents of the so-called anti-vaxxer movement mistrust vaccinations because of various (real or imaginary) medical, legal and ethical issues around them. Which would have been fine if the outcome of that kind of decision only affected the anti-vaxxers - after all, people should be allowed to choose what they put into their bodies. The trouble, however, is that the growing population of unvaccinated children and adults – i.e., those that are unprotected against well-known germs – is leading to contagious and dangerous diseases (like measles, for example) making a comeback in many communities (because, of course, those germs never really went away; vaccines had only kept them at bay). In other words, anti-vaxxers don't only put themselves and their own children at risk – they also put as-yet-unvaccinated infants in the vicinity in serious danger.

Sigh. Poor Edward Jenner must be turning in his grave at these developments, as also Louis Pasteur, Walter Haffkine, Jonas Salk and all those other vaccination stalwarts who worked so hard to ensure we wouldn't die like flies, or even have to suffer, from terrible diseases like smallpox, rabies, plague and polio. And Mum Nature is the one having the last chortle, as usual, as she strikes back at us in ingenious (devious?) ways, turning us against ourselves even as we hack into our very genomes in the great quest for immortality.

What is to be done then? With so much information and contrary opinion about health and wellness being slammed at us constantly, and given that there are no guarantees against disease and pain, how do we lead a life that is not only healthy but also, well, happy? Maybe the answer is to attempt to live as lightly as possible on the earth, in a way that causes the least damage to ourselves, the creatures we share our world with, and our environment, even as we seek single-mindedly to uncover life's most fascinating, most magical secrets. Maybe it lies in being mindful about not only what we feed our bodies with, but also what we feed our minds and emotions with. Maybe it's simply about being grateful for the things we have, instead of constantly chasing after something that we believe is shinier, bigger, better.

And maybe it's about trusting the universe, and our fellow humans, to do right by us. Yup, even when – *especially* when – they are doctors.

ACKNOWLEDGEMENTS

There have always been too many doctors in my family. But it was only after my older sister maxed her Grade XII board exams, entered medical college, brought a grinning skull home and made cadavers standard-issue dinner table conversation that my real fascination with the science of medicine began. For the five and a half years of relentless work it took for her to become a doctor, I pored over the beautifully illustrated diagrams in her copy of *Gray's Anatomy*, lapped up everything the textbook on forensic medicine had to say about entry and exit bullet holes, and marvelled at the selfless dedication the profession demanded, wondering what drove its practitioners to put themselves out, willingly, day after night after day, to helping their fellowmen heal. Three decades later, with mistrust of doctors becoming commonplace, I am still wondering. Ergo, this book, my little tribute to the profession and the fraternity.

It goes without saying that my project would not have come to fruition without a lot of help and guidance, and many thanks are due to those who provided it.

Some context-setting is in order, however. This book was first published by Puffin India, with a different cover and title, in September 2019 (a warm thank you to my editor Sohini Mitra and the entire Puffin team), mere months before the COVID-19 pandemic smashed into us like a sledgehammer, the sneaky, mutating virus responsible for it confounding the best doctors and scientists. But the same coronavirus also inspired scientists across the globe to collaborate and create a vaccine against the scourge in record time, apart from spurring healthcare professionals to willingly take on insane workloads, thus turning the tide of popular sentiment, and reinstating doctors and nurses as our society's real-life heroes.

This beautiful new edition that you are holding is published by Hachette India. I'm deeply grateful to the entire team at Hachette, but particularly to Thomas Abraham, Managing Director of Hachette, and my friend, mentor and editor for over three decades, Vatsala Kaul Banerjee, for putting their trust and energies into this edition. For the arresting new cover, which holds many secrets (how many did you find after reading the book?), many thanks to designer Pia Alizé Hazarika.

Fortunately for me – and the readers of this book – the clever, quirky, fun illustrations by the very talented Mihir Joglekar, which were part of the original edition, continue to illuminate this one.

A book like this, crammed with so many facts and information, and written by a non-professional, demands not one but several goings-over with a fine-toothed comb to catch errors, omissions and any kind of unintentional misinformation. Much gratitude, therefore, to my accomplished once-classmates and still-friends Dr Sanjay BS, cardiac surgeon at Fortis Hospitals, and Dr Sujai Hegde, surgical oncologist and founder-director of the Centre of Advanced GI Oncology at Kamalnayan Bajaj Cancer Centre in Pune, for taking the time out from their busy, busy, healer-lives to read the manuscript in minute detail and offer me very valuable feedback.

A big shout-out also to Amarnath Kamath, dear and valued friend of the family, who connected me to *his* dear friend, the very efficient Lakshmi Mani of Narayana Health, who personally carried the manuscript to Dr Devi Shetty for his opinion.

What can I say about the amazing Dr Shetty, who found the time, in between performing life-saving cardiac surgeries, helming his nationwide chain of multi-specialty hospitals and research labs, and overseeing the charitable work of Narayana Health, to read the manuscript of a book whose author he did not know, and not only give it his approval but also write a wonderful endorsement of it – *all within 48 hours*? Thanks so very, very much, Doc – you are a true rock star, but you knew that already, didn't you?

And finally, and most importantly, my deepest gratitude to all the seekers and dreamers mentioned and not mentioned in this book, for living lives that serve as beacons to others beset with the same insatiable curiosity about everything around and inside us, and the same consuming need to make the world a better place for everyone in it.